LIFE BEGINS AT 50!

CELIA ANDERSON

Boldwood

First published in Great Britain in 2024 by Boldwood Books Ltd.

Cover Design by Rachel Lawston

Cover Illustration: Rachel Lawston

A CIP catalogue record for this book is available from the British Library.

Paperback ISBN 978-1-83617-135-5

Large Print ISBN 978-1-83617-136-2

Hardback ISBN 978-1-83617-134-8

Ebook ISBN 978-1-83617-137-9

Kindle ISBN 978-1-83617-138-6

Audio CD ISBN 978-1-83617-129-4

MP3 CD ISBN 978-1-83617-130-0

Digital audio download ISBN 978-1-83617-132-4

Boldwood Books Ltd
23 Bowerdean Street
London SW6 3TN
www.boldwoodbooks.com

For Angie Crane: trusted confidante, amazing hairdresser and very good friend.

To change one's life:

1. Start immediately.
2. Do it flamboyantly.
3. No exceptions.

— WILLIAM JAMES

PROLOGUE

20 MARCH 1998

The disco ball is spinning and fractured shards of light are already turning the floor into a kaleidoscope. Kate hears the opening chords of the song that's been chosen for the first dance, and her heart sinks. Howard's still propping up the bar, schmoozing a gaggle of middle-aged men with pot-bellies. They remind Kate of a semi-circle of expectant mums, or maybe Moomins, sticking out their little round tummies so proudly.

As she watches, they all haw-haw-haw at the end of a very long anecdote. Howard joins in, louder than any of them. Kate knows he hopes they might be able to swing it for him to join the prestigious Meadowthorpe golf club. Whoopee.

'Off you go, love,' her dad says, giving Kate a little push towards the dance floor. 'Leave this to me. I'll round him up for you.'

'Good luck with that one,' Kate mutters, but she does as she's told. Ted Baxter squares his shoulders, loosens his tie and marches towards the bar. Soon the rather unsteady figure of Kate's brand-new husband is weaving its way towards her. Howard looks good in his hired tailcoat and waistcoat. He's ditched the top hat but he hasn't yet developed a rounded profile, so the waistcoat and trousers perfectly complement his slim figure.

'Go for it, my son,' one of the golfers cries. 'Give her one for me.'

Ted shoots the man a very dirty look and makes a move back towards the group at the bar but Kate shakes her head at him. This isn't the time to demonstrate how protective he's always been of his only daughter. It's not the Christmas episode of *East-enders* and her father is the local doctor. She doesn't want a fight. It wouldn't do Ted's image any good.

Not wanting to look less than the perfect bride, Kate pulls her stomach in and tries to stand tall. Moving into the flat above the Chinese takeaway with Howard has made her pre-wedding diet almost impossible, but she's managed to squeeze her naturally curvaceous 14/16 body into a pale green sheath of a dress. The heavily boned basque has helped.

Her mother wanted her to do the whole meringue thing with a big skirt and veil but the idea of trying to look like a virgin bride after six months of living in what her granny insists on calling 'sin' has put Kate off that idea. *Minty-frost* is the shade of the frock, according to the pencil-thin shop assistant, who worked hard to persuade Kate that it was only a tiny bit too tight and she'd soon drop a few pounds. 'All brides-to-be lose weight before the big day,' she'd said, with the confidence of someone who has clearly never polished off an entire Chinese dinner for two and still had room for the prawn crackers.

Howard reaches Kate and holds out his arms in an extravagant gesture that nearly topples him. She moves closer and lets him enfold her. At least that way he'll stand a chance of staying upright. They begin to sway to the music and the guests let out a collective *Aaaaah* as the words of the song become clear. 'Love

Me for a Reason' wasn't Kate's choice but Howard's mum loves Boyzone and neither Kate nor Howard had any idea what they should pick. A reason for love. That's an interesting thought.

Why has Kate decided to marry Howard? They were fine just living together. It was the messy student type of lifestyle she'd never had before, living away from home for the first time and only washing up when you ran out of crockery. No commitments. No rules. Providing a regular retreat for Kate's wayward brother Jamie into the bargain, for which her parents are more than grateful. Jamie's wild streak is a lot more manageable now Howard has introduced him to the delights of golf. Ted and Caroline are full of praise for the way Howard has transformed a twenty-year-old fireraiser into something resembling a grown-up. They are 100 per cent in favour of this wedding. Howard will be an asset to the Baxter clan, in their opinion. If only Kate felt as convinced.

'How are you doing, Mrs Brown?' Howard murmurs. 'This is a great party. Jamie's had a few too many but most people are holding their booze so far. Clive says it was a good move booking the golf club function room for the do. I think I'll be in there before Christmas. Full membership for me, and provisional for your little brother, if we can keep him on the rails.'

'Lovely,' says Kate, unable to focus on anything but the moment when they go upstairs and she takes off this bloody basque. She murmurs the thought to Howard as the music swells, and he sniggers.

'I can't wait either,' he says. 'I'm going to give you a night to remember, babe.'

Kate doubts this. He's already ticked her off for getting fake tan on his brilliant white shirt when they kissed for the photographer, so she'll need to have a long, hot shower before she gets into bed to get rid of any hint of tango. By the smell of the alcoholic haze that's surrounding her now, Kate guesses that as soon as Howard's stripped off his own wedding finery, he'll be face down and snoring on the rose-petalled four-poster before she's even left the bathroom. She closes her eyes and blocks out the uncomfortable image. This night is only laying the groundwork for the next stages, and there'll be plenty of time for the real reason she's marrying Howard after she's done her teacher training and had a few years getting established.

They shuffle to the music for a moment or two, then Howard bends to whisper in Kate's ear. His breath is hot and beery on her neck.

'Oh, while I think about it, I was talking to the guys about us buying a house,' he says, glancing over at the bar. 'I mentioned that you were interested in working in a school. Quentin's missus is the head teacher at the primary nearest to us. He reckons they're looking for teaching assistants. He can get you an intro.'

Kate's eyes are wide open now. She looks up at her husband. He's beaming, as if he's just given her the best news ever. 'You're joking, aren't you? I don't need a teaching assistant job,' she says. 'I'm going to train to be a proper teacher. We agreed.'

'I know we did, but that'd take ages,' Howard says, in the syrupy voice he always uses when he wants something badly. 'You've already wasted enough time playing at catering with your Aussie mate.'

'I haven't been wasting time with Sophie. We got our catering qualifications. I just didn't know then how much I wanted to teach.'

'Yeah, yeah, yeah. But if you got a teaching assistant post we could have a mortgage a lot sooner.'

'A mortgage on what? I don't want to live in a new house on a half-built estate in the middle of nowhere. I like our flat.'

'Oh, come on. That place was just to get us going, no more

and no less. Clive says his mum's just gone into a retirement home and she's selling up. She's got one of those little cottages on Fiddler's Row. That'd be more your style, wouldn't it? Cosy and old-fashioned.'

Kate guesses he means this to be a compliment, so she ignores the image it conjures up and focuses on this new thought. A house in that lovely terrace on the village green? That would definitely beat the flat.

'We couldn't afford it, though... could we?' she says. Already, the idea of living in such a dream of a place is winkling its way into her mind. Willowbrook village has always been her home, nestling in a generous loop of the Nene with water meadows stretching out into the distance and the wild sea marshes only a few miles away. Her parents live in one of the gracious riverside houses near the country park, bought as a near wreck when property was much cheaper, but Kate has always known that she and Howard would need to look for something much smaller when the time came to move.

'We might be able to manage it if you were working,' her new husband says. 'With two steady incomes, we'd be laughing. Also... I had a quiet word with your dad yesterday when we were doing the wedding rehearsal.'

'Oh, Howard. You haven't asked him for money, have you? Please tell me you haven't.' Kate can feel her face burning. Both her parents seem to think the sun shines out of Howard's neat little backside. They won't be so keen on Jamie's chief cheer-leader if he's going to start tapping them for cash.

'Not a hand-out. It'd just be a loan. Ted would love to have you living close by, where he can make sure I'm looking after you properly.'

Kate thinks about Fiddler's Row. The longing to live there almost takes her breath away. There are eleven houses in the terraced row that curves around two sides of the green with its three ancient willow trees. It's a beautiful spot, often photographed by visitors to Willowbrook. The lively little brook that gives the village its name wiggles right across the centre of the green as it makes its way down to the river. Fiddler's Row is directly opposite Kate's favourite pub and there's even a handy shop at the end of it. The river is only five minutes' walk away and Willowbrook Country Park with its lakes and woods is barely a mile from the cottages.

'But... what about my degree? I want to be a teacher, Howard, you know that,' she says, pushing the vision of her perfect home away.

He kisses the top of her head and gives her a squeeze. 'Be realistic for once, eh? It's time to knuckle down and earn some proper cash. You're twenty-four now, Mousey. Hey, I can officially call you Mousey Brown now. How cool is that?'

Howard laughs at his own feeble joke. Kate can smell whisky along with the beer now, and a trace of his spicy aftershave. The combination isn't alluring. She opens her mouth to argue, furious enough not to protest at the hated nickname.

'You can't say I've got to change my plans now, after all the times we've talked about it. You just can't. I've done all my research and the forms are ready to send off. It's agreed. I'm going to uni in September.'

'But think about it, Mousey. You can't live in halls like a normal student when you're a married woman, you've got me to think about. Plus, you'd feel like an OAP next to all those kids fresh from sixth form.'

'There'd be other students my age, I know there would. Twenty-four isn't old, Howard, and the university campus isn't that far away. It's on a direct bus route too. I can commute.'

They wobble to the music for a few more moments. Kate

thinks she might have won but then Howard plays his trump card. 'If you went to work properly now instead of just marking time in the bakery doing silly shifts and spending ages on teacher training, not only would we be able to buy that little cottage in one of the best locations in the village, but we could start a family even sooner. Babies, Katie. That's what you want, isn't it?'

And there it is, right in front of her. Love me for a *reason*. This is Kate's reason. Because the image of herself teaching a class of eager-faced five-year-olds is inspiring, but it isn't quite as tempting as the one of her cradling a lovely, cuddly baby in her arms, with a curly-haired toddler holding onto her legs and an older child... maybe even twins... playing with their Lego on the hearth rug. Her mum and dad are backing Howard as husband material largely because he's dragged Jamie back from the brink of being a full-time hooligan, but Kate knows in her heart she's chosen him because he's strong, fit and she thinks he'd make a great father for her future children. That's not a bad list, is it? Not everyone marries with a heart full of unconditional love, and stars in their eyes. This is real life, not a fairy tale.

A few braver or possibly tipsier couples have joined Kate and Howard for the slow dance but as it ends, the DJ switches to the disco playlist that Kate had prepared when she was trying to distract herself from going downstairs to the takeaway for three spring rolls and a bag of chips. The sound of the first dance track brings more people to the floor and soon there's a mass of waving arms and gyrating bodies as 'Hi Ho Silver Lining' gets the party started.

Howard gives Kate a pat on the arm and mutters something about going to have another word with Clive and Quentin. He heads for the bar, ploughing his way through the crowd as family and friends slap him on the back and tell him what a lucky man he is. Kate kicks off her hideously tight heels and throws them under a nearby table. A serious conversation with Howard about their future is looming, but for now there's dancing to be done. Sophie bursts onto the dance floor, sparkling in a very short, very sequinned dress. She grabs Kate by both hands and twirls her around to the music. Kate laughs out loud.

'Are you okay, darl?' Sophie yells above the din. 'You two looked as if you were having the sort of chat a loved-up couple shouldn't be having at their wedding do. I was watching you, and wishing I could magic us to the motherland. You need to get your old carefree look back again.'

'You know I've always wanted to tag along and go to Australia with you when you visit your folks,' says Kate, wistfully. 'I guess it'll never happen now.'

'Never say never, that's always been my motto. Look, I'm going to ask you the same question again. Are you okay? I saw a film once where the bride legged it from her own wedding do.'

'But that's mad. Weddings take ages to arrange and they're really expensive. Why would anyone do that?'

Sophie seems to be struggling for words, which isn't like her. 'Well, sometimes people change their minds, I guess. They get caught up in the buzz of the moment and then realise... Anyway, I just wanted to make sure...'

'I'm fine,' says Kate, as Sophie's words dry up. And suddenly, she really is. There's a reason for all this. Everything else can look after itself. What happens next doesn't seem to matter any more. So long as there are babies in her future, everything else will be just perfect.

Sophie frowns, but says no more and they dance until their feet ache. Howard's right in one respect, it really is a great party. Kate's prediction about his bedroom activities turns out to be almost accurate, except that he adds an extra element by throwing up in the sink before crashing out, but Kate doesn't worry too much. There'll be plenty of time for that kind of stuff when she's good and ready, and if they really can swing it, buying a house on Fiddler's Row will be a big step in the right direction. Perhaps her dream career was just that... a fantasy, along the same lines as the idea of travelling to Sydney with Sophie and backpacking around Oz. It's time to be a sensible married woman now. It's almost time to become a mum.

1

JANUARY, TWENTY-FIVE YEARS LATER

'So, come on then, what's stopping you? I've got the bleach in my bag. You've only got to say the word.'

Kate heard Sophie speaking through a kind of fog. She'd been miles away, lost in a prickly flashback of her wedding night, brought on by an excess of January melancholy. This March would have marked twenty-five whole years of being married, if Howard had still been around. Ever since they'd made their vows, Kate had found 20 March more significant than any other day of the year. It stood for hopes and dreams and future plans. To begin with she'd taken the time to produce an imaginative, hand-crafted card for Howard and source the traditional present for each anniversary, but gradually the effort dwindled to a shop-bought card and perhaps a voucher of some sort, if he was lucky.

Howard had never seemed to mind whether Kate remembered or not, and his own offerings, usually of rather tatty flowers, were spasmodic, so in the end Kate had decided not to mark the occasion. Even so, many of these anniversaries still managed to make themselves significant for one reason or another. Maybe if the marriage had lasted they would have had a party for their silver wedding. On the other hand, there was no reason why Howard would have had the urge to plan a celebration of all those years with Kate when he'd been sleeping with someone else for at least the last twelve months, even if sleeping had probably been the last thing on his mind. Although the new lady would have inherited the snoring part too, which was an excellent thought. Kate hoped Howard still sounded like an ageing warthog when he slept.

'What are you talking about, Soph?' Kate asked, dragging her mind back to the present. She rubbed her eyes and blinked at their reflection in the long mirror on the wall. Sophie was looking distinctly irritable. She must have been waiting a while for an answer.

'I had a feeling you weren't listening. Going blonde. You said you'd think about it last time I came to cut your hair. Come on, there'll never be a better opportunity. Your mum did it months ago, just before she left for France. *Good for you, Caroline*, that was what I said at the time. Blondes definitely have more fun, I reckon.' She laughed and ruffed her own short curls. 'I'm a prime example of that, aren't I?'

The image of Caroline Baxter living a carefree life in rural Normandy wasn't welcome. Her mother had made the move to live near Jamie and his family way too soon after her husband died, in Kate's opinion. They'd hardly had time to organise a decent memorial service for Kate's dad before Caroline had the house on the market and was ferrying numerous carloads of boxes and bin bags to the charity shops. It had been clear that the sudden departure of Ted Baxter the previous year had affected Kate and her mother very differently. Caroline's honey-coloured hair sometimes seemed like just another way of thumbing her nose to the past. There was no way Kate was going to go down the same road. It was quite enough to cover her greys with a box of medium brown dye every few weeks.

'Ah, well, I'll ask you again next time,' said Sophie. 'I just thought, what with Howard doing a bunk like that, the slimy toad... well, to be honest, I hoped you'd be ready to make a fresh start. He never did deserve you. Shagging someone else all this time, and then leaving you high and dry after you'd put up with him for years. What a dork.'

Kate winced at the word shagging. Sophie had always been blunt, and the picture this conjured up made her stomach churn. She wondered if Howard still left his socks on. Her friend was on a roll now and didn't notice Kate's expression.

'And what did he ever contribute in return, the useless drongo?' Sophie continued. 'All he did was go to work and play golf. He was a waste of space. Aunty Beryl always said so too.'

Sophie's clever hands were busy with the scissors and comb but she gestured with her head to the party wall that joined Kate's cottage to Beryl's mirror version of the same. Kate could hear the TV turned to top volume as the *Pointless* theme tune thundered out. Batty-Beryl-Next-Door, as Howard had called the old lady, was slightly deaf now at eighty years old but in no way batty, in fact she was probably one of the shrewdest people in the village. Kate wondered how many other locals considered her to have been Howard's doormat. Quite a lot, she imagined, including the two stalwarts who completed Beryl's gang, Anthea and Winnie. They were regulars at The Fox and Fiddle across the green, and also at any other village activities that involved bingo, raffles, cake and/or Prosecco. All three were now either widowed or divorced, and Beryl and her friends had developed a reputation for living life to the full.

Kate reflected sadly that those ladies would be quite right to think she'd been downtrodden for years. She had let Howard walk all over her for way too long.

'My aunty is one cool cookie,' Sophie said. 'She had a great time when she went to see Mum and Dad last year. She even talked about emigrating to join them, did you know that? It was only the idea of having Christmas dinner on the beach that put her off. She said turkey and sprouts wouldn't taste the same in the heat. Oh, and she couldn't persuade the others to come with her. She does love her old mates.'

'Beryl was going to move to Australia? She never told me.'

'Well, she didn't leave us in the end, did she? But she's visited loads of times since Mum met my dad back in the day and headed off out there. She's a right globe-trotter. So where have *you* been recently, Katie? Got any trips planned, have you?'

There was no need to answer this. Sophie finished her work and held a hand mirror up at the back for Kate to see the result. It was hard to spot any difference in the before and after viewings. The little pile of hair on the floor was never enough to suggest a major change had occurred.

'Lovely,' said Kate automatically. It wasn't, but it was neat and tidy and still long enough for her to tie back when she was at work in the café. Her hair had reached down to her waist when Kate had first met Sophie. Now it was just a hindrance if she let it get too long.

As if reading her mind, Sophie said, 'Still happy behind that counter at Pat's Place? Don't you miss being at the school?'

The lump in Kate's throat was making it difficult to answer. She swallowed hard.

'I do miss the kids,' she said. 'It was so hard going back to work after Dad died, though. I lost the plot for a while. The best thing all round seemed to be to have a completely fresh start.' Kate paused, collecting her thoughts. It had been a hideous time, and thinking about it still made her want to howl with pain. 'I had plans to get my act together and do some of the things I'd been putting off for ages. But then everything changed again,' she continued. 'When Howard left I got kind of... stuck.'

Sophie was silent for a few minutes, packing up her kit. The grandfather clock in the corner creaked, warning that it was about to strike the half hour. At least Howard hadn't tried to take the clock. It was the only thing Kate had managed to rescue from her parents' house when her mum had cleared the decks and sold up so speedily.

'I suppose if you'd had kids it would have been different,' Sophie said. 'You'd have had more of a focus.'

The silence that followed this bald statement carried on until the clock finally struck. Kate turned to look at Sophie, who was avoiding her gaze. 'But we didn't, did we? Have babies, I mean.'

'No.' The single word showed that Sophie realised she'd gone too far. This was a place where they never strayed. The longed-for babies were just another dream now.

Kate sighed and stood up, brushing the last remaining clippings of hair from her jeans. 'Do you ever regret not having children?' she asked, batting the ball firmly back into Sophie's court.

There was no hesitation. 'Never. There's Paul to think about, and neither of us ever got broody, luckily. We've got Ralph too. He's worse than any baby. He's probably winding Aunty Beryl around his little finger, I mean paw, right now. She loves dog-sitting when I'm working over in this neck of the woods.'

Kate considered this. Since Sophie and Paul had adopted their beloved pet, they had mellowed even more, if that was possible. Deciding to give a rather dishevelled rescue dog a home had been a bonus for them. Ralph, once he was properly settled and had stopped eating their shoes and barking at the neighbours for entertainment, had been a definite asset.

Sophie was clearly still mulling the subject over. 'We like our life just how it is, Kate. I'm so glad I've still got my gran's old cottage here. I wasn't sure what to do with the place when she left it to me but it's saved me loads of money in rent. Paul's got the little flat in London for when he's working and we give each other lots of time to do our own thing but when we get together we like to party. We go to the theatre, we see our friends, have fancy holidays.' Sophie put her head on one side, distracted. 'Maybe you should think about getting a dog?'

'I'd love to, but I can't right now,' Kate says. 'You know I'm out at work a lot. It wouldn't be fair.'

'I guess that's true, but it's different for us. Ralph fits in well with our lives and it's lovely to come home to such a warm welcome every time we go out. If we go abroad, he stays with our lovely neighbours or Aunty Beryl and everyone's happy. Kids use up lots of money and time and... well... headspace. You can't do fun stuff whenever you want to if you've got a houseful of the little buggers.'

'No, but...' Kate stalled. She couldn't begin to explain the gnawing grief she still felt at not becoming a mother. The sadness and secrets in her past were always waiting in the wings for her to drop her guard. One secret in particular haunted her more than most. She pushed it out of her mind. Only Howard knew the truth, and he wouldn't tell. He wouldn't dare.

2

Sophie hadn't noticed the fact that Kate was now staring into space, lost in her memories. 'Anyway, we didn't go down that road, the having-sprogs-thing, so there's no point in discussing it, is there?' she said, getting her phone out and flipping through her diary. 'Let's get the next appointment in the calendar before I go. It's a good job I make the effort to come here and tidy you up, because you'd never bother to find a new hairdresser if I didn't. You'd look like a yeti or Rip Van Winkle by now.'

'Cheers.'

'It's true. If you didn't have the job in the café, you'd probably never be out of your pyjamas.'

'I'm okay. Nobody needs to worry about me. I'm a bit lonely but that's par for the course after the last year. I'm still getting my head round losing Dad and then Howard going.'

'Yes, I know, but you should be getting out more now. You're popular, you always have been. I bet they miss you loads at the school and it wasn't just the children who loved you. The mums and dads at the school felt the same, you could tell. How many godchildren have you got now? I've lost track.'

Kate smiled. 'Oh, there are loads of them. Plus Elsie, of course. She's the one I see most often.'

'Elsie's Sam's daughter, isn't she? He did well to get custody of her when his girlfriend left him high and dry. He was only a kid himself at the time, to be fair.'

'He was seventeen. It was six years ago but it sometimes seems like only yesterday. He still looks like a teenager. Can't remember if I told you, but Sam works in the café with me now so it's easier for me to help out with Elsie.' Kate looked across at the wall by the kitchen door. From top to bottom it was covered in drawings and photos pinned to a giant cork board. 'That's my gallery,' she said. 'Most of the pictures are by Elsie but the others send me some now and again. I've got photos of them all up there too.'

Sophie reached out to give Kate a hug. 'You're an angel, that's what you are.' Still holding Kate by the shoulders, Sophie stood back to look at her. 'If only you'd just agree to smarten yourself up a bit, you'd be absolutely perfect.'

'Huh. I thought best friends were meant to like you how you are. And anyway, these are my favourite jeans.'

Sophie tutted. 'I'm your best mate whatever you're wearing, obviously, but those jeans are the darkest blue you can buy and I bet they've got a label on that says comfort fit. Yes, I thought so. And you've dug out that ancient blue T-shirt and the navy cardi again. You had those on last time I was here, I'm sure you did.'

'It's not navy, it's indigo.' Kate could hear the defensive tone in her voice. 'We can't all have your flair for clothes.' Today, Sophie was modelling her usual stylish collection, including sunflower-patterned leggings, a bright green sweatshirt and a diamante headband holding back her short white-blonde hair. Her multiple piercings glinted every time she moved her head, giving her an extra sparkle. Even her voice was exotic compared to Kate's, with its mellow Australian undertones that were only slightly diminished by her years in England.

Kate looked down at herself. 'I'm comfy. They're my at-home clothes.'

'Yes, and they're almost the same as the going-out ones, aren't they? If you ever did go out, that is. You used to love being colourful. I still remember that rainbow bikini and the matching sarong you had when we first met. Every time we went to the beach you turned heads. Let's face it, everything in your wardrobe is either black, grey or navy now.'

'Indigo.' But Kate could tell Sophie wasn't listening. She was glancing around the room and frowning.

'It's very beige in here, isn't it? The only splash of colour in this room used to be that lovely jade-green sofa. Where's it gone? Oh, don't tell me,' she said. '*He* took it.'

'It was on HP. Hire purchase, or actually, Howard purchase,' Kate added, seeing Sophie's puzzled expression. 'He's still paying for it. He chose it, after all.'

'And where's the great big flashy TV? Surely he didn't leave you without a telly?'

Kate automatically glanced over to where Howard's pride and joy had sat, completely dominating the little room. 'Again, it was his. Bang and Olufsen, top of the range. I didn't want it.'

Sophie's face showed her horror. 'But... what do you do in the evenings? The selfish git, how could he? You love watching TV.'

'I... well, I usually go to bed quite early these days and watch something on my iPad. I get lonely down here on my own in the evenings.'

The dismal words seemed to lie between them, making Kate feel even more pathetic than she did before. She knew Sophie would never stand for such behaviour from her partner, but her friend had always been so sure of herself. Paul and Sophie had met on the Gold Coast during one of her extended jaunts and Paul's only long-haul venture. They'd been married for the past decade after both had spent many years previously being contentedly single. They were even happier now than when their whirlwind romance took off. How did they do it? Kate wished, not for the first time, that she had some of Sophie's bottle. It was no fun being the eternal wimp in a relationship, and now it was way too late to do anything about it.

'What's your secret, Soph?' she asked. 'How come you and Paul are so blissed out all the time?'

Sophie laughed. 'You're joking, aren't you? We have our rows like everyone else. Anyone who says they never argue with their partner's either a liar or so wimpish they can't bring themselves to talk back.'

'But you're happy?'

'Yep, I guess so. Don't wanna tempt fate. You know, like in those *Hello* magazine interviews when the celebs go on and on about how much in *lurve* they are and the next thing is, you're reading about their divorce in the papers.'

Kate pondered on this for a moment. 'I think there must be some deep secret, though, something I don't know about.'

'To a good marriage, do you mean? Or any kind of long-term relationship?'

'Either. Both.'

'Seriously? I've got absolutely no idea.' She laughed. 'P'raps ours works because we spend so much time apart. Right, enough of this heavy stuff, let's think about colours,' said Sophie briskly. 'Do you really like indigo best these days, or is it just easier to blend in?'

'No, I still like lots of different shades. And before you say any more, this has definitely been an indigo kind of day but I *have* got other things I can wear.'

'I'm sure you have, but when are they going to see the light of day? I can come and help you, if you like? I'm really good at make-overs.'

Kate flinched. 'No, it's okay. I can do it myself. I promise I'll have a go at sorting out my wardrobe, just as soon as I've got time.'

Sophie picked up her hairdressing bag in one hand and gave Kate a hug with her free arm. 'Okay, I believe you... I think. Look, I'm going to have to dash. I told Aunty Beryl I'd cook tonight. She wants her favourite: chips, pork sausages with onion gravy and mushy peas,' said Sophie, shuddering. 'You've got to hand it to her, that woman's got the digestive system of a twenty-year-old. We can talk on the phone anytime about all this, though. You need taking in hand, girl. And Katie?'

'Yes?'

'It's all very well making sure all your godchildren are okay, but don't forget about yourself, will you? You'll be fifty soon.' Sophie looked down at her fingers as she counted, then said, 'September's only eight months away. It's probably time you took stock.'

'I really don't want reminding about the big birthday.'

'I know you don't, but think about what I've said, won't you? There's no need to go blonde just yet, but something's got to happen. You're stagnating.'

'Cheers. What a lovely thought.' Kate pulled a hideous face but Sophie didn't smile.

'I mean it. Next time I'm here I want to see that you've made some changes in your life, okay? And I'm giving you a deadline.'

'How do you mean?' This sounded serious. Kate's stomach fluttered alarmingly.

'This has got to be your year, right? By Christmas, you're

going to show me that you've left the past behind and started all over again.'

'Yeah, well, that's not as easy as it sounds.' Kate saw the look on Sophie's face. 'Okay, I'll try. I really will. I just wish we could meet up more often, Soph. You're always either working or off up to London to see Paul.'

Her friend regarded Kate, head on one side. 'My house isn't that far away, you know. It's twenty minutes' walk at the most, hardly even out of the village. You could visit me sometimes instead of us leaving it six weeks or more every time. Why not come and stay the night? A sleepover, like the kids say.' She waited for a response and when none came, she sighed heavily. 'But you won't, will you? You never venture anywhere further than Willowbrook Park café these days. How long is it since you had a holiday?'

'I... well...'

'Exactly. So shall we start to think about *you* for a change, darl?'

Kate couldn't think of a reply. Sophie checked her watch. 'Jeez, look at the time, I'm off. Those sausages won't cook themselves. Think about it, though. The spare bed's always made up. Just give me a few hours' notice to get the gin and tonic in and hoover round and you can come over anytime. I'll even lend you my second-best dressing gown. See you.'

With a final wave, Sophie left, stepping over the low wall that divided the tiny front garden from Beryl's. Kate watched her friend let herself in next door and then turned to look at the view that always soothed her soul, however ruffled she was feeling. The village green stretched out ahead, with its trailing willow trees and the brook that hopped and skipped over mossy rocks, giving local children the perfect place to play Pooh Sticks from the narrow wooden bridge that crossed it. The path that wound its way round in front of the houses led to The Fox and Fiddle where Kate had spent many sociable hours in the past, but hardly visited any more. A few early punters were already gathering for Happy Hour, and their voices rang out across the grass, making Kate think of chilled white wine and raucous pub quizzes.

Sophie's visit was always a breath of fresh air, but this time it had brought with it a turmoil of mixed feelings. Frustration at being put so firmly on the spot mingled with the very first stirrings of hope. It had been a difficult few months but for some reason, this chilly January Saturday felt like a new beginning. Kate couldn't quite face the thought of going over to the pub, let alone sleeping in a strange bed at Sophie's house, but change was in the air. Her indigo day must be the last one, at least for a while. From now on it would be brighter colours and a lighter heart. All she needed to do was to figure out how to begin.

3

Kate peered at her watch, hoping it would tell her that it was nearly bedtime. This had been happening far too often lately and she was ashamed of herself for wanting time to fly, but the days had sometimes dragged since Howard left. Although she hadn't particularly wanted him to return from work, it was a focal point. Dinner had to be thought about, which sometimes meant a quick dash to the shop on the corner if Kate hadn't planned ahead.

This was always a good chance for a chat with Mrs Nightingale who ruled the roost at Willowbrook General Stores, a grand name for the small shop at the end of Fiddler's Row. Mrs N (nobody except Beryl and her acolytes ever dared to call her Sylvia) was ferocious and prickly in equal measures but she'd known Kate for years and it was comforting to speak to someone who knew the Baxter family history inside out. Also, Mrs N had her finger firmly on the pulse when it came to village life and politics, which was helpful now Kate wasn't in the thick of the action at the primary school. Each visit to the shop was like a local news bulletin, complete with sniffs and folded arms if the details were salubrious.

Grabbing her duffle coat from the hook on the back of the door, Kate thrust her purse into her pocket and headed down the path to the shop. She was in dire need of either wine or chocolate tonight. Probably chocolate would be less likely to leave her with a feeling of self-loathing at three in the morning.

'Well, look at you with your fancy haircut,' said Mrs Nightingale as Kate approached the counter.

'I didn't think it looked any different, to be honest,' said Kate, glancing at herself in the mirrored wall tiles behind the till. 'I'm surprised you noticed.'

'You don't get much past me, dear. I saw Beryl's Sophie go by earlier. She did me a perm last time and it's still in good shape so I didn't need her this month.' Mrs Nightingale patted her tight grey curls proudly. Her hair was so stiff with hair spray that Kate knew it wouldn't dare to move, even if gale-force winds hit the village. The older lady pursed her lips.

'What are you after for tonight then? Bottle of Chardonnay, is it?'

'No wine, thanks. I'm just going to get some dark chocolate,' Kate said, choosing two bars of her favourite brand. 'There's a good film on later.'

'Life on the edge, eh?' said Mrs N, smirking. 'You want to be getting out more, dear. There are still some nice young men available. Well, when I say young...' She peered over her glasses at Kate. 'You don't want to push your luck. Isn't it the big five-oh this September? I always remember, because you're the same age as my Christopher and a couple of years older than our Lennie, isn't that right? All good chums together growing up.'

Kate decided not to put Mrs N right about these supposed close friendships. Christopher wasn't too bad but Lennie had always been a thorn in her side. She also ignored the reference to the birthday and cut to the chase. 'I don't need a man.'

'Of course you don't. Me neither, when I come to think of it. We're strong women, you and me. The kids keep telling me I should retire but I've got staff and family to help out. I can pick and choose when I work these days.'

'Lucky you.'

'I know. Well, enjoy your film. I'm going to shut up shop, soak my feet in a bowl of hot, soapy water and have a plate of fried onions later. You won't find a man who'd put up with that, I can tell you.'

'No, you're probably right.' Kate paid for her purchases, trying not to visualise the scene. She said goodbye and left the shop quickly, speeding up as she got closer to home. Suddenly, her little house felt very much like a refuge. She was glad she'd left a light on. It looked welcoming through the window and almost cosy, despite the lack of furniture. Kate's cottage, number six Fiddler's Row, was right in the middle of the terrace and she loved the symmetry of the curve of eleven cottages, each one with a small front garden, uneven roof tiles green with moss in some places and a variety of colours on the front doors. Some of these doors were smarter than others, with fresh paint and shiny brass numbers. Others hadn't stood the test of time so well or had been left to the mercies of the weather.

The door of number six was glossed in a tasteful mid-grey. Kate had chosen the colour and done it herself the year before. Beryl's door was much brighter, sporting scarlet paint, and had a large brass five by the side of it. In the summer, Beryl's huge hanging basket always provided a vibrant splash of clashing colours but for the moment, the purple and blue shades of the more subtle winter pansies were lingering until the weather was warm enough for the new planting of the spring.

The brilliant white of Beryl's double-glazed windows made a startling contrast to her door, and the whole effect was kept sparkling by the regular cleaner that Sophie and her parents clubbed together to pay for when the old lady had begun to fret about letting her standards slip. Kate suspected that the reluctance to clean was more because it took time away from Beryl's hectic social life, but who could blame her? Beryl and her friends had much more going on than Kate did, and none of them would see eighty again. Sophie was right. She really needed to take stock of her life if the local octogenarians were leading the way when it came to fun.

It was still too early to cook the simple pasta dish that Kate had lined up for this evening and she really mustn't start on the chocolate yet. Maybe she should attempt some experiments with food that took more time to get ready. At least then the rest of the evening wouldn't go on so long. As she pondered on this idea, Kate's phone buzzed with a message from Sophie. Her eyes widened as she read it.

> Hey, mate. Aunty B's just told me that the Meadowthorpe Morris Men are at the pub tonight. They don't usually go out much in January but they're doing a special fund raiser. Do you fancy going over? I could murder a pint. They're a great bunch, do you remember last time? X

It had been a while since Kate had ventured into The Fox and Fiddle, partly due to her general lack of enthusiasm for socialising these days but also because it had been her dad's local, and being there made her miss him more than ever. Did she want to go over to the pub with Sophie? She certainly did remember the last time she and Sophie had seen the MMMs, as they were known locally. It had been a riot of laughter with too much beer, but that night was not long before her dad had died and so the memories were bittersweet. He'd been an enthusiastic part of the group for years, whacking sticks and jingling bells with gusto. After a moment, Kate typed her answer back.

Can't face it, sorry. Too soon after Dad.

There was no response for at least five minutes, and Kate was beginning to worry that she'd offended Sophie when the next message pinged into view.

And you think he'd want you to sit at home and moulder? Get your best jeans on, eat something to line your stomach and try and find a jumper that isn't navy. I'm calling for you at 7 on the dot. Beryl and her sidekicks are coming too. They're always good for a laugh.

It was too much of an effort to say no again, and Kate sensed a flicker of something that felt almost like enthusiasm. She stashed her chocolate in the fridge, put the pasta on to boil and went upstairs to rummage in the wardrobe drawer.

An hour later, dressed in jeans and an over-sized burgundy sweater that could almost have been described as jolly, Kate had finished her dinner but still had a little while to wait. She made herself comfortable on the bed and spread out the handful of photographs she'd unearthed along with the jumper. They were all from the era when Sophie had burst on the scene, fresh from Sydney after a passionate but disastrous relationship with a surfer dude called Jason. Her parents had thought a few weeks with Beryl would take their daughter's mind off her problems. Sophie initially rejected this simple solution to her woes but to everyone's surprise, she'd fallen in love with English village life and opted to stay with her equally rebellious aunt long term.

'Beryl's the naughty sister,' Sophie told Kate soon after they met at the pub. 'She really gets me, and she's happy if I stick around a lot longer. Hey, I've had a thought. You and me could do something together. How do you fancy catering college? There's one in the town, Beryl says. Meadowthorpe, isn't it? I love cooking. Or have you got other plans?'

As it happened, Kate was drifting at the time, unsure whether to bite the bullet and head for university or to mark time and carry on aimlessly finding casual work for a while. Catering college sounded like a good halfway house. Her father was cranking up the oh-so-subtle pressure for her to stay locally. For a pragmatic medical man in his working world, Ted was the worst kind of worrier when it came to his daughter and hated the idea of Kate flying the nest. Also, Kate's mother, Caroline, had almost reached the end of her tether trying to keep tabs on Jamie, who seemed to find new trouble to get into with every week that passed. If Kate signed up for a local course, she should probably try to give her mum some much-needed back-up to get her younger brother back on the rails.

As it turned out, Jamie had other ideas about being sensible, and by the time Kate and Sophie's course finished he was on the verge of sliding into even more dangerous waters. And that was where Kate's future husband entered the picture. A novice golfer himself, if Howard hadn't got involved in the nick of time through a new scheme run by the golf club to encourage teenagers to get off the streets and onto the green, Kate knew Jamie's story could have panned out very differently.

At this point, everything changed for Kate, because Sophie decided to take a long break to visit her mum and dad in Australia before settling permanently in Willowbrook and Howard made it clear that he wasn't just hanging around the Baxter home to keep an eye on his protégé. To begin with, Kate was flattered that he obviously lusted after her so desperately but soon found a tug of war going on with herself right in the middle.

Kate picked up one of the photographs and studied the body language. In it, she was sitting on the swinging seat in Beryl's garden on a bright summer's day, sandwiched in between Howard and Sophie. Jamie was lying on the grass at their feet smoking something dodgy, as she remembered. All of their faces were sullen. Kate remembered Beryl getting her camera out and bellowing 'smile'. Nobody complied.

'Why won't you come to Sydney with me, Katie?' Sophie had wailed, just before the photo was taken. 'You know you want to.'

'Who says she wants to?' Howard snapped. 'Kate's better off here. I know for a fact Ted doesn't want her to go with you.'

'Ah, phooey,' Sophie said. 'He just likes her being where he can keep tabs on her all the time. I'm sure it's not natural to be so clucky about your kids.'

'He ain't clucky about me, though,' Jamie said. 'He leaves all the flapping to Mum.'

'I know. You're the lucky one,' said Kate. 'It seems as if Dad's obsessed with the fear that I'll get murdered, or worse, if I go far from Willowbrook.'

'What's worse than being murdered then?' Jamie chipped in again from the floor, and was rewarded with three icy glares. 'Just asking,' he mumbled, rolling another tatty cigarette.

In the end, Howard had won the argument. Of course he had. He'd played his trump card by booking a trip to Portugal for himself, Kate and Jamie in a holiday complex right next to a golf course. Howard explained that he would coach Jamie by day while Kate saw the sights, sunbathed and swam, and at night they'd all go out on the town and eat delicious local food. Ted approved of Kate being supervised and Caroline sighed with relief at the thought of some respite from worrying about what Jamie might do next.

When the three returned, Sophie had already left for her own holiday, still furious with everyone, especially Kate. She was away for several weeks and by then, Jamie had thoroughly got the golfing bug, Kate had accepted Howard's very romantic proposal of marriage and she'd also decided to follow her original plan of applying for a university place to train as a teacher. Her ultimate aim was to have as large a family as she could manage, but there was plenty of time for both. It took a long time for Kate and Sophie's relationship to settle into its previous comfortable pattern, because Sophie had never been one of Howard's fans, but eventually they'd clawed back their equilibrium.

Kate was still lost in her memories of that torrid time when she heard three loud raps on the front door as it was flung open and Beryl's voice calling, 'Come out, come out, wherever you are! Sophie's sent me and the girls to make sure you don't back out of tonight's jolly.'

When Kate reached the top of the stairs she saw three upturned faces, all beaming.

'You look almost cheerful in that sweater, dear,' Beryl said. 'It's nice to see you with a bit of colour on for a change.'

'You can say that again,' said her friend Winnie. 'But showing a bit of boob wouldn't come amiss.' She glanced down at her own ample cleavage, proudly on display in a clinging crimson top. 'If you've got it, flaunt it, that's what I always say. That's a very high neckline you've got there.'

'Either legs or boobs, you need to make the most of your assets, Kate,' said Beryl. 'I've gone for legs tonight. Some people say you shouldn't wear tight trousers after a certain age but these ones do wonders for my bum, I reckon.' She did a twirl and Winnie applauded.

Anthea, whom Kate always thought of as *the posh one*, nudged the other two as Kate came down the stairs. 'Give her some space, you're crowding the poor treasure,' she said, stepping back onto Winnie's toe.

As Winnie hopped up and down, swearing under her breath, Kate viewed the three ladies, wishing she had a pair of sunglasses handy. Nobody could ever call *them* drab, she reflected, half admiringly and half in mild horror. Winnie, the most outrageous of the three, was resplendent in her red top, which she'd teamed with a long sparkly skirt and brilliant white trainers. A multi-coloured head wrap finished the look. Beryl was slightly less dazzling in purple velvet trousers and a pink tunic with sequins around the neck and hem, whereas Anthea looked almost understated compared to her friends, wearing many linen layers of aubergine, scarlet and silver-grey with at least five matching necklaces dangling over her ample chest. All three sported bright red lipstick and enough eyeshadow and liner to grace the cast of a high-quality drag show. They were stunning.

Linking arms with each other, the four women crossed the village green. Kate was glad her sweater was a warm one as the chill of the evening hit her. They met Sophie outside the pub, hopping up and down on the spot to keep warm. 'It's nights like this when I want to be back home and sitting on the beach, with the smell of the barbie in the air and my bare feet in the sand. Ah well, I can dream, and I've got to say they don't have entertainment like this back home. Are you ready for a great night out, Katie?'

Kate didn't answer because her attention had been caught by

the group of men standing by the pub's porch, underneath a swinging sign showing a wicked-looking fox playing a violin.

As the women approached, several heads turned.

'Katie,' called the nearest man, coming forward. 'We were just saying we wondered if you'd make it, ducky. Your dad would be really glad you did, I'm sure. Dr Ted was a real one-off. We do miss the old boy.'

'Hey, not so much of the old, Pete,' said one of the others who had an impressive white beard. 'I've got five years on The Doc and I'm definitely not old.'

'Come here and give us a hug, Katie. Ted was taken much too soon. We're going to do a little tribute for him later,' said Pete. 'And our fund raiser is for the heart ward at the hospital where he was... where he...'

'...died,' Kate completed the sentence. She hated all the euphemisms, such as 'passed' and 'gone to sleep'. Her father had been beyond treatment by the time he reached Meadowthorpe Infirmary but the staff had been wonderful. Ted had worked there as a young man and it had been clear he was still well-respected even in death. Kate was glad the coronary ward was getting some sort of recognition for their gentle care of her family in the immediate, nightmarish aftermath.

'See, told you it was the right thing to come over,' said Sophie, as Kate was enveloped in one bear hug after another.

'Lucky, lucky, lucky – that's what you are, girl,' hissed Winnie. 'I wouldn't mind a squeeze from some of these boys, I can tell you.'

Anthea and Beryl nodded. 'Me neither,' said Beryl. 'I'm partial to a bloke with a decent beard, so long as there's no food stuck in it.'

'Don't remind me,' said Anthea, shuddering. 'There was that

night when...' She broke off and whispered to Beryl who hooted with laughter.

'Yes, you dodged a bullet there. Anchovies, wasn't it?' she said, pulling a face. 'Never go for a pizza with a man who's got a beard, that's been my motto ever since.'

Kate let the hug-fest run its course, thinking it was best to get it over with now rather than when she'd had a drink and might be even more prone to tears. They finally made it into the pub, where the landlord greeted them at top volume.

'Blimey, the Three Witches have got back-up tonight,' he boomed. 'You're a brave lass, Kate. These girls will most likely drink you under the table. You should see them on quiz nights. It's a wonder they can see the answer sheet to write on by the final round.'

'Pipe down, Ned, and less of your cheek. Don't forget I used to change your nappies when you were a nipper,' said Winnie, reaching over the bar to poke him in the chest. 'Many a time you've peed in my eye, because you always used to fiddle with your...'

'I don't think the punters want to hear about that,' said Ned, holding up a hand and blushing.

A few guffaws from nearby drinkers made him redden even more, and Beryl came to his rescue.

'No more smut, Winnie,' she said. 'For now, anyway. Going back to what you were saying, Ned, we've decided we need a new name for our quiz team. The Three Witches makes us sound like nasty pieces of work. Any ideas?'

Ned put his head on one side, considering them. 'Fun Girl Three? The Three Degrees? Ladies Who Lunch?' he suggested.

Beryl, Winnie and Anthea looked at each other and shook their heads.

'How about The Lager Louts?' Ned said. 'No, that's no good

because you girls always drink fizz. Hey, I've got it. The Saga Louts.'

'What's that supposed to mean?' Sophie asked.

'Well, they're always planning holidays, aren't they, and they like the ones that are... you know what I mean... aimed at the...'

'Go on, spit it out,' said Anthea. 'The older clientele? And what's wrong with that? We know what we're getting with a Saga holiday, don't we, girls?'

Beryl nodded. 'We do. And we always liven the old dears up. You should see some of the poor souls. They don't even get up off their backsides for the disco night. What right-minded individual can sit still when the DJ's playing "See My Baby Jive"?'

'The Saga Louts. I like it,' said Winnie. 'You're not as daft as you look, Ned. Put us down for a table for the next quiz. We'll knock the spots off the other teams.'

That important matter settled, Sophie put in the order for herself and Kate, Beryl's gang having decided to get their own round in case they wanted to go on to a bottle or two of Prosecco later.

'Cheers! You're out of the house at last,' said Sophie, handing Kate a brimming pint of bitter. 'I knew you could do it, with a bit of a nudge.'

'Talking of houses, this round's *on* the house, for Ted,' said the landlord. Sophie flashed him a smile.

'When does the dancing start?' Kate asked, looking over at the door, still unsure whether she was looking forward to or dreading the performance.

'Good question. Right now, as it happens. Morris time,' Ned bellowed. 'Outside, everyone, and don't you three hog all the patio heaters this time,' he said to Beryl as she urged her friends forward. 'You should have put your coats on if you're cold.'

'And deprive the clientele of all this magnificence, darling?'

said Anthea, doing a twirl and almost capsizing Kate's pint as she left the pub.

Obediently, the rest of the customers trooped onto the green, glasses in hand. There was a babble of excited conversation as they formed a wide circle around the dancers who were already in place, with their snowy-white shirts and black knee britches. Each one was wearing pristine knee-length white stockings and black shoes. They had yellow sashes around their chests and clusters of bells at their knees and looped into their shoelaces. Kate's eyes instinctively searched for her dad before the realisation hit her that he'd never dance with his friends on the green again. Instead, in Ted's usual place was a smaller, more wrinkled man and over on the far side of the group, the two other very large newcomers shuffled their feet nervously. Kate avoided looking at them as much as possible, unreasonable resentment making her hot with grief.

As the accordion player struck up the first tune and the resident fiddler raised her bow, Pete stepped forward. 'Take it away, Martha,' he said to the woman with the violin. 'This one's for Dr Ted.' The others all looked towards Kate and bowed their heads slightly. 'We loved him, we miss him, we wish he was here. It was one of his favourites because wherever we were performing around the country, he said it reminded him of home. "The Willow Tree". For Ted and for Willowbrook.'

As one, the men nodded to Kate and began the dance. At first her eyes were too full of tears to see much, but when Sophie slipped her hand into Kate's and gripped hard, she at last started to enjoy herself. The swirling accordion, the leaping melody of the fiddle, the thump of the wooden staffs and the jingling bells were all immensely comforting. By now, a small crowd had gathered, and Kate noticed one man standing slightly apart from the others, arms folded. He was bearded, like most of the Morris men but taller than the rest, and wearing a long black overcoat that made him look vaguely like an undertaker. As Kate observed him watching the dancers, a serious expression on his face, his eyes met hers and he smiled as if he knew her.

'Who's that?' whispered Sophie, following her gaze. 'I thought he looked a bit grumpy but he's a cracker when he smiles.'

'I'm not sure. I hope he isn't going to come over.'

'And *I* hope he is. Loosen up, Katie. The night's young.'

Kate ignored her friend and the man turned his attention back to the entertainment. The dance was now in full swing, and as her sadness retreated, Kate felt overwhelmed with relief that she'd made it to the pub at last.

'Thanks for bringing me,' Kate whispered to Sophie. 'This is perfect.'

'Yep.' Sophie leaned closer. 'I know you've still got a few issues to get over with your mum, and maybe even with some stuff to do with your dad too. Cut them both some slack, Kate. They only wanted the best for you. Get your memories out, deal with them and then put the buggers to bed, yeah?'

Kate didn't answer for a moment or two. She was well aware that her relationship with her parents and brother had been complicated. She'd struggled to find a balance between a mother constantly jittery with anxiety for her son and a father hell-bent on wrapping his daughter in what felt like way too much cotton wool. Jamie's early behaviour problems at school and subsequent pushing the boundaries to breaking point had put a huge strain on any brother–sister friendship they might have had in the early years. Now, he was living in France with their mum on hand, a glamorous wife and three adorable children. It was hard not to be envious.

'What did I do wrong, Soph?' she asked eventually.

'Nothing at all, darl,' said Sophie, downing the rest of her pint. 'Let's have another one. The night is young and... hey, I think Anthea's pulled already.'

The two of them looked across to where Anthea was exchanging hot glances with one of the burlier new dancers, causing him to miss his partner's stick and swipe the unfortunate man on the head.

'Oopsy,' said Anthea, winking at Kate and Sophie.

Giggling, Kate picked up her own and Sophie's empty glasses and headed for the bar. This was no time for introspection. Soon she might well do some serious thinking about her life, but for now, the music, the laughter and the jingle of the bells was making her giddy with what felt almost like hope. Tonight was for dancing. Time enough for soul-searching tomorrow.

4

A fresh breeze whirled a few wet leaves around on the grass down by the water. Kate shivered and wrapped her scarf more closely around her neck as she flopped down on her favourite bench at the country park. So far, February had been disappointing. She'd checked today's weather forecast on her phone and was hopeful that although it might be chilly there would be some sunshine by now, but that hadn't happened yet, although the billowing clouds definitely looked as if they might part soon.

Kate's decision to take Sophie's advice about the year of changes hadn't come to much so far, apart from a solitary online purchase which was still making her feel slightly edgy. Choosing a bright yellow raincoat was easy, but wearing it with panache was proving to be trickier, even though there had been a long stretch of January and early February when torrential rain and high winds had swept the country. The news had been full of awful reports of flooding and none of the villagers had ventured far from home unless they'd had no choice. Sophie had cancelled all her hairdressing appointments and stayed in London so there was no opportunity for a team talk and Kate had easily slipped into torpor again, only leaving her house in her old blue waterproof to work in the almost-deserted café and scuttling home as soon as her shifts were over.

Now, the rain clouds were clearing at last and Kate had no excuse to stay indoors. It was time to take stock and give the new coat a proper airing. Thinking back to the night in the pub left Kate feeling gloomy. It had been fun, if emotional, but it was a one-off. She needed to stir herself and make a start on her next steps before Sophie descended again to check up on her friend's progress. Or lack of it. A stroll around the rolling, partly wooded expanse of Willowbrook Country Park was always a good way to cheer up, and Kate only needed to walk the mile across the village green, up the lane and over the bridge that spanned the River Nene and she was there, right by the tarmacked track that led to the main car park and the café known as Pat's Place.

The café, where Kate now worked, was housed in one of the stable blocks that had originally belonged to Willowbrook Manor. The grand old house had been destroyed by fire many years ago and now its grounds were open to the public, with the other outbuildings having been turned into a visitor centre and education rooms. Kate's shifts varied from week to week and she still had plenty of time before today's stint in the café began, even if the weather was too chilly to sit around for long, but her yellow coat was fleece-lined and she was armed with a flask of hot chocolate, so was soon feeling cosy and a lot happier. All of the memorial benches in the country park were fine places to sit when you wanted to have a good think. Within five minutes of finding a place to settle, her spirits always lifted.

You couldn't be sad when you were looking at views like these, thought Kate, with the rippling waters of the lakes and the quacking of the wildfowl who were going about their busy lives everywhere. There were plenty of benches to choose from here and Kate liked to be fair. She'd sat on them all at one time or another since she'd started working at the café, but the most recently installed one had the best view of the lake and the small island in the middle where the swans liked to nest when the time was right. She could see them circling at the moment, wondering if it was worth following the ducks to see what was in Kate's rucksack.

'I can't wait to see your cygnets when you get round to it,' she told them. 'This is my favourite time of year. New life, and all those fluffy feathers. Maybe if Howard and me had...'

The next words stuck in her throat. It was best not to say such things out loud. The four lost babies were just a memory now. One after the other, disappearing along with her hopes as Kate watched Howard getting more negative each time, his passion for golf increasing as his interest in his wife waned. Was that any different to the way other marriages functioned, though? Nobody knew what went on behind closed doors in other people's houses.

Since her time with Sophie, Kate had made a tentative start on the reorganisation of her life by listening to a series of podcasts on depression. They hadn't helped much yet, but she was persevering. The latest one advised being more forceful with your memories. She wasn't sure if that meant she should do what Sophie had instructed and face them, or the exact opposite. At the moment, Kate was working hard at keeping all anxious thoughts at bay. To distract herself from anything unsettling, she stood up and turned to read the inscription on the bench again.

In memory of Frances (Frankie) Clifford, our sunshine girl

10 February 1987 – 1 December 2022

Four Seasons in One Day

Not for the first time, Kate wondered about Frankie's short life, but her attention was soon caught by a man approaching from the end of the lake nearest to the water sports centre. He was even more warmly wrapped up than Kate, dressed as if for an arctic winter rather than a brisk morning in February, with a woolly hat pulled down firmly over his ears, and a scarf tucked into the neck of his jacket. One of his thickly gloved hands clutched a bunch of bright yellow roses. He stopped walking when he saw Kate sitting on the bench and did an abrupt U-turn, striding off in the opposite direction on the path that would take him right the way round the smaller lake.

Kate watched the man go. He seemed vaguely familiar, and not just because she'd seen him in the café a few times over the last couple of months. He'd usually been alone, but now and again he had an older lady on his arm. Kate guessed the woman must be his mum by the way she ticked him off when he forgot to get the kind of jam without seeds that she insisted on having with her scones, but she'd never seemed particularly affectionate towards him.

It occurred to Kate that the man had probably been heading for this very bench. What if he was here for a purpose? It would explain the flowers. Oh, good grief, the first date on the bench was actually... today. Mortified that she must have got in the way of an emotional pilgrimage, Kate gathered up her flask, her tin mug and her sandwich box and bundled them into the rucksack. It was time to leave, but something stopped her from disappearing completely. She strolled past the next two benches to the left, reading each inscription as she passed as a mark of respect, and then climbed the hill. There was another seat right at the top that provided a view of most of the park and there was still half an hour before she needed to be at the café.

Ten minutes later and feeling rather windswept, Kate spied

the man coming nearer again. He must have done a complete circuit of the lake at great speed and the brisk walk had obviously warmed him up because he'd ditched the gloves, undone the jacket and taken off his hat and scarf. Closer to, she could see that he was broad shouldered and well over six feet tall, with the kind of beard that always reminded her of Richard Osman from all those game shows that were so soothing to watch. She gave him a few brownie points for not stooping. Her mother had always drilled into Kate that people who stooped were at an instant disadvantage because everyone would think they were ashamed of their height. There hadn't been much point in this advice in the end because Kate, as in most other areas, was seen by her family as average. Medium height, mid-brown hair, hazel eyes that fell short of Ted's chocolate-brown ones and a tendency to panic in exams so that her results were uninspiring.

The man's short dark hair was standing on end now and above the beard, his cheeks were flushed. His pace slowed as he neared Kate's new favourite bench and glanced around, after which he sat down, placing the roses on the seat. He took off his black-framed glasses and pulled out what looked like a very clean white handkerchief. Watching as the man proceeded to carefully polish his spectacles, Kate marvelled that some people still carried proper cotton hankies. Her father had never gone out without one, freshly laundered by Caroline and neatly pressed, but nobody else she knew bothered with them. Fascinated, though not wanting to intrude, Kate tried not to stare but her quarry was too preoccupied to look around and spot her so she felt quite safe to stay put. With his back to the bench, he put his glasses back on and began to speak in a deep, carrying voice, the stiff breeze carrying the words up the hill.

'Hello, Frankie,' he intoned.

'If you were here
I'd buy you a beer,
But instead I've brought this
to toast you, Sis.'

Kate reflected that this was probably the worst poem she had ever heard. It didn't even scan properly. Fascinated, she leant forward to see what might be going to happen next. The man reached into an inside pocket and brought out two items. It was hard to see exactly what they were but after a moment, Kate realised that one was a phone and the other a quarter bottle of champagne. She heard the pop of the cork, and as the man raised the bottle to his lips he must have pressed a button because even at this distance she could hear the sound of the unmistakeable introduction to one of her favourite Abba songs. It was 'Dancing Queen'.

As the music played, the object of Kate's interest stood up, put the bottle on the ground and peeled the wrapping from the flowers, spreading them out across the bench. He picked up the champagne again and poured a few splashes of it over the brass plaque before solemnly bowing his head.

Kate put a hand up to her mouth to stop a sob coming out. The poor soul. Maybe she should go over and say something sympathetic. The man was drinking the rest of the champagne now, in thirsty gulps. Kate hoped he wasn't going to be driving any time soon. Just as the thought crossed her mind, a loud pipping noise came from the direction of the car park and he pushed a sleeve up to check his watch. Slipping the empty bottle inside his coat, he headed off at a fast pace, leaving the flowers strewn across the bench and one very curious woman looking down from the hill. As he left, he stuffed the plastic wrapping from the flowers into a nearby bin. Kate nodded her approval.

One of her pet hates was people who left floral tributes around to rot, still swathed in cellophane.

'Well, fancy that,' said Kate out loud. She heard the bleep of her phone alarm reminding her it was time to go over to the café. The day seemed rather flat now, although as she made her way down the hill, she registered that the splash of buttercup yellow the flowers made was a cheerful sight, just like her new coat, which was beginning to feel less like a beacon attracting attention and more of a hopeful step into the future. She hoped the man would come back soon. There was something touching about him... something vulnerable and yet he was... the word that came to mind was *substantial*, which didn't sound all that appealing, but summed him up pretty well. He was good-looking in a rugged kind of way but she had a feeling that he was the sort of man who probably didn't realise it.

As she pondered all this, it dawned on Kate where she'd seen the man before, apart from in the café. Of course! He was one of the customers who'd been standing quite near to her and Sophie outside The Fox and Fiddle, also watching the Morris dancers. She remembered now how he'd towered over the others around him and had glanced across at her a couple of times, almost as if he was going to say something, but then changed his mind. It seemed odd that she hadn't recognised him at the time, but Kate supposed that the emotion of the evening had pushed everything else out of her mind, plus the long black coat he'd been wearing was very different to his usual garb of jeans and a battered leather flying jacket.

The memory of the man looking so tentative rather than trying to strike up a conversation that night made her decide that he probably wouldn't be super-confident and therefore too scary to talk to. It would be nice to speak to him if he called in again for coffee. They'd exchanged wary smiles a couple of times when she'd served him so perhaps they were already part-way there, but Kate quailed at the thought. She wouldn't want to risk a rebuff. Even so, there was the tiniest spark of hope inside her that she could be brave enough to give him a better welcome next time he was in the café.

Maybe she would find a way to say hello, perhaps even strike up a conversation. It could be that this man needed a new friend just as much as Kate did. An unthreatening person to chat to on a bench. The thought of this prospect warmed Kate as she jog-trotted towards the café, boots clunking on the tarmac path. The seeds of the dream had been sown. Now it just remained to be seen if they would grow.

5

20 MARCH 2001

Kate is sitting in the rocking chair gazing out of the front window. She's in the living room of the home she shares with Howard and her hands are clasped over her stomach in the age-old protective gesture of women who suspect they might be about to be stepping into a whole new world, one that's full of cribs and nappies and broken nights and tiny woolly cardigans. Can it be true?

She looks at the pregnancy test she bought from the chemist in Meadowthorpe this afternoon. Mrs Nightingale's shop doesn't stock them and even if it did, Kate wouldn't want her news being broadcast to the whole village. Not yet, anyway. She's been putting off getting a test because it seems like tempting fate, after all the months when nothing has happened. It would really be better to wait until tomorrow morning when the results should be stronger and more accurate, but it's no good. She needs to do this now, before Howard gets home from work. There can't really be any doubt. She's been feeling very queasy and her breasts are so tender that lately she's been avoiding going to bed until

Howard's safely asleep, because even if he only rolls against her by accident, it's too painful to bear.

The lavish bunch of lilies her husband presented her with this morning is already scenting the room with its heavy fragrance. Three years. It's not a perfect marriage but they get along reasonably well for most of the time. Kate's assistant job at the school is fulfilling, but the longer she works there, the less likely it seems that she will ever bite the bullet and go to university to get her qualifications. She's seen the teachers' workload increase almost daily and the recent Ofsted inspection has put a massive strain on all the staff. Better to stay put.

And now, there's this new excitement to take on board. If Kate *is* pregnant, she can work until nearly the time when the baby's born and then take maternity leave. There are plenty of others who are longing to step into her shoes. Teaching assistants' roles are like gold dust. The school holidays make the hours ideal for working mums. She might not even go back to work afterwards. More children could follow in quick succession, if she's lucky. Kate has no fear of taking charge of a whole brood of them. It's what she does best.

Leaving the comfort of the chair, she gets to her feet. Her whole body trembles with anticipation. It's not far to the bathroom but today it seems like a long way away, even though the house is what her mother calls *bijou and compact*. It's plenty big enough for the two of them. Kate loves its cosiness, but of course they'll need to upsize if the family expands and it'll be worth it if there are babies. They might move out into the local countryside. So long as Howard's near enough to the golf club to carry on with his main obsession, he'll agree to a bigger mortgage.

Kate is already halfway up the stairs with the pregnancy test in the pocket of her cardigan when an excruciating pain causes her to double up in agony. She sinks down, holding her stomach as the cramp takes hold. *No, no, no,* she screams silently. *This can't be happening.* But the cramps are getting worse, coming one after the other in quick succession. She crawls up the last few steps and collapses onto the landing, hearing Howard's key turning in the lock as she rolls herself into a tight ball. The last thing she remembers thinking as she drifts into unconsciousness is that the lilies are making the house smell exactly like a funeral parlour.

6

Milo turned his back on the lake and the distant bench and clambered back into the taxi that he'd booked both to bring and wait for him, nodding to the driver that he was ready to go back to Meadowthorpe. He couldn't bring himself to speak yet, but luckily Bob, who'd introduced himself at the outset and done his best to bond with Milo on the way to the country park, was oblivious to the problem. He prattled on happily about his grandchildren as Milo stared miserably out of the cab window, watching the tree-lined lane widen into the major road that would take him back to the office.

The champagne had left a sour taste in the back of Milo's throat. There hadn't been enough in the bottle to even blunt the edges of the pain he was feeling and playing her favourite tune had pushed him even further back down into his pit of grief instead of being the joyful celebration he'd hoped for. Memories of Frankie crowded in as they joined the dual carriageway and the car picked up speed.

'You okay, mate?' Bob said eventually as the silence became

oppressive. He peered at Milo in the rear-view mirror. Horrified, Milo realised that tears were pouring down his face.

'Yeah, yeah. Just... just had a bit of a bad day,' he croaked, wiping his eyes on the sleeve of his coat.

'Gets you like that sometimes, don't it? Life's a bitch and all that. About a woman, is it?'

Milo wondered how to answer this one. A woman, yes, but not a wife or a lover as the man probably imagined. The heart-rending grief was for his younger sister who often had all the capricious whims of a little girl and went away without saying goodbye, leaving a tornado of mixed feelings behind her. Remorse that he hadn't somehow managed to prevent her death was predominant today, along with a hefty dose of survivors' guilt. Frankie had been so much more charismatic and talented than Milo, in his parents' often expressed opinion. Whenever he saw the elderly, now-frail couple, he knew that however often he visited them, he could never make up for the yawning gap left by the loss of their treasured daughter. Every subject they talked about seemed to end up provoking tears from his mum and a sorrowful silence from his dad.

Unwilling to articulate any of this to a stranger, Milo just nodded again and got out his ear buds, tuning in to the playlist he'd made for today. Might as well have a good old wallow while he was at it. Bob shrugged and turned his radio up. The rest of the journey passed with them both in their separate bubbles of music. Milo's was mainly cheerful and upbeat, but when he got to the slower track about fields of gold he was very glad to see they'd reached a junction near to his flat.

'Here's fine, just drop me off, please,' he said, getting out his wallet and adding a generous tip to the already colossal amount on the meter. Who cared? It was worth it not to have to think about driving safely on a day like this. It had been risky to come here for this anniversary because it was bound to plunge him into deep sadness, but it was important to mark the occasion. Today would not only have been Frankie's birthday, but it was exactly a year since he and his sister had gone for their last run together. An unenthusiastic jogger, Milo had been persuaded to join Frankie before tea when they'd both been visiting their parents and, as always, had needed some space away from them.

'Come on, Moggers,' she'd said, knowing that the old nickname would most likely tug on his heartstrings. 'You're always saying you need more exercise after you've sat on your backside behind a desk all day and if last year's anything to go by, you're going to be eating your body weight in birthday cake and trifle later. Get your trackie bottoms on and let's get moving.'

Milo had rummaged in the random heap of clothes left behind years ago when they had both departed the family home. The result was a baggy pair of sweatpants and a T-shirt with an ancient gravy stain still visible. Frankie had looked him up and down, and giggled.

'Good job one of us has still got it,' she said, doing a twirl so he could admire her designer gym clothes and bright yellow trainers. 'Let's do this before you decide it's your nap time, you poor old sod.'

They'd taken the track that led to the river path. Milo had puffed and panted alarmingly to start with but after a mile or so he'd got into his stride and had almost been able to keep up with his sister, only skidding once and managing to right himself before he hit the ground. They ran alongside the river, which was in full spate after heavy rain. Milo was too breathless to chat for most of the way but Frankie had glanced over her shoulder every now and again to check he was keeping up and each time had rewarded him with one of her beaming smiles.

The memory of the last run was fresh in Milo's mind when

he'd woken up that morning. The only time he'd been back to the river since then was to support his parents as they scattered Frankie's ashes, so today he'd decided to go to the bench instead. At least there he might find some much-needed peace.

Calling in at his flat, Milo exchanged his jeans and jacket for the more formal clothes he wore to work, adding the long black overcoat that made him feel like the responsible financial advisor that he was, rather than his alter-ego of an over-aged teenager with a passion for eighties rock music, sizzlingly hot curries and collecting Terry Pratchett novels.

Back in the office, after putting in a few hours doing the most basic, mindless jobs he could find while his partner, as usual, picked up the showier front-of-house tasks, Milo felt justified in going home, although the place that went by that name these days didn't have any of the comforts you'd expect a successful financial advisor to have achieved. Since the depressing day when he'd moved into the sixties apartment block, he'd secretly thought of it as The Lime Green Palace. Whoever had lived there previously had had a taste for this shade, and the futon, the one easy chair and all the kitchen utensils that came with the rented flat matched each other in an intense blast of seventies kitsch. There were a few flashes of orange here and there to break up the acidic green effect but these only seemed to make the place more mind-blowingly like the beginning of a migraine, or a tropical fruit salad on speed.

Milo's marital nest had been in a quiet close of semi-detached Mock Tudor houses near the golf course. His ex, Marianne, had her eye on a much more upwardly mobile lifestyle for them both and wanted him to join her in taking up the sport but had soon realised he had neither the aptitude or enthusiasm for spending the day flicking a small white ball into the undergrowth and then wandering off to hunt for it. His wife had made her own friends at the club, one of whom had now offered her a bigger place with a jacuzzi and an outdoor pizza oven on the opposite side of the course. Tempted by such riches, she left without so much as a backward glance, taking their seventeen-year-old son with her.

The ending of the marriage was tough in some ways but the only real casualty in Milo's opinion was the fractured relationship he was now enduring with Luka. Over the years, the boy appeared to have swallowed all his mother's woes about Milo being a workaholic who had no time for his wife and child. This was true to some extent, but largely brought on by the fact that Marianne wanted the sort of luxurious lifestyle that could only be provided easily if both partners worked. She chose not to.

Milo's flat was in darkness by the time he got home but as he walked towards it he saw that there was someone waiting below his first-floor window, huddled in the porch. To begin with, alarm bells rang in his head. There had been a spate of robberies lately and one of his neighbours had only just replaced the locks on her front door. When he realised that the dark figure was no sneak thief but was son-shaped, his heart rate steadied and his spirits rose hopefully. Luka stepped out of the shadows when he spotted Milo.

'I've been here over an hour,' he said. 'I thought you'd be home by now. Mum said she'd heard you're not putting the stupid hours in any more. I don't suppose you need to, now you haven't got us to support.'

Milo sighed. 'Are you coming in?' he asked.

'Well, I'm not waiting here to give you a hug and go home,' Luka said. 'Too right I'm bloody coming in.'

The chilly air and stale smell of the shared hallway greeted them like the unwelcoming porch of a pub just before opening time, but they were soon through the foyer, up the concrete stairs and into Milo's apartment, which had a much more pleasant aroma of the spices he'd used to make last night's curry, complemented by a lingering hint of his favourite minty shower gel. Milo turned on the overhead light and Luka flinched. In the brutal glare of the high-watt bulb, Milo could see that his son's face was pale and drawn, with a vaguely green tinge that actually toned quite well with the furnishings. A sudden pang of protective love nearly floored him, but he pushed the feeling away and exchanged the main light for a couple of table lamps. The room immediately looked cosier as the lime greens faded in the soft glow. At least it was warm, and the futon was large, if hideously uncomfortable. Luka flopped into it with a grunt of relief that immediately turned into a wince.

'Aren't you feeling well?' Milo said, going through to the kitchen end of the room to put the kettle on.

'I'm fine,' Luka said. 'Just thought it was time I came to see where you were holed up?' He hiccupped and put a hand up to his mouth.

'Luka, have you been drinking?' The words were out before Milo could stop them.

'What if I have? What's it to you?'

Wordlessly, Milo carried on with his usual soothing coffee-making ritual, taking great care with grinding the beans and letting them steep in the pot. By the time he carried it over to Luka on a tray with two mugs, a plate of cookies and a sugar bowl, his son looked as if he was almost asleep. Milo busied himself pouring coffee and then reached the awkward moment of not knowing if his son took sugar these days. Saving him the bother of asking, Luka leaned over and added two heaped spoons to his mug, grabbing three biscuits with the other hand.

'I'm starving,' he muttered.

'Well, I can rustle up a bacon butty if you like,' Milo said, mentally going through the contents of his fridge. There were a couple of eggs, and if he toasted the bread Luka wouldn't notice that it was a bit past its best. Luka shook his head, munching cookies as if he hadn't eaten for weeks. 'Don't bother yourself,' he said, through a mouthful of crumbs. 'I guess you've forgotten I don't eat animals.'

Without asking permission, Luka stretched out a hand and took the TV controls. He flipped through several programmes at an annoying rate and then chose a channel playing a very old episode of *Top of the Pops.*

'Look at the state of that lot,' he said, grinning. 'Was that how they used to dance in your day? Really?'

Taking a large swig of coffee, Milo focused on the screen. There were girls in tank tops and hotpants swaying from side to side self-consciously, their long hair looped behind their ears. The band were wearing silver platform boots and had a heavy spattering of glitter on their cheeks.

'I'm only fifty-one, Luka,' he said, with mild bitterness. 'This is the seventies. I'd have been in primary school.'

Luka shrugged, clearly unconvinced. Milo wished his son didn't seem to either despise him or see him as an ageing joke. Over the years, their initially joyful relationship had slowly worsened. Since the split he'd sent various messages asking Luka over to the flat but all of them were ignored. If only Luka had given him some warning that he was going to drop by, Milo could have made the place seem more welcoming, cooked dinner, filled the fridge with... but again, the knowledge that he didn't know his son's tastes any more hit him hard.

'Does your mum know you're here?' he said eventually, kicking himself as he saw Luka's expression harden. Why hadn't he kept it light?

'Nah. She doesn't worry about me much now we've moved

into the big house,' Luka said, taking another couple of cookies and dunking one in the remains of his coffee. 'She's training for a golf tournament. Gym in the mornings, practice in the afternoons. It's serious stuff. They... she really wants to win this one.' He paused and then blurted out, 'I hate living there. Brad usually ignores me, even though Mum tries to make us like each other. I stay in my room most of the time.'

The spectre of Marianne's new partner, golf and otherwise, seemed to hang in the air. Luka's cheeks had a faint flush now, which made him look almost healthy. His long, lean body reminded Milo of himself at that age, although the shock of auburn hair was all from Marianne. His head was shaved at the sides and back but the top was a riot of mad curls. Over his nose, the smattering of freckles he'd also inherited from his mother stood out strongly. The combination of bright hair, pale skin and long-lashed green eyes was startling.

Luka had been rather a red baby, a chubby toddler and a gawky adolescent in turn but now Milo could see that his son was fearsomely attractive. When did that happen? It had only been about six months since they'd last met, but to be fair, that occasion had been so fraught with emotion that Milo probably wouldn't have noticed if Luka had grown an extra arm. He'd been moving out after weeks of long silences punctuated with ferocious rows, and Marianne had made the event as tricky as possible, arguing the toss about shared belongings she'd barely noticed before until the very moment that the van had finished loading the few items he'd cared enough about to fight for.

'So anyway, I bet you're wondering why I've rocked up here tonight?' said Luka, draining his coffee in one gulp. He looked a bit less unhealthy now, Milo thought with relief, although in his opinion his son was much too skinny.

'You know you're welcome any time,' Milo said, ignoring the

challenging tone of the question. 'I've invited you often enough. I would have liked to cook you dinner but I haven't been shopping yet this week.'

'Oh, you *are* still busy at work then?'

The sneering tone was getting stronger. Milo stretched his tired body, rolling his shoulders to relieve the ache that was spreading down his back. It had been a long day, and all the emotion at the country park was taking its toll now.

'I've been to Frankie's bench, actually,' he said at last. 'Are you planning on going there, or are *you* too busy?'

With the onus back on him, Luka looked thrown for a moment. 'I... well, I probably will. I could cycle over. Look, Dad... I'm sorry I didn't make it to the funeral.'

'It's okay. You were away with the sixth form, weren't you? A residential?'

Luka looked down at the shabby rug at his feet. He seemed suddenly fascinated by its pattern. He cleared his throat. 'I got back home the day before. I could have come. Mum didn't want me to, and I... I bottled out, to be honest. I've never been to a funeral.'

Milo tried to take in this varied information. 'Your mum didn't think you should go?' he said eventually, picking out the most significant point. 'Why on earth not? Frankie was your aunt. You were close at one time, weren't you?'

'There's no need to make me feel worse than I do already,' Luka burst out, getting to his feet. 'I know I should have been there.'

The pause stretched.

'Did you come here tonight for a reason, son, or was it just to touch base with me?' Milo said, cringing at himself for trotting out one of his partner Max's corporate phrases. He hated them all, along with 'Let's run that idea up the flagpole and see who salutes' and 'We need some blue-sky thinking here, guys'. Luka was looking at him with the usual derision in his eyes now.

'It doesn't matter. I just wanted to...' he mumbled, before breaking off and picking at a loose thread in the tattered sleeve of his hoodie. Milo remembered with a pang how Luka had always had a habit of ragging his cuffs when he was anxious. Marianne had hated it.

'Wanted to what?' he prompted, when no more words were forthcoming.

'Oh, nothing. It doesn't matter now. I'm going. We haven't got anything to say to each other really, have we?' He lumbered to his feet, and Milo did the same, both swaying slightly as they got their balance after the intense hit of the coffee and all the pent-up emotion.

Milo reached out a hand to try to stop Luka as his son turned on his heel but he wasn't quick enough. In seconds, Luka had reached the landing and was clattering down the stairs to the front door. Milo walked over to the window and watched the tall figure swing down the road, breaking into a trot as soon as he reached the entrance to the recreation ground. He disappeared between the trees and Milo was left with a heap of crumbs, two empty mugs and a cloud of desolation. Even more concerning was that unfinished sentence. He'd wanted to... what, exactly?

7

The next time Kate saw the man who she hoped would be her new friend, spring was firmly in the air. The weather had taken a turn for the better and he was walking towards her along the lakeside path, wearing khaki cargo shorts and a baggy, faded T-shirt. Kate pretended not to notice him as she steered her young goddaughter towards the play area. It was her day for doing the school run so she'd already collected Elsie, given her a snack, taken her to see her dad, who was doing a late shift in the café, and now they were attempting a circuit of the whole country park before tea.

Elsie was riding her pride and joy, a small fluorescent-pink bicycle with stabilisers which were definitely not as stable as they should be. It was one of Kate's regular slots for looking after Elsie and she found the responsibility quite terrifying sometimes, even after years of experience with children of various ages. Elsie was a force of nature. You could never be quite sure what she'd do next, but Sam was so grateful when Kate took over, especially if it coincided with his café shifts, and Kate adored the little girl with her sparkling brown eyes and hair the colour of ripe apricots which was usually tied up in two uneven bunches but today was hidden under a wildly patterned cycle helmet. The helmet was a great idea in Kate's opinion, because Elsie hadn't developed much awareness of danger yet.

As they approached the man, a teenage boy on a very flash mountain bike screeched past them, narrowly missing Elsie, who cried out in alarm, lurched across the bank and slid neatly into the lake. The panic that followed was out of all proportion to the depth of the water, but Kate was in loco parentis and an inch of lake full of weeds was as terrifying to her as a complete lagoon. In seconds, the man had stepped into the muddy shallows and lifted Elsie up, still attached to her bike, depositing her in a safe place on the bank. Her screams alerted a nearby elderly couple who bustled over, and from somewhere in a voluminous shopping bag produced a towel to mop the little girl up, which was then passed to her rescuer. He dabbed at himself perfunctorily, saying he was fine and that a bit of water never hurt anyone.

'Mother always carries a small towel with her, don't you, pet?' said the older man. 'Especially when we come here. You can't go wrong if you've got a towel, that's what I always say.'

'It stems from the days when our three were forever leaping into the lakes for a paddle,' said his wife. 'Holy terrors, all of 'em. You had to have eyes in the back of your head when they were on the loose. Our Malcolm once jumped in and landed on a moorhen. I don't know which one of them was the most surprised.'

Elsie was listening now, dampness forgotten for the moment. 'Did it get deaded?' she asked.

'Oh... oh no, ducky. It swam off quite happily. Malcolm was always the skinniest of the three. No harm done.'

Kate saw the couple glance at each other and then at the lake and wondered if this was quite true. She hoped Elsie wouldn't ask any more questions. Fortunately, the older man was now rummaging in his backpack, and soon produced a fistful of chocolate bars with a flourish reminiscent of a conjuror. 'Emergency supplies,' he explained, handing them over. 'Now, you three take yourself to the nearest bench and have a little sit down while you all recover. Not easy being grandparents, is it?'

'But we're... we're not...' Kate exchanged embarrassed looks with Elsie's rescuer and tried to interject more but it was no good. The other man was still in full flow.

'It's a nightmare being left in charge, isn't it? You worry more than you ever did about your own kids. Still, grandparenting's the finest job in the world. And you know what they say. The best part is that you can give them back at the end of the day.' He laughed heartily at this and his wife joined in with a gentle titter. He put an arm around her shoulders. 'Come on, Mother, let's go and have a cup of tea.'

His wife beamed up at her husband and then at Kate. 'Don't I know you?' she asked. 'Oh, I've got it. You're the lovely lady who serves in the café, aren't you? Such a friendly place. We'll get ourselves over there right away, Trevor. I've worked quite a thirst today, what with all this extra excitement on top of our walk. Might even treat ourselves to a toasted teacake or even an ice cream. The weather's better this week, even though it's only the middle of March. Look, the sun's trying to come out at last.'

They waved as they walked away, arm in arm. Kate thought how wonderful it must be to have a partnership like that, where all you need in life is each other and maybe a buttered teacake each. Elsie had recovered quickly and was picking bits of water weed out of her socks. 'Can we have the chocolate now, Aunty Kate?' she asked hopefully, eyeing the three bars. 'This man prob'ly needs one. He's all wet.'

Kate glanced down at his feet. 'Oh, for heaven's sake, look at the state of your trainers. They're full of mud. I'm so sorry.'

'It's fine. The sun will dry them soon enough. This is turning out to be a much better kind of day than I was expecting, to be honest, and that towel mopped up most of the sogginess.' He grinned at Elsie. 'Maybe we should all carry one in future. And emergency snacks too, obviously.'

Overcome with shyness now the crisis had passed, Kate wasn't sure how to release their saviour from having to sit on a bench and eat chocolate with two complete strangers, but luckily he took over.

'We should probably introduce ourselves first. I never eat KitKats with strangers, and I'm sure you two don't either. I'm Milo.'

'I'm Kate, but I expect you already know that,' Kate said. 'What with Elsie saying it, and also because...'

She left a pause to see if Milo realised where else they'd seen each other before, apart from the café. He didn't disappoint her.

'You're Ted's daughter, aren't you?' he said. 'You were really brave to come and see the MMMs at the pub. It must have been hard for you.'

'Did you know my dad then?' Kate asked.

'No, I never met him, sadly. He sounds like a great bloke, though. Everybody's favourite GP, by all accounts.'

'Yes, it was a shame he couldn't look after himself better in his retirement,' said Kate bitterly. It had been a bone of contention between them that Ted's cholesterol level was sky high but he'd refused to cut down on any of the fatty foods he adored. None of his friends had realised that he'd had health issues and that was the way he wanted it. 'Life's for living, love,' he'd been fond of saying to Kate. Until it wasn't.

'Physician, heal thyself?' Milo suggested.

'I suppose that old saying sums it up. Anyway, this is my goddaughter, Elsie,' said Kate, beginning to walk towards the nearest wooden seat. 'Her bike's new. I don't think she's quite got the hang of it yet.'

'I had it for my birthday,' said Elsie. 'And the helmet. I don't like wearing the helmet, though. Can I take it off for a bit, Aunty Kate?'

'Yes, just while you have your chocolate. But it needs to go straight back on afterwards.'

'Okay. I was six last week,' Elsie continued, to Milo. 'We had a party. There was jelly and cake.' Her bottom lip wobbled as she looked down at her shocking pink treasure, now being wheeled along by Kate. 'I hope it's not all scratched.'

By this time, they'd reached the bench and Milo sat down and started to examine the bike while Kate finished removing pondweed from Elsie's once-white socks.

'The bike's fine,' he said after a moment. 'No damage. Now, about that chocolate...'

Kate handed the bars out and they sat in a row munching happily, for all the world as if they were what the elderly couple assumed, two grandparents having a breather and a snack with their much-loved granddaughter.

'This is kind of bizarre, isn't it?' Milo said, licking the last remaining smears of chocolate off his fingers when he'd finished eating. 'I've never been a grandpa before.'

'I've never even been a mum,' Kate blurted out, before she'd had time to think that this was probably too much information.

'You're my nice god-mummy instead,' suggested Elsie. 'Can we go on the play area now? There's swings. You can come if you like,' she added to Milo as she slid off the bench.

Kate opened her mouth to start thanking him for his help

and to say that of course he must be keen to be off on his walk that they'd interrupted, but Milo was already on his feet.

'Going to the swings is something I've not done since my son was small,' he said, grinning at Elsie. 'That sounds like a great idea.'

Elsie clipped on her helmet again, jumped back onto her bike and wobbled slightly. 'How old is your little boy now?'

'Seventeen. His name's Luka and he's nearly as tall as me these days. He used to like the slide best.'

'I do too. Come on,' she said, forging ahead and getting her balance at last.

Kate and Milo followed behind, Kate hovering as closely as she could to avoid any more mishaps. Milo put a hand on her arm and the reassuring warmth of it seemed to go right through her body. 'Give the child some space,' he said quietly. 'She's getting the hang of it now.'

'Right. Point taken. I'm sorry you got dragged into our drama, though.'

'It's not easy standing back, but everybody needs to take risks sometimes,' Milo added. 'Elsie's doing well and there's no harm done. Also, the bonus is chocolate on a sunny afternoon and making two new friends. I'm also road-testing my new contact lenses and neither of them have dropped out.'

Kate had noticed he wasn't wearing his glasses. She'd liked them, but it was easier to see his expression now his eyes were more visible, and they were extremely expressive eyes, sea green, with thick lashes and heavy, rather sleepy-looking lids. They gave the impression of this man being thoughtful and... yes, sensual. She wondered, with a shiver, if that was an accurate description.

'Why have you ditched your glasses?' she asked, to distract herself from the intrusive thoughts.

'It's part of my new campaign to try different things. I might get rid of the beard next. Like I said, bonus new friends too. I call that an excellent result.'

'With a daring rescue thrown in. What was the alternative going to be? I bet it didn't involve pond weed.'

He thought for a moment. 'I was going to have a few moments sitting on my sister's memorial bench and then give my father a call. We've not been getting on too brilliantly since she... since Frankie... well, we had a few disagreements, Dad and me... Hey, I don't know why I'm telling you all this. I don't usually share stuff with strangers. Or friends, for that matter,' he added under his breath.

'Is... I mean *was* your sister the sunshine girl?'

'Yes.' The stark one-word answer touched Kate's heart. She waited for more but none came.

'I like to sit on Frankie's bench too,' Kate said eventually, when the silence became uncomfortable.

'Do you? Were you a friend of hers?'

'Oh, no, but I've been intrigued by the unusual wording on the plaque, and obviously sad because she was so young. I've read all the benches, but hers is my favourite.'

'That's good to hear. And you're local? I've got a flat near my office in Meadowthorpe at the moment so it's too far to walk here for me.'

'Your office? What do you do?' Kate asked.

'I'm a financial advisor, but my speciality is helping people to get out of debt. I'm in partnership with my old friend Max, but I'm beginning to think... anyway, enough of my worries, are you a local? My flat's in Meadowthorpe to be near work, but Willowbrook's a great place to live, I'd imagine.'

Kate started to answer but Elsie had reached the play area now and dismounted by tipping herself sideways. Milo leaped forward just in time to catch her. He set her on her feet and she rushed away.

'One thing this place has in spades is seats,' he said. 'Let's sit on this one near the slide. We can supervise Elsie, you can tell me what it's like to be a fairy godmother and I'll explain about the significance of the words on Frankie's bench. It's basically about packing a lot into a short time. How does that sound?'

Kate smiled. It sounded like the perfect way to while away an afternoon. She settled herself where she had a good view of the little girl and tried not to flap. Elsie was now standing right at the top of the slide, poised to launch herself down. The blaze of delight on her face was beautiful to see. Everyone needed a bit of freedom sometimes, Kate told herself firmly, and at this moment, Elsie wasn't the only one. It was another kind of freedom to let yourself make new friends and not worry what they thought of you. She turned to Milo and prepared to do just that.

8

20 MARCH 2003

Kate manoeuvres the bulky pram around a corner in Mothercare, narrowly avoiding demolishing a stand of brightly coloured wellies. The slight jolt makes the baby inside jump and Kate holds her breath, but the tiny boy only snuffles in his sleep and finds his fist, sucking fiercely.

A young girl with a red-faced baby strapped to her chest in a sling nudges Kate sharply as she bends to look at the disposable nappies. She doesn't apologise, and the baby lets out a squeak of protest as he's dangled horizontally over the shelves. Kate thinks that if the child was hers she'd be a lot more careful. She watches, burning with indignation on the baby's behalf as the girl leaves the shop and stands outside to light a cigarette, not seeming to care that the smoke is drifting right across the sling.

Turning, Kate now spots a buggy with a wailing child inside it. There's no parent to be seen and the toddler, who can't be much more than one year old, is waving his fists as tears spurt from his tightly closed eyes. Kate looks around. Surely somebody is going to come to his rescue. She wheels her own pram over to see if she can help. As she bends to try and soothe the child, she hears footsteps behind her and someone taps her on the shoulder.

'Wotcha think yer doin'?' says a youth in a baseball cap with the word *stud* on the front. 'Leave my kid alone. I've seen you in 'ere before, staring at the babies. You're a pervert, that's what you are.'

By now, the young girl with the infant in the sling is back inside the shop and she marches over to Kate. 'What's up, Darren? Is she bothering our Terence? She was gawping at me, an' all. She's a right weirdo.'

Kate's so shocked at this onslaught that she can't speak. The girl takes hold of the buggy and rushes out of the shop, muttering to herself. The boy gives Kate one last filthy look and follows. Shaking now, Kate looks around. Has anyone heard all this? An anxious-looking assistant comes over to check on her.

'Are you okay?' she says. 'Take no notice of those two. We try to ignore them usually. I always say it's a good job they found each other. At least they're not spoiling another couple.' The assistant laughs rather bitterly. 'Do you want me to get you a drink of water, love? You look a bit flummoxed.'

'No, it's okay. I... I didn't do anything, honestly. I was just seeing if anyone was with the toddler because he was crying,' Kate manages to say.

'I know. I'd have done the same. Don't worry. Look, I've got to go and serve a customer. Give one of us a shout if you need to have a sit down.'

Kate watches the woman go. It's all very well saying don't worry, but the assistant has no idea what was going through Kate's mind when she bent over the buggy. She'd wanted desperately to take that little boy home with her, and the baby in the sling too. Why should people like that pair be able to have children if they can't or won't look after them properly? If she hadn't had the pram with her, Kate might have given in to temptation and at least saved the toddler from his tears. It's a dangerous, sickening feeling, this overwhelming urge to have a baby of her very own. Kate knows for sure that she would be a better mother than some of these others who don't look as if they care whether they have kids or not. She wishes she could talk to someone about the red mist that comes over her when she sees a child looking unloved, but she's afraid anyone else might say she's unhinged.

Swinging the pram around, Kate moves slowly towards the outer door. The place suddenly feels full of shoppers. She feels as if everyone's staring at her. They must all think she's a weirdo too. Why did she decide to wear her red coat? It makes her stand out way too much. Looking down at her coat with revulsion, Kate resolves to put it in the ever-growing pile of over-bright clothes destined for the charity shop. Blending in is much safer these days. As she reaches the entrance to the shop, a kindly-looking lady leans over to look into the pram, cooing as she sees the fleecy-wrapped bundle.

'He's a darling, isn't he?' she says, giving Kate the benefit of that particular look that mums and grannies often share, or so Kate has observed over the years. 'What's his name?'

'This is Felix,' Kate says, inching towards freedom as she speaks.

'How old?'

'What?'

'How old is the little man?'

'Oh... about six weeks.'

'He's a bonny baby. Is he your first?'

Kate debates her answer. It's so tempting to lie just to be part of this exclusive fellowship of child-bearing women but in the end, she just can't manage it.

'He's not mine,' Kate says, blinking hard. 'I haven't got any children. I'm just looking after him for a friend.'

The lady pats Kate's arm. The fellow feeling between them hasn't gone away. 'Your turn will come, dear,' she says. 'You've got a very motherly face. Just be patient.'

As the woman walks away, Felix opens his still partly unfocused blue eyes and attempts a smile. Kate sighs. Be patient? For how long? Her patience is starting to wear extremely thin now.

9

The meeting with Milo stirred something in Kate. It was hard to pin down this fluttering feeling but it was almost as if she was anticipating a holiday, or even Christmas. This was odd because as Sophie had reminded her, it was a long time since she'd had any time away from home and Christmas didn't look as if it was going to be much fun at all this year.

By nine o'clock on the evening of the pond weed experience, Kate was still unsettled. She decided that if sleep wasn't going to be easy to find tonight, she might as well go the whole hog and dig out a few more of the old photographs that had sparked so many memories on the night of the Meadowthorpe Morris Men. Heading upstairs, Kate showered, changed into her comfiest pyjamas and reached into the wardrobe drawer to pull out another random selection. She really ought to organise all the photos into an album if she was going to keep them, but for now, a handful would do. The grandfather clock downstairs was striking the half hour as she looked down at the first snap. That summer when Sophie had only just arrived in Willowbrook had been strangely magical. Looking back, the warm weather seemed even balmier and the days had stretched out in front of the two of them, endless and golden. The photographs told the story of a glowing time, bronzed and free, and Kate's rainbow bikini now seemed to sum up that season of freedom.

The nearest beach was only a twenty-minute bus ride away from the village, and when Sophie realised this, she wanted to go there as often as possible. Kate's skin gradually darkened in the sunshine until she was almost as brown as Sophie, and still between jobs so with more time on her hands to swim, sunbathe and drink endless cans of diet cola, Kate began to really relax for the first time in years. She'd been an anxious child, almost school-phobic at times and easy prey for any bullies looking for entertainment. Her brother Jamie was the extrovert, annoyingly cute as a little boy even when he was behaving like a prima donna on speed. Kate had wished she was more like him, at least until the real trouble started.

For a while, Sophie helped a lot with Kate's confidence-building, encouraging her to join in pub quizzes, discos and persuading her to attend live gigs at various venues around the area. That had all ended when Howard put the sparkling diamond ring on her finger. Howard had very different plans for their social life.

Determined to focus on the future and not waste time looking back over her shoulder at the wilder days, Kate threw herself into marriage with as much gusto as she could muster. Her work as a TA was intensely satisfying, and without all the extra admin to fit in at home. Gazing at the young, tanned girl in the snapshots, Kate hardly recognised herself, but there was no point in dwelling on the past. She'd had plenty of good times over the years, even if life hadn't panned out quite the way she'd expected it to. Leaving her job at the school had been hard, but the café was proving to be a great way to earn a living, and Pat was a good boss and definitely appreciated Kate's earlier catering qualification.

Childless or childfree? That was the burning question she must ask herself. The years of agonising over the lost babies had taken their toll on her mental health. Surely now was the time to put all that sadness behind her. Sighing, Kate rubbed her eyes. If only life was that simple.

Enough was enough. No more nostalgia tonight or she'd never sleep. Kate debated going downstairs and putting the photos in the bin but in the end she decided they were a part of her history that should be preserved, even if she never looked at them again. Perhaps she'd keep one out to frame, and be a constant reminder of the Kate who was colourful and carefree. Selecting the best of the rainbow bikini snaps, she went along to the small bedroom and stashed the rest in what she'd always called The Cupboard of Doom. In there were things that hadn't seen the light of day for years. Closing the door on her memories, Kate went back to bed with the knowledge that she'd faced them and emerged virtually unscathed, although a mug of hot chocolate wouldn't go amiss. If only all life's demons were so easily dealt with.

10

April arrived without the usual visit from Sophie, who had been tempted away by the offer of a hairdressing booking on a month-long cruise.

'I couldn't believe it when I got the email,' she told Kate breathlessly, when she called to postpone their appointment. 'Paul's just landed a job with the cruise company working on the sound systems for the entertainment, and he managed to get me in too. I'll see you as soon as I'm home. How's the rejuvenation programme going?'

'Oh, ticking over nicely,' Kate hedged, wondering if going out with Beryl's gang a couple of times counted as a step forward. They had been riotous nights, though, to be fair.

'I heard you'd been on the lash with The Saga Louts,' Sophie said, grinning. 'You're a brave woman, Katie. Beryl wants you to go to Bingo Night at the church hall with them, and then on to the pub quiz afterwards tomorrow night. Are you up for it?'

Kate considered this. 'I might be,' she said eventually. 'Oh, what the heck. Yes, I blooming well am.'

The previous outing had been bingo too, an eye-opener in

many ways. This time, as before, Beryl called for Kate, escorted her to the hall and presented her with a special pen to mark the card. Sitting at a table with Beryl and Winnie, plus Sylvia Nightingale from the shop, Kate was once again alarmed to see the intensity of their expressions.

'Where's Anthea?' she asked, glancing around.

'Oh, she thinks this kind of thing's beneath her,' said Winnie, with a sniff. 'Didn't stop her sharing the bubbly I won last week, though, did it? She's meeting us at the pub later.'

'It's meat bingo tonight,' said Mrs Nightingale. 'I've got my eye on that pack of pork chops. How about you, Beryl?'

'Steak,' was the one-word answer, and Winnie nodded in agreement.

Kate began to feel vaguely nauseous. She'd never been tempted to be vegetarian apart from a couple of months as a teenager, but now the array of joints, liver, chops, sausages and steaks was making her wonder if a nut roast might be nice for the weekend.

'What about you, Kate? I suppose you haven't got much use for a hearty rib-eye steak now your man's done a runner,' said Mrs Nightingale.

Beryl and Winnie both shot the shopkeeper looks that could have felled a lesser woman, but Mrs N was coolly organising her bingo slips ready for the big moment, and ignored them.

The ladies on the next table overheard this comment. 'A bit of sausage won't go amiss though, will it, ducky?' one called, and they all cackled.

Kate could feel herself blushing. If only she'd listened to her common-sense voice and stayed at home. This was hideous, and the smell of blood from the top table laden with prizes was getting stronger.

'I think I'll...' she began, planning her escape, but just then a loud voice called for silence and the real madness began.

The bingo caller was clearly an old hand, shouting out the numbers along with the standard patter (*legs eleven* and an accompanying wolf whistle, etc.). To her surprise, now she was more acclimatised to the pace, Kate found herself getting caught up in the excitement of the moment and when she did indeed scoop a large pack of pork sausages, she gave the ladies on the next table a thumbs up before collecting her prize and holding it aloft while everyone clapped.

By the end of the night, Kate had won a further prize of a beef joint, which she donated to Winnie, and was soon following the other two across the green to The Fox and Fiddle.

'Hey, ladies, you made it just in time. I've saved you your usual table,' Ned said. 'Are The Saga Louts up for the challenge? I'm warning you, there are some tough questions tonight.'

'We're The Saga Louts plus The Junior tonight,' said Beryl, pointing to Kate. 'Last time we fell down on the hits from the eighties and some ridiculous question about phonics, whatever that is, but Kate's our secret weapon.'

Kate bought a bottle of Prosecco for them all to share, hoping it would give her inspiration. The only time she'd ever been part of a quiz team before at a school fund-raising event, she'd let her much more youthful team down badly when she'd failed to come up with the answer to the tie breaker. Who knew Elton John was christened Reg Dwight? Well, the winning team did, obviously. You could see why the poor bloke had changed his name.

They settled themselves at the only remaining table and Kate filled their glasses just as Ned rang the bell for round one. For the first ten minutes, Kate sat with her mouth open, amazed at how much general knowledge the three older ladies had between them. Anthea was a whizz when it came to geography. 'I worked my way around the globe with a number of different men before I finally married one of them,' she said under her breath, when Kate expressed her admiration in a pause between rounds.

'She was auditioning them to choose a prime stud with good staying power, that's what we heard,' said Winnie, laughing so hard that her necklaces rattled and her chins were set wobbling.

'And I found him. Sadly for me, he was still going through an auditioning process of his own. Hey ho, you win some, you lose some. At least I got plenty of great sex along the way.'

Unfortunately, Ned had just rung the bell for silence at this moment, and several interested faces turned towards Kate's table, some of them disapproving. Anthea smiled back innocently and raised her glass to them all in a toast. 'Frigid, the lot of them, I'm guessing,' she said, in what was possibly meant to be a stage whisper.

Kate was relieved when Ned started reading the next questions and even answered a few in the education round, but it wasn't until the final pop music set when she realised how much her team were relying on her.

'We can do most of the earlier stuff, dear,' said Beryl. 'Beatles, Stones, Motown and all that, and a bit of anything that I've noticed when I'm dancing round the kitchen to Radio 2, but the rest's up to you. I think we're in with a chance of winning the top prize tonight. It's a cheese hamper. I do love a bit of Stilton. No pressure, though.'

Kate took a deep breath as Anthea scribbled down the first four answers and then sat back as Ned asked them to name the three members of Bros. 'Go on, Kate,' she said, handing her the pen. 'It's your turn. I've got no idea.'

'Oh, goodness,' Kate breathed, racking her brains. She'd

loved Bros. She could do this. Aha. *Matt Goss, Luke Goss and Craig Logan*, she wrote quickly.

Beryl punched the air as the next three questions came and Kate answered them just as easily.

The final question of the round involved not the Beatles themselves, but their various wives, so Winnie took over. 'I loved all those boys,' she explained. 'I was hoping to marry Paul but he always seemed to pick the white girls. He'd never met me, though,' she added thoughtfully.

While the results were being totted up, Beryl fetched another bottle from the bar and Kate began to relax until she felt Winnie nudge her in the ribs. 'It's neck and neck for the winner, I've just heard Ned say,' she said happily. 'Between us and The Gremlins. I can't be doing with them, the smug lot. They won last time too. We just need to answer the tie breaker and we're home. Could be anything. You have to speak up as soon as you know it, nice and clear.'

Ned cleared his throat and the chatter died down. 'For the cheese hamper, folks, here we go. Alison Moyet and Vincent Clarke were part of which eighties band?' he said.

Kate leapt to her feet. 'Yazoo!' she shouted, causing Beryl to choke on a gulp of Prosecco and Winnie to raise both arms in victory.

'Correct. Game, set and match to The Saga Louts and The Junior!' Ned yelled back, as the pub erupted in applause. The Gremlins' table was the only place where gloom had descended and the team soon shuffled out, without so much as a 'well done' to the winners.

'Miserable buggers,' muttered Ned, as he presented the prize to a beaming Beryl. 'It's about time someone took them down a peg or two. Well done, girls.'

As they finished their drinks, shared out the cheese and

congratulated each other, it dawned on Kate that for the first time in months she hadn't felt her age. It was great being the junior member of the team.

'I need to know something, girls. How did you all feel about turning fifty?' she asked the others.

Three heads looked her way, each with a different expression. Beryl was the first to speak.

'It was a pretty lousy time for me,' she said. 'Not because of the particular age, but my mum was dying and my dad had dementia. Being fifty didn't seem important one way or another. It was when I was sixty that I really let my hair down and celebrated, and I've never looked back since. Life's for living, and while we're on that subject, we need to get our next holiday booked, ladies.'

Winnie looked at Kate with her head on one side. 'I didn't like the actual birthday much,' she admitted. 'I was between jobs and pretty miserable after I was made redundant, but then I got lucky. The best jewellers in Meadowthorpe was advertising for staff and they chose me. I ended up as manager. After that, my age didn't seem to matter.'

'How about you, Anthea?' asked Kate, when the last of the three still hadn't replied.

'I loved it,' Anthea said. 'I was more bothered about being thirty, to be honest, because I was stuck in a bit of a rut then. Forty was fine but fifty really felt good. I was fit and healthy and happy, and I still am. Why? Are you worried about the big birthday coming up, Kate?'

Kate looked at them all, still glowing from their quiz victory and the Prosecco, all unselfconsciously dressed from head to foot in whatever colourful clothes they chose to wear.

'Well, I was, kind of,' she said, grinning. 'But somehow the idea seems much less depressing now.'

'Depressing? No way,' said Beryl. 'Do we look tired of life? As if!'

Kate started to laugh at the outraged look on Beryl's face, and the others joined in. Soon they were rocking back and forth in their chairs, tears pouring down their faces.

'I don't know why that was so funny,' gasped Beryl eventually when they'd all calmed down. 'It must be the fizz that's gone to our heads.'

'No, it's not the fizz,' said Kate, wiping her eyes. 'It's just that you lot are high on life, and that's exactly how it should be. I'm going to try and take a leaf out of your books. Bring on the celebrations – I'm ready!'

11

The next morning, somewhat sore of head, Kate viewed herself critically in the mirror as she got ready for work. Much overdue a trim with Sophie away, her hair was badly in need of attention and she'd had to start putting it up for work, which along with a pair of new cerise leggings and some dangly gold hoop earrings she'd found in a drawer had actually resulted in a lot of compliments from the café customers, so that was a bonus. She'd even started using tinted lip gloss and a lick or two of mascara.

Kate yawned as she laced up her trainers. Tonight was mercifully free of invitations from The Saga Louts and was going to be a stay-at-home one because Elsie was arriving soon. It was fun looking after her goddaughter in the daytime, but Kate had always found the sleepovers even more precious. Sam had very little social life as a rule, having taken full charge of his baby daughter when he was only seventeen and using all his available childcare so that he could work to support himself and Elsie, but now and again, Kate persuaded him that he needed to kick back for a night and catch up with his old friends. When this happened, Sam would usually drop Elsie off in good time for tea and then the two of them would cook together and eat off trays on their knees and watch something they both liked.

This was trickier since Howard had taken the jade-green sofa and the TV, but Kate still had her iPad. They could watch their favourite films with it balanced between them now, because since Sophie's latest visit and pep talk, Kate had browsed the local charity furniture shops and managed to find a replacement sofa. It was a lot less stylish than the original and definitely not the shade she would have chosen but was huge and comfortable. More to the point, it was the only one she could afford. She couldn't wait for Elsie to see it for the first time.

'I'm here,' Elsie shouted as she barrelled through the front door after only the briefest of knocks. 'What are we having for our tea tonight, Aunty Kate?'

Sam followed her into the living room more slowly, pulling an apologetic face at Kate. 'Maybe say hello properly first, chick?' he said wearily. His normally delicate cheekbones looked even more hollow than usual, Kate thought, feeling a rush of concern. Out of all the young people who'd passed through the school while she was working there, Sam held a special place in her heart and he still felt child-like to her, at twenty-three. She had taken him under her wing at school and he'd flourished, showing huge potential, especially in art, but instead of taking this further and going to college in the town as everyone expected, Sam had fallen into the web of one of the scariest girls in the local secondary school when he was only sixteen. Lara Shaughnessy, red-haired siren and more beautiful than any teenager had a right to be, in Kate's opinion, had reeled Sam in and he'd appeared to revel in her attention. The fling might have run its course with no harm done, but Lara, making one of her few slip-ups in life so far, had got pregnant.

In those days, Kate hadn't been sure which road Sam was

going to follow when it came to his sexuality. His flamboyant style of dressing and long blond hair had triggered a few raised eyebrows in Willowbrook, where conventionality ruled, and his skilled use of eyeliner and nail polish had caused Beryl to wonder if Sam was 'a bit too fond of the ballet, if you know what I mean, Kate.' Even so, Lara had obviously overcome any doubts Sam might have had and they had been inseparable for weeks. Sam had regularly sported a fine collection of love bites and had seemed completely besotted with his ever-expanding lover. He'd attended antenatal classes with her, even though she wasn't keen on the idea, borrowed numerous books about childcare and fatherhood from the library van that visited the village every week, and had even taught himself to knit when Lara refused to consider making small cardigans and bootees.

However, when Elsie was born, Lara had left town as soon as she was able, abandoning her daughter to Sam seemingly without a backward glance. His parents, who had never seemed particularly keen on Sam anyway, had been adamant that they weren't up for life with a tiny, colicky baby but, undaunted, he'd eventually managed to secure a council flat not far from Kate's house and had made a home for them both with a lot of help from the local church, whose members immediately organised gifts of furniture and so on.

'How's it going, love?' asked Kate, flipping the kettle on to make Sam a mug of his favourite camomile tea.

'Fine, thanks,' said Sam, watching Elsie warily as she dived onto the new sofa. 'Careful, Else, you'll be over the back of there if you don't watch it.'

'This is so cool,' said Elsie, now stretched out with her head on a fat cushion. 'Did you get it just for us?'

'Pretty much,' said Kate. 'What do you think, Sam?'

He viewed the sofa with his head on one side. 'Well... it's very...'

'Purple!' shouted Elsie. 'It's pretty. Nearly the same colour as my new unicorn. Look!'

She fetched her overnight bag and pulled out a large stuffed unicorn with a long silver horn. 'She's called Horny,' Elsie said proudly. 'I heard Daddy say that word when he was on the phone before we came out.'

Sam's eyes met Kate's and his lips twitched. '*Sorry*,' he mouthed. Kate tried not to giggle.

'What a lovely name, Elsie,' she said.

'Yes, and she's almost as purple as the sofa.'

'Actually, the label says violet,' said Kate. 'I know it's a bit bright but it was the squishiest one they had and we can't eat our tea sitting on camping chairs any longer, can we?'

'No, we can't. They were really uncomfortable. Are you going now, Dad?'

'Yes, I'm off to paint the town red. Don't make me any tea this time, thanks Kate. I'm late already. See you tomorrow, sweetie. Look after Horny.'

Sam leant down to give his daughter a hug, kissed Kate on both cheeks and left before there could be any more questions.

'Why has he got to paint the whole town red?' Elsie asked, frowning. 'He's only just done our living room. I don't like red. I thought he was going out with Dippy Den for a pint, not painting.'

'He is, it's just a figure of speech,' Kate said.

'What's a...?'

'Look, I've bought the ingredients for making pizzas,' Kate interrupted, before things could get any more complicated. 'Do you want anchovies on yours?'

This proved to be an excellent distraction as Elsie made

vomiting noises and ran into the kitchen. 'They stink,' she shouted. 'I'd rather eat a slug.'

'I've got some of those in the garden too, so no problem there. Right, wash your hands, put your pinnie on and let's get started.'

The pizzas were a great success, heavily loaded with mozzarella, fresh basil and tomatoes. Elsie decided they should watch *Cinderella*, and they curled up on the purple extravaganza with Horny until the little girl's eyelids began to droop.

'I wonder if Daddy's in bed yet?' she said, yawning. 'There won't be anyone to read him a story tonight, will there?'

'That's your job, isn't it?'

'Yes, we take turns. I'm allowed to pick two and then he chooses another one. I hope he's not lonely.'

Elsie always settled well at Kate's and never asked to go home but this was a conversation that was repeated every time she stayed over, with variations. Kate had a sudden vision of the father and daughter curled up under Elsie's *Frozen* duvet cover happily reading to each other. Sam had worked hard at helping Elsie to begin to read independently even before she started school and now she was confident enough to manage quite a few of her books. The mental picture of the loving relationship the two of them shared was beautiful but Kate couldn't avoid pangs of envy.

'Is it time for my bath?' Elsie's voice cut into these dismal thoughts and Kate stirred herself.

'You bet it is. Crazy foam tonight? Pink or blue?'

There was no answer to these questions because Elsie was already galloping towards the stairs. Kate followed more slowly, still thinking about dashed hopes and disappointments. Still, at least she had all her godchildren to love, and knowing Elsie made up for an awful lot of sadness. Now she'd faced the challenge of the photograph album it was time for Kate to make a better job of counting her blessings and get to work on what might happen next. The purple sofa was only the beginning. Next job, the contents of her wardrobe. Out with indigo, in with violet and scarlet and vermillion and all those colours that she'd avoided for years.

'Sod you, Howard Brown,' Kate muttered as she headed up the stairs. 'The Saga Louts have definitely got the right idea about living it large. I'm going to be fifty and fabulous and I'll definitely bring the colours back, just you watch me.'

12

20 MARCH 2005

Kate stands at the kitchen window looking out of the tiny, windswept patch of garden. She hasn't even had the heart to clear the tubs of dead plants yet, let alone sweep up the fallen leaves from the few shrubs, so they sit, getting more and more soggy and slimy, all around the back door.

'It's my wedding anniversary, Barnaby,' she says to the cat. 'Seven years ago I was signing my life away.'

The cat scratches behind one ear and views her without blinking.

'You must be suffering from the seven-year itch,' says Kate, grimacing at her own joke. 'I don't think you're the only one, though. Howard's usually back by now. I think he's forgotten the date again.'

Barnaby yawns and begins to wash his bottom with what seems like excessive care. Kate shrugs and is about to rummage in the fridge to see if there's anything for dinner, having hoped until the very last minute that she'd be taken out to eat this year, when she hears her husband's key in the door.

'Honey, I'm home,' he shouts, as if this old joke will make up for the fact that he's at least an hour late.

Howard comes into the kitchen and Kate stares in amazement, because he's almost hidden by the most enormous bunch of flowers she has ever seen. The scent of them is already travelling across the small room, the delicate fragrance of stocks and old-fashioned roses mingling with eucalyptus and mint. This is no garage shop last-minute purchase.

'Happy anniversary, my cherub,' Howard says, handing Kate the flowers and bowing low.

'B... b... but... I thought you'd forgotten,' Kate stammers, burying her face in the bouquet. He's even remembered how much she hates the scent of lilies. What on earth is going on?

'Forget? Not on your life. Why would I do that? Off you pop and get yourself smartened up,' Howard says, grinning at her. 'Why don't you wear that cute little black dress I bought you?'

'I thought I'd get my nice mustardy-yellow one out for a change,' says Kate, slightly nettled at being told what to wear when she doesn't even want to go out tonight.

'Nah. Makes you look sallow, that one. Black's the thing for a swanky restaurant. Come on, hurry up. We're going out to celebrate together, for once. Seven years of marital bliss with you and...' he pauses as if waiting for a drumroll. '...a fantastic deal with Gerard and Sons, signed and sealed this very afternoon.'

Aha. It's all becoming clear. This longed-for transaction means that Howard will be even more firmly entrenched in the camaraderie of his beloved golf club.

Suddenly weary, Kate puts the flowers down on the table and without meaning to, places her hands on the small of her back. Since the second miscarriage last Christmas she's not felt like celebrating anything, but tonight... maybe, just maybe it's going to be a new beginning for the two of them.

'Are you up for driving tonight or shall I order a cab?' Howard says, already on his way for a shower.

'I don't mind driving,' says Kate. There's a very good reason why she won't be drinking this evening. It's too soon to hope really, but she still does. Perhaps this time everything will be okay.

13

Kate leant on the café counter and glanced up at the clock on the wall, considering whether her overall would manage to get her through another day. She was trying to restrict her laundry because the washer was on the blink again and she had a horrible feeling that this time when it conked out, it would be forever. Dreading big bills was a new and worrying part of Kate's life. Having somewhere to live was one thing, but keeping the place going on her own was another matter.

'Could you provide me with another of those delicious toasted teacakes, my dear?'

The dapper elderly man at the counter was a regular customer, and Kate took his order with a smile. She watched him go and sit back down in the corner seat next to the sofa and the table of magazines and paperbacks that she kept replenished. Kate and Pat had decided that this wasn't going to be a selection like the typical ones at their local dentist which usually consisted of half a dozen dog-eared copies of *Horse and Hound*, *Country Life* and one about cross stitch.

The man rootled in the heap and dug out a book that Kate

had placed there only the day before. She nodded her approval. It was a thriller with a subplot about late-in-life romance. She wondered if he'd be taking a few tips from the story, although to be fair, he seemed perfectly happy to visit the café on his own.

The café was quieter now, and the eclectic mix of rustic tables and mismatched chairs were nearly all empty. Large, leafy plants were placed here and there, and each table had a small flower arrangement in its centre, also placed there by Kate. The scent of freshly ground coffee beans mingled with the warm smell of the teacake toasting. Green and white gingham curtains framed the windows and their pattern was matched in the fat cushions on the sofa. It was a peaceful scene, and one that Kate never tired of, although today she was definitely a little more jaded than usual.

It had been one of those nights when sleep just wouldn't come. Memories kept flooding in and try as she might, Kate couldn't chase them away. It was as if finding the photographs had unleashed a past that she wasn't yet ready to deal with. Finding a frame for the rainbow-bikini girl had only been the start of the wave of nostalgia, and now the photo greeted her every morning from the mantelpiece when she came downstairs. That girl had had no idea that one day Kate would long for her blossoming body, large with pregnancy, to make skinny bikinis a thing of the past. She stretched her shoulders, rubbing the small of her back with both hands, in an unconscious echo of how she'd felt all those years ago when babies were still possible and a new life was, briefly, growing inside her.

'Get yourself a coffee and have a sit down, lovely,' shouted a voice from the kitchen. 'It's going to be a long day and you're on clearing-up duty tonight, remember.'

Kate replied that she'd just wait five minutes so Pat had chance to nip to the loo first. Her boss was an old friend and Pat's

Place had been a saving grace over the months since the split. Walking to Willowbrook Park this morning and hearing birdsong and the whoops of a couple of early-morning paddleboarders, Kate had felt an overwhelming gratitude for being able to enjoy working in such a beautiful spot.

She was about to set the coffee machine in motion when the bell pinged as the café door opened, and in walked a very familiar figure. Beryl was looking very smart today, dressed in her favourite orange jacket, and Kate could see that she was wearing her new false teeth for the occasion, the ones that were very shiny but a bit too large, as if she was breaking them in for someone else. As Kate watched, she removed the jacket and tidied her hair. Underneath, she had on a pair of black leggings and a long cream top. Her small feet were encased in rainbow-striped pumps.

'You're looking good,' Kate said, beaming at her friend. 'This is a nice surprise.' Her neighbour usually let her know if she was planning to call in for a coffee and sometimes timed it to get a lift back so they could go and do their supermarket shopping, so today's visit was unexpected, although the other two of The Saga Louts were already installed at their favourite table, so this wasn't such a surprise after all.

Beryl waved to her friends, who were sitting in a corner eating cakes. 'Morning, ladies. I can see you've both got your usual? I thought you'd have eaten enough carrot cake last week when we went on the coach trip to Bath. You know what they say: *a moment on the lips, a lifetime on the hips*.'

'We weren't expecting you today, but I'm sure Pat's still got a piece for you, darling,' said Anthea.

'Anyway, *you* can't talk,' said Winnie. 'You ate that tearoom in Bath out of clotted cream. I thought you said you were going to rejoin the slimming club at the village hall this week?'

Beryl snorted. 'The feeling's worn off now,' she said. 'I decided life's too short to count calories. That's why God made leggings. Anyway, I'll be with you both in a minute. I just decided to come in on the spur of the moment, dear,' she said, turning to Kate.

'Really?' Kate made Beryl's latte and passed it over, unconvinced.

'Yes, it's such a lovely day.'

Kate looked Beryl straight in the eye and waited.

'Well, okay, you've rumbled me,' the older lady said. There was another short silence, which Kate forced herself not to break.

'I was going to try and catch you before you left for work,' said Beryl eventually. 'But I was just about to set off for my laughter therapy session.'

'Your... what?' This was a new one on Kate, although she remembered Sophie telling her that one of Beryl's hobbies was joining new clubs and classes.

'Laughter therapy with a touch of yoga.' Beryl pulled a face when she saw Kate's expression become even more incredulous. 'I know, I don't look very bendy but it's the seniors' class so they're not expecting us to stand on our heads. And then we laugh and laugh. It's amazing. You should try it, Kate. I'm kind of road-testing the class for the other two.' She gestured towards Anthea and Winnie. 'Anyway, have you got time for a quick chat or are you too busy?'

Pat, who always appeared to have the supersonic hearing of a bat, called from the kitchen, 'Yes, she has, I've already told her to have a break. Move it, Kate, or you'll miss your chance.'

Kate did as she was told and they both took their drinks over to a table by the window. Winnie and Anthea looked somewhat mortified that Beryl hadn't joined them but she gave them another wave and indicated that she'd see them shortly by means of a bizarre kind of semaphore involving much pointing at her watch and miming.

'So, what's all this about?' Kate said, sitting down. 'Come on, spill the beans, as Sophie would say.'

Beryl sighed. 'As a matter of fact, it was our Sophie who suggested I had a chat with you. She said you'd been on her mind ever since the last time she did your hair. Did she bully you? She can be a bit too forceful sometimes, just like her mother.'

Kate laughed. 'Only a bit, and I guess I needed it. She wants me to smarten myself up and get into the habit of wearing bright colours again. I've made a start.' She indicated her speedwell-blue dress, patterned with white daisies. The skirt and sleeves were just visible under the overall. The dress was an old favourite but with a wash and press was looking quite fresh again.

Beryl nodded her approval. 'Nice frock, and I like your hair up, it really suits you. Shows off that slender neck. You're lucky, mine's more turkey than swan these days. Just give me a minute to do justice to this magnificent snack.'

Beryl started to eat the large slice of carrot cake that Pat had fetched from her secret stock for favoured customers. She sighed happily as she finished it. 'Perfection,' she said to Kate, using a paper napkin to wipe a bit of frosting off her chin. 'How do you manage to work here and not put on half a stone a week? I wouldn't be able to resist this stuff.'

'I suppose I haven't got much of a sweet tooth these days. I still get guilty pangs if I eat too much cake. Howard thought it would be a good idea for me to watch my weight after Dad died because I was comfort eating but I never seemed to lose more than a couple of pounds and then I put it straight back on. Then he left and I kind of lost my appetite for a while.'

'Maybe it's time to loosen up a bit. Like I said, life's too short to feel guilty. Well, about cake anyway. Why did the silly man think you should diet? You've always looked lovely as you are.'

Kate shrugged. 'Oh, that was just Howard. He always liked to keep in shape for his golf and he thought I'd be happier if I was thinner.'

'I know someone like that,' said Beryl thoughtfully. 'She went on one of those crash diet things years ago. Ate nothing but cabbage soup for ages. She thought it'd make her husband love her more.'

'And did it?'

'I don't think so, not particularly. She just broke wind a lot. He left her for another man eventually. I don't think it was just the farting to blame, but that's another story.' Beryl chortled, and finished her coffee. 'There must be a lesson there somewhere. My Len liked me as I was. I wouldn't have thanked him for trying to change me.'

The café had started to fill up now, and despite her boss shaking her head, Kate moved over to the counter to give Pat a hand with the brief rush. When she came back, Beryl hadn't gone to join her friends but was sitting waiting.

'Did you want to say something in particular to me?' Kate said, sitting down again.

'Not really. Well, yes. And no.'

'That's covered all bases,' said Kate, grinning. 'Go on, let's get it over with.'

Beryl began to fidget with her bag. Kate wasn't used to seeing her neighbour unsure of herself. She began to feel uncomfortable. Just as she was about to nudge her again, Beryl said, 'I wouldn't normally interfere but it was something Sophie said. She was moaning about Howard being a... well, I'm not going to repeat the word, dear, it's not one I use. Anyway, I wanted to say that he wasn't all bad, even if he did have funny ideas about you getting thin.'

Ah. Thank goodness. Kate's heartbeat gradually began to return to normal. She made herself rally quickly before Beryl could register her momentary panic.

'And the fact that he'd been having an affair for months. There was that small thing too,' she said, wondering where on earth this was going, if it wasn't going to be the drastic unveiling of secrets she'd dreaded.

'Yes, there was that. No excuse for treating you so badly. Although I don't know if you realised it, but Howard often did little odd jobs around the house for me. You know the sort of thing, changing light bulbs, repotting plants and so on.'

'Yes, I know he could be useful, but that didn't make him a saint.'

'No, that wasn't my point. I wanted to say that one time, when he was mending my fridge door, I could tell he was very agitated, which wasn't like him. I asked what the problem was, and told me... he told me...'

Beryl reached in her bag for a perfectly laundered cotton handkerchief and blew her nose. When she'd collected herself, she continued. 'He told me about you taking that baby.'

Dumbfounded, Kate stared at Beryl. So she'd been right in her first terrified guess. It was the big one after all. She shivered, even though the café was cosy and warm. A sick feeling curdled her stomach. 'What? He... but why would he do that?'

'Howard was worried about you. He thought you were on the edge and you might do it again. I said I could call round and keep an eye on you if he wanted me to, but Howard said you wouldn't welcome it. He reckoned you'd just send me away with a flea in my ear.'

'It sounds as if you two were proper mates.' Kate couldn't keep the bitterness out of her voice, but Beryl didn't seem to pick up on it.

'We were. He called me Batty Beryl. And I called him Horrible Howie. We used to have a right old giggle.'

'I bet you did.' Kate's mind was reeling now. Howard was worried about her? But surely telling their neighbour was a kind of betrayal? How awful that Beryl knew her most shameful and terrifying secret, and not only that, had known for a long time by the sound of it.

'So when Sophie said all that nasty stuff about him, I thought I'd just have a word in your ear,' Beryl says. 'Howard wasn't all bad by any means. Yes, he did the dirty on you, but he did care. And actually, you're going to be a whole lot happier on your own. Perhaps you just had different ideas about marriage, and so on. Anyway, I've stuck my nose in enough. I'll leave you to get on with your work. I'm going to ask Anthea if she can give me a lift into town when we've finished here. Between you and me, her driving leaves a lot to be desired these days, especially when she forgets her glasses, but if I can't take a risk at my time of life, when can I? Everybody's got to die sometime.'

With that, Beryl gathered her belongings and joined the other two ladies who were already on their feet. Kate watched them go, Beryl's bright jacket making a dramatic contrast to Winnie's fuchsia anorak and Anthea's floor-length camel coat as she followed her friends down the path to the car park. Kate made her way towards the kitchen, her thoughts still in turmoil. Beryl knew about the baby and even with that knowledge, she still seemed to like Kate just as much as she had done before. This would have to be talked about again, and soon, but the warmth of Beryl's friendship stayed with Kate, giving her a glowing feeling of security.

14

20 MARCH 2010

Kate stares at the baby lying on his back in the pram. He looks back at her, blue eyes still unfocused. At least he isn't crying now. His piteous wails had caught at her heart and she'd had to rock him for at least five minutes before he stopped.

'It's not your fault,' Kate whispers to him. 'You didn't ask to have useless parents, did you? I bet your nappy's soaking wet too, isn't it?'

She reaches into the pram to confirm her suspicions, but that's not a problem. There are disposable nappies upstairs because Kate keeps a stock of everything she might ever need in the childcare line, ready for when she looks after her friends' babies and her godchildren. Everyone comes to Kate. They trust her. But would they feel the same if they knew what she'd done today? Maybe she should just change the baby's nappy and when he's comfortable, take him back again. 'They don't deserve you,' she tells the baby. 'Why couldn't you have been born here and not down the road? I wanted to be a mum so badly...'

She hears the front door open and stops speaking abruptly.

Her hands instinctively reach towards the baby but before she can pick him up, Howard comes into the living room and stops dead.

'Not another one. Why, oh why do you keep letting people dump their kids on you, Kate? They see you coming, they really do.'

'It's not what you think. This isn't one of my friends' babies. This one's staying with us. I found him, Howard. He's mine. He needs me.'

The awful realisation of what's happened is now hitting her husband. She wonders if he's been afraid of something like this all along. 'You can't mean that. What the...' he begins, but Kate holds a hand up.

'Don't say any more,' she says. 'He was crying. They don't care about him. So I've brought him round here.'

'You... you took someone's baby? Kate, what's going on?' He peers into the pram and the little boy waves his fists happily.

'See, he likes us,' Kate says, but she knows this happy moment is about to end. Her head is starting to pound, veins throbbing in both temples.

'Where did you take him from? Tell me, quickly. We've got to get him back. Someone's probably calling the police right now. Kate. Tell me.'

The baby starts to whimper as Howard's tone becomes louder and more frantic. Kate sighs.

'Now look what you've done, you've upset him. He belongs to that girl in the flats at the end of the road – the one who shouts a lot. She's got a dog that barks day and night too. It's a wonder the poor child ever sleeps with all that racket going on, and she's always leaving him out there in the communal gardens. I was just passing down the back lane on my way to the shop...'

But Howard has gone, wheeling the pram out of the back door so fast that he scrapes it all down the passage, leaving flakes of paint on the carpet. Kate hears him trundling down the garden path towards the gate at the bottom that leads to the alleyway. She flops down on the sofa and starts to cry. By the time her husband is back, she's sobbing so hard that she hardly notices when he comes to sit down beside her.

'Thank goodness I came home when I did,' he says. All the anger has gone from his voice. 'She can't have even noticed the baby had gone. I wheeled him into the garden of the flats and parked him under the cherry tree. I've seen the pram there before.'

'Did... did anyone notice you?'

'I don't think so. I thought that nosy woman at the shop did for a minute but she was just staring out of her back window at something else. She didn't even register me going past.'

Kate tries to control her tears but it isn't until Howard puts a tentative arm around her shoulders that she manages to stop hiccupping. It's not like him to hug her. His warmth makes everything seem less awful.

'You have got to listen to me now, Katie,' Howard says, quite gently. 'You've been acting weird ever since Christmas. You know they wanted you to take some time off school and I think it was a mistake going back straight after...'

His words dry up and Kate looks at him. Is he actually crying? Howard, who's breezed through her four miscarriages without acknowledging anything but a brief disappointment? Her husband blinks and rubs his eyes.

'That last one was especially tough, being on Christmas Eve, and everything,' he says. 'And you were four months along. I really thought we were going to get to the final hole this time.'

The golfing analogy grates but Howard's not finished.

'Kate, if I hadn't come home when I did... you could have been in really serious trouble. I can't believe you think it's okay just to help yourself to someone else's baby, just because we can't have one of our own. What on earth got into you?'

Kate tries to explain that the Easter holidays have given her way too much time to think and that this morning, she has taken her beloved Barnaby to the vet's and he's had to stay in. He'll probably have to be put to sleep tomorrow. It all just suddenly seemed too much and then hearing the baby crying... she just couldn't bear it. Howard listens, but she can see by his face that the shock of finding the baby in the house has thrown him completely.

'We need to get you a doctor's appointment,' he says eventually. 'I'll ring now.'

'I'm not taking any tablets,' says Kate.

'I think they need to decide that. You could lose your job if this gets out, and that girl could still go to the police if anyone saw you and tells her.'

Kate shrugs. She can't bring herself to care really.

'This has got to stop, you know that, don't you?'

'What do you mean? I'm not going to go round stealing babies, Howard. I was only helping out, to stop him being upset.'

'No, I mean the whole pregnancy thing. We're going to stop trying now. It's too much. We're not meant to be parents. We can be okay as we are. I know – I'll get you a puppy. You love dogs, don't you, and if Barnaby's not going to be around, it'll be company for you.'

Kate stares at Howard. Does he really think adopting a puppy will make up for the loss of all her dreams?

'And I won't tell anyone about what you did today if you promise to go see a doctor,' he continues. 'If you don't go... well, I'll have to mention to your boss at the school what happened.

You shouldn't be in charge of children if you're mentally unstable, should you?'

Kate feels the last vestiges of hope drain from her soul. He'd do it, she knows he would. She's stuck here now, with a man who could make her leave the job she loves and won't even carry on trying to give her the baby she longs for.

15

Milo began to make tentative plans to call at Willowbrook Park again during the coming week. When he was sitting on Frankie's bench, it was getting slightly easier to think about his sister and to mull over the deep sadness and regrets she'd left him with, although away from it, he was still struggling. Also, it would then seem quite natural to drop into the café and see if Kate was working. There was something about Kate that Milo just couldn't get out of his head. Perhaps it was because she'd seemed so calm and tranquil once the brief crisis with Elsie was over. For Milo, peace was hard to come by at the moment. Kate's warm smile and sparkling eyes had made him feel as if he was safe, but also had an unnervingly tingling effect on his senses. When they'd said goodbye, he'd had an overwhelming urge to wrap his arms around her and kiss her. There was only one way to find out if this was going to be something special or if he was just a vulnerable man with a ridiculous crush.

Frustratingly, just as Milo had decided when he could visit Willowbrook Park, events conspired against him. An urgent message reached him early the very next day to say that the senior member of staff at his firm's sister office in King's Lynn had been taken ill and was now off sick, possibly long term.

'You'll have to go over there,' his partner said, when Milo arrived at work for an emergency meeting. 'They can't cope until we find someone else to hold the fort, and you know they always help us out when *we're* having staffing problems. Us small businesses need to stick together.'

'But Max, I was going to... to do some other stuff. Why don't you do a stint there yourself?' Milo suggested.

Max raised his eyebrows. 'Good suggestion, and normally, I'd jump at the chance but I can't leave Deirdre at the moment. She... well, I should probably have told you this before but quite frankly, she's been struggling lately. The poor love doesn't want anyone to know. She's having some treatment for her bouts of depression at last but we're a long way from a place where she can be on her own in the house. I've even hidden all the tablets... Look, I'm sorry, but you really are going to have to take one for the team this time.'

'But that's awful. I didn't realise Deirdre was in a bad way. She seemed fine the last time I spoke to her. How long has this been going on?'

Max didn't answer for a moment. Then he said, 'I don't want to talk about it just now, okay?'

Resigned, Milo went back to the flat and made the necessary arrangements to leave. Max was one of his oldest friends and he couldn't let him down. Their partnership had saved Milo from having to apply for jobs much further away and he'd always been grateful that he'd been able to stay close enough to his parents to keep an eye on them, even though they'd never made that task easy.

Once he'd packed a small case, Milo texted Kate, thanking goodness they'd already exchanged numbers. If he couldn't casually call in at the café, he'd need to make another plan. He pondered for a moment and then began to type.

Hello, Kate

Really enjoyed chatting to you the other day. This might seem a bit sudden but I was going to see if you wanted to come to the theatre with me one night, or maybe a matinee? There's a great musical on in town. Will have to be on hold though because I'm off on a mission of mercy to save the day in King's Lynn. More soon, although this could turn out to be a long job. I'm hoping to get things under control this week, but it's not looking good right now.

Looking forward to seeing you asap,

Milo

He considered adding a kiss but decided against it and pressed send before he could mess about with the wording. Her reply pinged almost immediately.

A mission of mercy? Intriguing. White charger stuff, I hope. You seem to make a habit of rescuing people, don't you? No problem, will look forward to the theatre. I think I read in the paper that they're doing Oklahoma. See you soon, hopefully, Kate

No kiss there either, but he didn't really expect one. Somewhat reassured but still disappointed, Milo locked up and headed for his car. As he drove, Milo's thoughts irresistibly turned back to Kate but before he could begin to wonder if she just saw him as a potential friend or if there might be a spark there one day, his phone bleeped with an incoming WhatsApp message. He resisted the temptation to try and read it while he was driving, but soon spotted the sign for a roadside café where he'd stopped previously for coffee. He pulled off the road and parked up, not anticipating anything other than a last-minute instruction from Max, but when he opened his message, Milo was amazed to see it was from his son.

Luka hadn't been in touch since the day he'd called by the flat, and previous to that visit he'd only communicated if he needed something urgently, usually cash. Their relationship had never been straightforward and the recent meeting hadn't helped. Milo had absolutely no qualms in blaming Marianne for this. She'd never understood the overwhelming compulsion he had to get everything finished at the end of the day and Milo knew for a fact that she'd used his long working hours against him, although he'd tried his best to make time for Luka at weekends.

> Hi Dad, I dropped in to see you because I was near the office but the other bloke says you're away for a bit. Can you give me a call? L

Desperately needing caffeine, Milo made his way into the café and ordered a double espresso. Luka, calling in to see him at work? Something must be badly wrong. Was he ill? He'd definitely looked dodgy when he called at the flat. Milo paid for his drink and chose a table as far away from the counter as possible before phoning his son's number. Luka answered on the second ring.

'Dad? That was quick.'

'It sounded urgent. You okay?'

'Yeah, I... just wanted to talk to you. Where are you?'

'On the way to King's Lynn, I've got to take over at the office there for a little while. Erm... talk to me about what? I mean. Of course you can, but I won't be home for a while, I guess.'

'I could come over as soon as you're back?'

Milo was really mystified now but Luka's voice sounded much more cheerful than the last time they'd met and to be having an actual conversation with his son without arguments was heart-warming. He cleared his throat.

'Are you thinking next week? You're not at school?'

'Got study leave, but to be honest, I'm revisioned out. Can I come then?'

There was an echo of doubt in Luka's voice now and Milo hurried to reassure him. This was too good an opportunity to miss, whatever the reason.

'Course you can. Are you sure there's nothing wrong?'

'Nah, all good here. I wanted to talk to you about some stuff I've had on my mind. It's about... where I want to live. I'm going to uni in September, so it won't be a problem for long but I wondered...'

'You wondered?' Milo's heart was beating very fast now. Was this about what he was guessing? Surely not.

'I want to come and live with you until I go. Is there any chance? I don't mind having the sofa, or an air bed or something...'

'Oh, Luka, I'd love to have you. Leave it with me, okay? Are you sure you can stand it there just for now?'

'Yeah, I'm cool. Text me when you're home again. See you soon. Oh... and...'

'Yes?'

'I'm... sorry about how I was last time... at the flat. It was a bad day.'

'Hey, no problem. We all have 'em.'

'Cheers, Dad. I'm looking forward to seeing you, yeah?'

'Me too, Luka. Me too.'

They disconnected, and Milo finished his coffee, gazing out

of the window at the traffic flashing past on the main road. This was all very strange but it was a whole lot better than what had gone before, even if his flat was really too small for two leggy adults. Milo had pondered for a long time on Luka's throwaway remark as he'd left the flat the last time they met but he'd hardly dared to hope that this would be the issue that was preoccupying his son.

Milo stirred himself, conscious that these next few days were going to be very busy. He pushed his worries to one side and got on his way, putting his foot down to overtake a line of lorries and singing along to the radio. It was an old song by the Byrds, one of his mum's favourites called 'Turn, Turn, Turn'. The words echoed the ones on Frankie's bench. A time and a season for everything. As he drove towards the big, blue skies that told him he was on the way to Norfolk, even with the shadows that haunted his mind at the moment he felt more positive than he had for months. Maybe it was the right time for Luka to draw nearer to him. Milo hoped so, with every beat of his heart.

16

With Milo away and consequently with no prospect of him dropping in at the café, Kate's mood fluctuated between wanting to prove to herself that she wasn't reliant on a man to keep her looking forward to her working day and sadness that the delicate new friendship between her and Milo now had no chance to grow and develop.

The warmer weather was strangely unsettling and there was still no sign of Sophie to discuss everything with. The cruise had turned out to be a fantastic opportunity, and both Sophie and Paul had been offered the chance to move straight on to another one, this time around the Canary Islands. Kate knew it was good news for Sophie, but she couldn't help feeling a pang of envy. She was even beginning to think she might like that sort of experience for herself. Maybe she could start with a river cruise, on a much smaller boat. The thought was exciting and terrifying in equal measures, and she shied away from it, for now at least.

Returning home from work, the sounds of Beryl, Winnie and Anthea having a slightly drunken tea party in Beryl's garden floated over the dividing hedge. Kate couldn't see them through the thick foliage, but their voices rang out clearly in the still air.

'Top-up of Prosecco, girls?' Beryl asked.

'Oh, go on then. Bottoms up,' Winnie said, with a hiccup.

'I was beginning to think this was a dry do,' Anthea drawled. 'My last-but-one ex was like that, especially with champagne. He'd give you a small drink and then hide the bottle for himself. Loaded, but selfish, that was Tarquin. I screwed him for lots of lovely alimony, though, so he lost out in the end, the mean sod.'

Winnie's giggle was infectious, and Kate couldn't help smiling. She knew that if she called over the hedge, Beryl would invite her round to join them all, but something held her back tonight. She decided it was high time to bite the bullet and take stock of her life. A list was what was needed. Everything was always better with a list. There was a solitary bottle of merlot in the cupboard (Howard had taken the wine rack, which was just as well because Kate would have found its emptiness depressing) and she fetched it out, rummaging for the corkscrew at the same time.

Was it best to eat first or get straight on with the job in hand? Kate compromised by putting a ready meal in the microwave and uncorking the bottle. While she waited for it to heat up to tongue-scalding point, she poured herself a large glass of wine and found a notebook and pen. She debated going into the garden to eat, but it was starting to get chilly and the thought of overhearing more jollity from next door made her think that inside might be better tonight. As Kate went back out to fetch her cardigan, left slung over a garden chair, she heard the ladies next door expressing similar views about the weather.

'Blimey, it's dropped cold all of a sudden,' said Winnie. 'Let's go and line up a nice rom-com to watch and get the fire on. What time's the takeaway being delivered, Beryl?'

'In half an hour. I'm glad we're all having a night off cooking tonight, although I'll miss your jerk chicken. It's on Anthea this time. What film do you two fancy?'

'Something with bare bums,' said Winnie, decisively.

Kate leaned closed to the hedge, intrigued. She wasn't sure if she'd heard that last comment correctly, but Anthea was guffawing.

'You're absolutely right, Winifred,' she said. 'Men's back views are so much better than the front. All those unfortunate dangly bits are off-putting. Give me a well-muscled backside anytime.'

'Ditto,' Beryl chimed in. 'And a decent pair of legs, not too hairy, and none of those lumpy calves with knots on them, like cyclists get. They make me queasy. What do you reckon, Anthea?'

'Couldn't agree more, not to mention the sweaty Lycra shorts that cling to every curve and bulge. Mind you, I suppose that way you at least know what you're getting in advance.' Anthea let out a loud snort. 'Bring that bottle with you, darling. I put another couple in the fridge and the cash is on the worktop for the curry. Let's get this show on the road, girls.'

The voices became more distant and Kate went inside, grinning. What a great bunch these ladies were, and they seemed to be able to talk to each other about anything and everything. It made her own evening look very dull by comparison. She heard the microwave ping and her stomach rumbled hopefully. Taking the piping-hot risotto from the microwave, she loaded it onto a tray with her glass and the bottle and carried it across to the purple sofa.

As Kate sat down, sinking into the soft cushions, and peeled the top off the carton, her phone bleeped. She rolled her eyes, expecting to see Pat's name displayed. There had been talk of doing a deep clean at the weekend and Kate wasn't looking forward to the prospect. Instead, the number on the screen was unfamiliar. She clicked to read the message.

> Hi Kate. We haven't met yet but I'm the new headteacher at St Jude's. We're in a bit of a mess regarding our summer fair and some of the staff told me you might be able to help. I hope you don't mind me messaging you? The person who was going to face-paint for us has dropped out suddenly and they tell me you always used to do a sterling job on that stall, when you worked at the school. The fair is three weeks on Saturday, it'll take place on the village green if the weather's good or in the school if not. Is there any chance at all that you could help? I'd be eternally grateful. Yours, in hope, Richard Blackshaw

All of a sudden, Kate's appetite disappeared and she looked down at the risotto with revulsion, her stomach churning. Up to now, she'd avoided any contact with St Jude's, still feeling deep sadness that she'd had to leave all her friends on the staff, and the children who she'd watched grow and learn. The previous head had been a good friend but had now moved on to a bigger school which had made the thought of going back to visit even more daunting. Now, the thought of facing everyone again was painful. Should she do it?

Pushing her microwave dinner away, Kate reached for her notebook and pen. It was time to do this thing properly. The message was a huge nudge to decide what her next priorities should be. In true to-do list style, she decided to include some of the things she'd already started on, so that she could show the whole thing to Sophie the next time they met. Kate took a huge gulp of wine and began to write.

Kate's master plan for turning fifty and making life better:

- *Order some brighter clothes*
- *Get new cushions for the purple monstrosity and make the living room more cosy*
- *Join a club, or a class, something that's fun and different*
- *Go on a journey alone*
- *Stay over at Sophie's house*
- *Reconnect with friends from St Jude's*
- *Go on a date with Milo, even if it's just as friends*

So far so good with the first one, thought Kate. I already have the yellow raincoat and my new jeans and leggings. It's a work in progress, though. Summer clothes next, mainly new T-shirts. My old dresses still fit, luckily.

She ran her eyes down the list. The sofa cushions would be easy. She'd visit the market next week, and lighting a fire would instantly make the living room more cosy. Maybe a few candles too. As for joining something, maybe Beryl could advise on that one, although some of her choices were a bit off the wall in Kate's opinion. Standing around in a room and laughing for an hour seemed an uncomfortable idea. A dance class, though – that would be different and good exercise too. Salsa? No, she'd need a partner. Kate shelved the idea for now and considered the next points.

Go on a journey alone

Hmm. Not sure where or when. Pondering this one. Train?

Stay over at Sophie's house

Think it's time to fix this. Will ring her when she's back.

Reconnect with friends from St Jude's

Message just arrived from the new head. Must decide whether or not to help at the summer fair.

Go on a date with Milo, even if it's just as friends

He has asked me to go to the theatre but he's not been in touch since. Still busy with work, I guess. I'll go if he asks again.

Hungry again after all the brainwork, Kate picked up her fork and began to eat the barely warm risotto. It wasn't bad, but she knew she could have made something better. She added an extra item to her list, and then thinking about the ladies next door happily watching a film, she scribbled down one more after that.

- *Try out new recipes, ones that take more preparation time*
- *See how much a decent TV would cost if I paid monthly*

Now for the fire. Kate finished her dinner and took the tray to the kitchen, promising herself another glass of wine later. Fetching the log basket from the shed, she filled it with the chunks of wood, breathing in the resiny scent. There were only a few left when she'd finished. She added some smaller pieces of kindling and a newspaper from the pile she'd collected from the café when they were discarded by customers.

Back in the living room, she set about constructing the 'paper sticks' that her dad had always made for the open fire at home when she was growing up. Each double sheet had to be tightly rolled up and then wound around the fingers, with the end tucked in to secure the little bundle. Then Kate scrunched up more newspaper and built a little pyramid with a few paper sticks topped with a wigwam of kindling. Striking a match released the sulphuric scent that took her back to childhood even more than making the fire already had done. The paper caught immediately and tiny flames began to lick their way up the pyramid.

Kate carefully placed three smaller logs on top of the heap and sat back to watch. The glow from the burgeoning fire warmed her spirits as much as her body and she realised how much she'd missed this primaeval comfort. It had seemed too much effort to light one just for herself but for goodness' sake, why shouldn't she? Howard had always sorted the ordering of logs but that was no problem.

Back on the sofa, Kate reconsidered her list. She could hunt for candles next, there were plenty stashed away upstairs, given as gifts at the end of term over the years from grateful children and parents. Howard had hated her burning them because he said she was prone to dripping wax around when she blew them out. It didn't matter now. Finding the candles took less than ten minutes, and Kate brought her treasure box downstairs to unpack. When the lid was opened, the mingled fragrances made her giddy. Bergamot, vanilla and lemon mingled with camomile, frankincense and sandalwood in a wild bouquet of scents.

Selecting a fat candle that claimed to be 'soothing and calming', she lit it and closed the lid on the others. The delicate aromas of lavender and cedar wood gradually filled the room. Kate turned off the bright overhead bulb and sat in the firelight, letting her senses appreciate the new cosiness. This was much better. A couple of lamps would complete the ambience and make evenings much more relaxing. Annoyed with herself for not making these simple changes sooner, Kate made some additional notes on her list to show that she had done all she could tonight.

Now for the trickier items. A solo journey could wait. Kate was too busy at work this week to think about planning that one, and a visit to Sophie couldn't happen until her friend had finished gadding off around the world. As for Milo, that was another waiting game. The school summer fair, however, was a different matter.

Kate thought back to all the times she'd sat watching the queue of excited children line up to have their faces painted in a wide variety of styles. It had been fun, but doing it again would mean facing everyone from that part of her past all in one go. She'd seen a few of them around the village but this would be overload. On impulse, she threw another two logs on the fire, picked up her phone and dialled the number that Richard Blackshaw had texted from. He answered on the second ring.

'Hi, Richard, it's Kate Brown. I'm just responding to your message. Can you...'

'Oh, Kate!' he interrupted. 'It's so good of you to call. I can't tell you what a relief it would be if you could join us and do your usual fabulous work. You... you will, won't you?' A note of doubt had crept into his voice. 'It was just that the staff all said how brilliant you always were and I...'

Richard stopped speaking. He seemed to be lost for words. Kate was hit by the realisation that she was needed, really needed. Visiting the school had seemed an impossible hurdle if she was dropping in to say hello, but if she had a proper job to do, and most likely it would be out in the sunshine, maybe it'd be okay.

'Of course I'll help. I'd love to,' Kate said, without giving herself time to mull the idea over any more. 'Text me the details. I expect you've still got all the paints.'

'Yes, everything's here, and we'll set the stall up ready for you on the day, weather permitting. You can even have the one nearest to your house, if that's more convenient. I'm told you live in a prime spot right near the green?'

'That would be lovely,' Kate said. They chatted for a few more minutes and then she ended the call, feeling the tension gradually leave her shoulders.

That's another one to tick off the list, Kate said to herself as she settled down again in front of the now-roaring fire. The soft candlelight added to the soporific effect of the flickering flames in the hearth. Sipping her red wine, Kate admired the rich crimson colour as she held the glass up. The reflection of the candle and the flames made the wine look like a huge ruby, gleaming and precious. Tonight had been a big step forward. Hearing the faint sound of laughter through the wall, Kate giggled. Maybe, like Beryl and co, a good dose of bare bums and well-muscled legs (not too hairy) would be a perfect end to a successful evening. She'd finish her drink and then fetch her iPad downstairs so that she could find a good film to watch. This was one more example of the gang of three leading the way to a new kind of life. Kate's fiftieth birthday wouldn't be an excuse for doom and gloom, it'd be a celebration of future fun and possibilities, Saga Lout style!

17

Home again at last, or what passed for it, Milo stared at the letter that he'd just dropped onto the kitchen worktop. A heap of post was waiting for him when he got back from his trip to King's Lynn but this one had been hidden under a pile of junk mail and he'd shelved the job of sorting it all until this morning, thinking there was nothing significant to bother with. Now he wished he hadn't. There was a lot to think about here.

The letter had landed in a small pool of spilt coffee and the brown stain was gradually seeping into it but Milo didn't feel inclined to move it. *Notice to quit the premises,* he read. The words blurred in front of his eyes. His landlord was giving him a month to find a new home. The building was being demolished to make way for a community health centre and hospice. Milo cursed himself for not committing to a longer rental agreement. Would that have made a difference? He'd only paid for the next four weeks and put off the decision to sign up for more because it was impossible to feel anything but vague acceptance for this place. It had occurred to him at the time that it was unusual for a landlord to agree to such a short-term contract but he'd been so keen to move that he'd ignored the alarm bells.

The flat had done the job while he got used to the idea of leaving Marianne and Luka, but even with a few personal touches, it wasn't very welcoming. Even so, the thought of starting flat hunting all over again made his heart sink. These uninspiring rooms suddenly looked more appealing, even if they weren't really anywhere near big enough to house both himself and Luka if that plan came off. Milo screwed up the letter and hurled it into the bin. His practical, financially focused brain told him it would be pointless to appeal against this decision, considering the scale of the new development and the fact that it was massively needed around here. What should he do? He wouldn't get a chance to go online and search for another place until much later.

The only thing that Milo could think of that might lift his pessimistic mood was a chat with someone understanding, and the person who sprang to mind immediately was, as always, these days, Kate. She'd struck him as the ideal person to talk to when you needed a sympathetic ear. More to the point, he was longing to see her. It was no good trying to kid himself any more. This was so much more than a crush already. It was scary, but also as exhilarating as standing on top of a high mountain where the air was like champagne.

Shelving any doubts about whether Kate would want to hear about his troubles, Milo made the snap decision to go straight to the country park after work. He still wasn't sure exactly which days she worked or even if she had regular hours, but he'd just have to risk it. He wondered if it would seem weird to wait for her to finish her shift in the café and then ask if he could take her for a drink so they could talk. Surely that was a bit heavy. Maybe if he dropped in as if he was just passing and then floated the idea, she'd think it was a spontaneous suggestion. She'd already agreed to the theatre trip, which was promising.

The day dragged. Milo ate some cheese straight from the fridge, made himself a pot of strong coffee for sustenance and ploughed on. On the dot of four o'clock, thanking his own presence of mind for suggesting the idea of flexi-time to Max, he took a couple of painkillers, changed into shorts and a T-shirt and left the building with a spring in his step. Time to put himself first for a while. It wasn't far to his car, which he'd managed to park under a tree for once. Even so, the heat as he opened the door was intense. Winding down all the windows, he turned on the radio and sang along at the top of his voice to an old Billy Idol song about it being a nice day for a white wedding. He guessed it probably would be, if you'd found the right person.

The drive from Meadowthorpe didn't take long and the entrance to Willowbrook Park was soon in sight. The winding, tree-lined drive to the car park nearest to the benches was cool and shady after the open road and traffic noise. Milo switched off the radio and luxuriated in the bird song and the drifting scent of newly shorn grass, at peace for the first time that day. There was a distant hum of a mowing machine and as he got out of the car, he could hear the splash of oars as the local rowing team geared up for their weekly practice. Milo quickened his pace as he headed for Pat's Place.

* * *

The cheerful ding of the bell on the café door caused Kate to look up from serving a customer, who appeared to be just finishing telling Kate a long and sorrowful tale. The smile that lit up her face when she caught sight of Milo looked perfectly genuine, and he told himself to stop being paranoid about whether she'd want to see him. They were already friends. New friends, for sure, but it was fine to come and say hello. It was perfectly okay.

Kate patted her customer's hand and murmured a few words of encouragement. The woman brightened up and thanked her, saying she'd be back next week to provide an update. When she was safely in her seat tucking into a buttered scone, Kate smiled at Milo.

'Have you come for a walk or to sit on the bench?' she said. 'I expect you'd like a cold drink first?'

'All three of those, really,' he said, beaming back at her, unable to hide the lift of joy her rosy-cheeked face and happy smile gave him. Kate's hair was scooped up into a large clip on the back of her head, leaving her neck bare and strangely vulnerable-looking. Her wide hazel eyes were fringed with lashes even longer and more luxuriant than his own and her eyebrows were natural and well-defined. Milo, after years of living with a wife who had the biggest selection of cosmetics ever known to mankind, could tell that this was a woman who didn't feel the need to wear make-up, apart from a dash of lip gloss that accentuated her gorgeous cupid's bow of a mouth.

'You look lovely,' he blurted out, and then stared at the floor, overcome with embarrassment, instantly turned back into the awkward teenaged boy he once was. Not spotty any more, but with no social skills whatsoever. Totally out of practice at the flirting game, if he'd ever been any good at it.

Kate laughed. 'You're the first person to tell me that for a long time,' she said. 'You must be a fan of the *end-of-a-hot-day-in-a-steamy-place* kind of look. I can't wait to get out of here and go home for a shower. What can I get you?'

'Oh... erm...' Milo tried to stifle his disappointment that the chance of Kate wanting to go for a pint was looking slim. 'Actually, hold the cold drink, I'll have a double espresso, please. Could do with a caffeine lift. When do you knock off work?'

'In ten minutes time,' she answered, busy with the coffee machine. 'It can't come soon enough.'

'So... I don't suppose the thought of an ice-cold beer in a shady pub garden would tempt you away from going straight home?' Milo said. He held his breath, convinced she'd say no, but it was surely worth a try. Kate didn't answer for a moment. When she'd given him his drink and taken the payment, she looked him in the eye.

'Why?' she said, rather tersely.

'Why what?'

'Why do you want to take me out for a drink when I look like a sweaty scarecrow?'

Milo gazed at Kate in amazement. 'I told you, you look lovely,' he said. 'Maybe I like sweaty scarecrows.'

She rolled her eyes at him and then, to Milo's relief, laughed. 'It's a look I've perfected since this mini-heatwave started,' she said. 'People have been asking me how I pull it off but I'm keeping my secret safe. When the trend really takes off, I can say I was the first.'

A couple more customers now stepped forward to claim Kate's attention, so Milo took his coffee to a nearby table and sat down. He wondered if he'd blown it, but when she finished serving them, Kate took off her overall and hung it on a hook.

'I'm leaving now, Pat,' she shouted over her shoulder.

Pat bustled out of the kitchen and gave Kate a brief hug. Her short black hair was plastered to her forehead, without any of its usual bounce. 'Off you pop then,' she said. 'Did I just overhear that you're off out for a pint? Lucky you, wish I could join you. I'm melting.'

Kate opened a hatch in the counter and came towards Milo,

who was already on his feet. She smiled up at him. 'Yes, I've been approached by this strange man who apparently has a thing about red-faced, shiny women. Only one drink, mind. I really do need to get home and shower. It's been a bit of a day.'

'Have one for me,' said a lady sipping an iced coffee over by the window.

'And me,' several more customers chorused.

Milo took in his audience. Had the invitation been overheard by the whole café? It certainly looked that way. Most of the occupants of the tables were waving to Kate as she approached the door.

'That was surreal,' said Milo, as they walked back towards his car.

'What was?'

'The way everyone was listening and they all acted like they know you and they have the right to earwig on your conversation.'

'Well, that's because most of them *do* know me, and you weren't exactly whispering. Unless someone's muttering under their breath, other people's chats are fair game in a café. There are a couple of local authors who spend a lot of time in there doing just that. They listen, they absorb the atmosphere and then write it down, or so it seems.'

'And do they all tell you their troubles?'

'Quite a lot of them do, yes.'

Milo looked down at Kate as she strolled along the path. He could completely understand why everyone and his dog wanted to bend her ear with their problems. She had the sort of motherly air that made you want to bare your soul and be made better, and yet there was something else about her, well-hidden but definitely there. Something almost unbearably exciting and tempting. What an odd mixture she was.

He thought about telling her this amazing fact but couldn't think of a way to put it nicely. Nobody wanted to be thought odd.

They'd reached Frankie's bench by this time and Milo paused. 'Can you stand putting off the beer for five minutes?' he asked hopefully. 'Only, this seat was taken when I came by earlier and I like to at least say hello to my sister.'

'Of course.' Kate sat down. 'Oh, but do you mean you want to be on your own? I'm sorry, I didn't...'

'No, not at all. It's good to have your company,' Milo reassured her, touched to see how flustered she was. 'I'm sure Frankie would have liked to have met you. Perhaps she came into the café at some point but you didn't know who she was. No reason why you should.'

Milo could hear himself rambling, and stopped talking abruptly. The two of them sat quietly, watching the ducks weaving around each other on the lake and the swans taking three cygnets for a swim, every now and again dipping their beaks into the water as if instructing their offspring how to find all the best snacks.

'Have you got a photo of Frankie?' said Kate, breaking the silence. 'Only if you want to show me,' she added hastily.

Milo reached for his wallet and slid his fingers into a side pocket. The tiny snapshot was tattered around the edges but his sister's face smiled up at him, still clear and bright. He carefully passed the photograph to Kate and she took it from him with equal respect. Milo leaned back against the plaque and watched her face. The tension he'd been feeling all day melted away as Kate studied the picture. She turned to him and her eyes shone with unshed tears.

'What a beautiful girl.'

Milo was deeply grateful for this simple, heartfelt statement.

After a while, he said, 'It's hard to get over the aching. I miss her so much.'

'I don't know if people do ever really get over such intense grief. That's not how it works. It's more a case of working around it and living with it, I reckon.'

'You sound as if you know what you're talking about.'

Kate looked up at him. 'My dad died, remember?'

'Oh, hell, I'm so sorry, of course he did,' Milo said, wishing he'd never started this conversation. 'I tell you what, let's go and get that drink. I think if we go any further with this conversation we'll both end up blubbing. I know a pub with an orchard next to it. The outside tables are all amongst the trees and there's a little stream running through the beer garden. It's not far.'

Kate slapped her forehead. 'Oh, for goodness' sake. I must be barmier than I thought. I've just realised I've got my car here too. I often walk but I was going to go shopping on the way home today because the supermarket's so nice and cool. I usually take my neighbour but she's feeling the heat today. Shall we do this another time when I'm not driving?'

Milo shook his head. He couldn't bear to put her off, it might never happen again.

'How about if I followed you home and wait outside? You can even have a quick change if you must, although as I said...'

'I know, I look lovely,' Kate said with a smile that didn't quite reach her eyes.

'But that sounds as if I'm trying to find out where you live. I didn't mean that.'

'I'm not worried about you being a crazed axe murderer, if that's what you're hinting at,' Kate said. 'But this is getting complicated. You're all ready and changed and I'm just... not.'

Milo sat very still and willed her not to change her mind. He could see why she wouldn't want to risk him following her home when she hardly knew him. Or was there another reason? His mind dredged up all sorts of possibilities in the minute or two it took Kate to ponder. Was there a husband there? She wasn't wearing a wedding ring but after all, lots of married people didn't. Kate surely must have someone who loved her, she was so easy to get on with. And if she had, he should back off right now. Eventually Kate stood up.

'Right, this is what we'll do. You can drive over to this amazing-sounding pub. When you get there, text me the name of it and the postcode. I'll have the quickest shower ever and get a taxi to join you. How does that sound?'

Milo was on his feet too now. 'Brilliant,' he said. 'Thank goodness one of us is a dab hand at making a plan, at least.'

Kate grinned and began to walk away. After a moment she turned back. 'I *will* come and find you, Milo,' she said. 'You're looking doubtful, but when I say I'm going to do something, I don't go back on it. Ever.'

She waved to him and despite the heat, set off at a cracking pace towards the café. Milo watched her go, and replayed her words in his head. It was the sort of promise his gut feeling told him he could trust. But why didn't Kate want him to go to her house? He was going to have to come straight out and ask her if she was already in some sort of a relationship. There was no way he'd be going behind someone's back, even if it was just for a sociable drink in a crowded pub. He pushed all these unsettling thoughts away and turned to face Frankie's bench.

'Do you think Kate's lovely too?' he said. 'You never liked Marianne, did you? You said I was a bad picker. And I'd reply something about pots and kettles, remember? I was being perfectly honest today. Even after a day in a hot café, she still looks beautiful to me, but I'm terrified of frightening her off and I don't even know if she's free. Wish me luck, Frankie.'

Glancing around, Milo reassured himself that nobody had witnessed him addressing a wooden bench, and strolled back to his car. He didn't intend to text Kate too soon and make her think she was being rushed, but the prospect of her company for at least part of a warm evening in such an idyllic setting made him want to run and jump. Today had started badly but it was improving all the time. All he needed now was somewhere decent to live and to get to know Kate a whole lot better. Of these two tasks, he had a feeling that the first was going to be by far the easiest.

18

Kate climbed out of the taxi, glad she'd decided to change into a summer frock. To begin with, she'd automatically pulled out a navy linen shift dress from her wardrobe. It was an old favourite and skimmed her curves, making her feel slim for once. Then, an echo of Sophie's voice rang in her ears. No more indigo. Taking a deep breath, she'd rummaged further and found one that was just as cool and comfortable but a pretty shade of turquoise. It was a sundress with broad straps. The downside for Kate was that the skirt only reached to just above her knees, making her feel unusually exposed.

Her shower had been taken at what felt like the speed of light and Kate was still slightly clammy when she got dressed. Now, she was finding it difficult to exit the cab without revealing a ridiculous amount of leg, but at least she'd shaved them yesterday so that part of her body was sleek and presentable. She was even wearing strappy sandals with heels. It was good to feel as if she was going to meet someone who seemed to really want to see her. The few times that Howard had arranged a get-together after work, she'd arrived at the chosen venue to find several of his golfing cronies already downing pints as if their lives depended on it.

The pub sign was swaying back and forth in a sudden and very welcome breeze. Kate tried hard to pluck up the courage to go inside. She could hear the happy sounds of customers enjoying the warm evening in the garden around the back. The thought of walking right through the crowded bar was daunting, so she made her way under a wooden arch covered with trailing clematis and down a rutty path through a small apple orchard towards the noise. She crossed her fingers. Hopefully, Milo had had the same thoughts and bagged them a table in the shade.

Kate noticed her host immediately because he leapt to his feet as soon as she emerged from the trees. The smile on his face made her previous panic worthwhile and she swayed towards him, trying to avoid getting her heels stuck in the grass. Leaning down, Milo kissed her cheek; the hint of five o'clock shadow brushed across her flushed skin sending shivers down Kate's spine.

'You made it,' he said, with obvious relief.

'I told you I wouldn't stand you up.' Kate's earlier qualms disappeared like butter in the sun when she saw the shyness and lack of confidence revealed in that moment. Milo's even worse than me, she realised with surprise. I need to help him to trust me. He must have had some bad experiences with women to look so concerned that I wouldn't show.

Now that Kate had given herself a task, everything was much easier. When Milo returned with a chilled glass of wine for her, she regaled him with a story the taxi driver had told her about his online dating experiences.

'The poor man had eight dates in the last two months,' Kate

said. 'And they seemed to get more disastrous every time. He finally twigged the problem was that he hadn't specified an upper age limit. He was sixty-three but the last two were over eighty and neither had their own teeth or hair.'

Milo spluttered into his beer. When he recovered himself, he says 'Didn't that come over in the pre-meeting chats online?'

'Apparently not. And they'd used photos from years ago on their profiles. Mind you, both of them brought him offerings of cake, so there was an upside, I guess. One had even made him some marmalade. Erm... Milo... have... have you ever done the online dating thing?'

Kate waited with trepidation for his response. What if he was working his way through all the eligible women in a thirty-mile radius? Milo was quite a catch, she could see that even more clearly now he was relaxed and peaceful. A financial advisor, presumably with his own place, a decent car and the sort of rugged, slightly vulnerable good looks that would appeal to a great deal of single females.

'I wouldn't have the nerve, even if I wanted to go down that road,' Milo said, pulling a face. 'How could you ever get out of the situation without feeling mean if it turned out to be a disastrous evening? I'm such a wuss that if I did end up having dinner with an octogenarian I'd probably accidentally agree to another date and end up enrolling her in my mother's bridge circle.'

Kate agreed that she'd probably be in the same boat. 'Although I do love talking to the older people when they come into the café,' she said. 'They have such interesting tales to tell when I'm not too busy serving. Sometimes I sit and chat with the lonely ones if we're not busy. Pat's signed us up for a befriending scheme where we're going to have a specified table at quieter times with a little notice on it to say you should sit there if you're on your own and you really want a natter. She's going to put me in charge of it.'

Milo reached over and took Kate's free hand. Her stomach flipped and she hoped against hope her fingers weren't all sweaty.

'That's a lovely thought,' he said. 'I hope more places take the idea up. You know what our problem is, though? We're just too nice. Maybe we ought to give each other lessons in being more forceful. I have no difficulty dealing with difficult clients at work but in my private life... well, just call me Mr Pushover.'

Kate laughed and finished her wine. She got to her feet. 'Ms Pushover here, saluting you,' she said. 'Let's drink to that. I'm going to have another glass of that sauvignon blanc and then we'll make a plan to toughen up. I see you're on Coke but you can probably have just the one proper drink?'

Milo wasn't keen on letting Kate get the next round in but she refused to listen to his protestations and took his order for a very weak shandy before heading for the bar. In truth, she needed a few moments away from him to cool down again. This hand-holding stuff was all well and good, but it played havoc with her composure. She half hoped he wouldn't do it again, but also... kind of wished he would.

When Kate returned with a tray containing her wine, a pint of shandy and some crisps to share, Milo was looking serious. Oh dear.

'What's up?' she said as breezily as possible. 'You're frowning.'

'Am I? I didn't realise. I was just thinking about the dating thing.'

Kate sat down and handed him his beer. 'In what way?'

'Well... I wondered... are you seeing anyone? Have you got

what they call a *significant other*? I really hate that phrase,' he added.

'Me too. And no, I haven't, as it happens.'

The relief on Milo's face made Kate smile, it was so obvious. 'That pleases you, I'm guessing?' she said. 'Did you think there might be some hefty bloke about to turn up and punch you on the nose?'

He laughed. 'No... yes... maybe. I can usually stick up for myself but I don't want to get blood on this T-shirt. It's my favourite. I used to go to a lot of gigs but this one's special. Do you like The Who?'

He'd neatly changed the subject but Kate wasn't in the least ready to let it drop yet. 'What about you?' she asked.

'Oh, yes, they're my favourite band. Never the same without Keith Moon but still brilliant.'

'You know that wasn't what I meant.'

Their eyes met and Milo smiled. 'Right. Well, I was married for a long time and we have a son called Luka. I saw him this week as it happens. We've not been in touch much lately, so it was particularly great.'

He paused to drink some shandy. Kate waited. No way was he getting off the hook that easily.

'But his mum and I decided to call it a day last year, although I didn't actually move out for a while,' he carried on, when it was clear Kate wasn't going to reply. 'Well, to be perfectly accurate, she made the decision. She'd found someone else. And that's all I want to say about that for now, if that's okay? It's a depressing story. How about you?'

Kate regarded Milo dispassionately. As far as she knew, although Howard was a natural flirt, he'd never been unfaithful to her until he'd met his new lady. Even so, Kate had often felt used. Now, belatedly, she was realising that by letting Howard call all the shots, she'd wasted an awful lot of time when she could have either been finding someone who valued her or having a life where she depended on nobody but herself for contentment. She wasn't at all sure how much, if anything, she was ready to share of her time with Howard. Maybe a one-liner would be enough.

'I'm not with my husband any more, because it turned out that he'd found somebody he liked a lot better than me,' she said eventually. 'Let's talk about something else, shall we? That's enough of the heavy stuff.'

Milo was still frowning, and Kate had no idea how to get them out of this trough. All the talk of broken marriages and fractured relationships had really ruined the gentle, almost flirty atmosphere that was just starting to grow between her and Milo and she very much wanted it back.

'Let's change the subject and play threes,' she said. 'It's what I used to do in school with the children who weren't great at conversation, and that's us tonight. Name your three favourite foods that start with the same letter. I'll give you a... C. Quickly, go on, without thinking.'

Milo laughed. 'I've got too many to choose from, but hey... I guess... chicken pie, chocolate cake and cheese. Your turn. Erm... three favourite seaside places in the UK, starting with the letter B this time.'

'That's easy. Bridlington, Brighton and Babbacombe. Now you need to tell me a secret.'

'Really? What happened to the easy questions? Oh, okay. Well, nobody else knows this but I like to eat pepperoni pizza in the bath. Your go. Tell me a secret.'

'I once stole a baby.'

The words were out before Kate could stop them and she put both hands over her mouth in horror. In the extended pause that followed, she squeezed her eyes shut and longed for a thunderbolt to strike her. Why, oh why had she drunk that second glass of wine so fast? Eventually, she heard Milo say, 'Kate? You're joking, right?'

He was offering her a way out. Could she get away with it? Worth a try. She laughed, hearing the breath catch in her throat. 'Of course I am. I was just... you know... inserting a bit of drama into the game. I used to do that with the kids too... only not with that line, obviously.'

Kate opened her eyes to see Milo looking at her intently. 'You didn't run a drama group with the kids by any chance, did you? That was definitely a showstopper.'

'I did, as it happens. It was the best part of my job. Well, that's put an end to my ice breaker. I'm not with a shy group of ten-year-olds now. I should remember to...'

The sentence was left hanging because Kate had no idea what to say next. She stood up and reached for her bag. 'I think I'm going to call a cab,' she said.

Milo was on his feet now. 'I've had enough too,' he said. 'I'll run you home, if that's okay?'

Kate looked up at him and her heart melted. She desperately wanted to escape this awkward situation of her own making but Milo didn't deserve a brush-off. 'Go on then, if it's no trouble. Although I'm warning you, I won't ask you in for coffee.'

She didn't expand on this bald statement and Milo made no comment. Kate wasn't about to explain to him that not only was she horrified at having blurted out something so awful, but if Milo saw the inside of her house he would realise that it was still sparse in places because Howard took all the best furniture when he left and she was only just starting to replace it. She was still on the hunt for decent lamps and the TV search hadn't got past the online browsing stage. If Milo could see number six

Fiddler's Row later in the evening with the candles and the fire lit, it would be a different matter, but that wasn't going to happen. Only the closest of friends had seen the place after the stripping of its assets and having her once-comfortable home denuded of so many of its basic items still caused her pain. Perhaps that was a conversation for another day. Or maybe not.

19

A couple of days later, after having agonised into the small hours over what the rules and etiquette of dating might now be, Milo decided he'd waited long enough to get in touch with Kate again. He texted her as he ate his cereal, pulling a disgusted face at the bowl of soggy bran flakes that was all he had left in the cupboard. He really should go shopping today, whether Kate agreed to the idea he'd planned or not. He rattled off a brief message without giving himself time to stress about the wording.

Are you working today? M x

Sod it all, if he wanted to send a kiss, he damn well would. He held his breath. If Kate was busy she might not be able to look at her phone for a while, but luckily for his blood pressure, she replied within five minutes.

Yes, until 4 p.m. Why?

I have a cunning plan. How do you feel about picnics?

Well they've never done me any harm, if that's what you mean? There's obviously the wasp issue... *smiley emoji*

Haha. So would you like to meet me at Frankie's bench for tea?

Ooh. Sounds great. I haven't got Elsie today or you'd have to provide jelly and cupcakes.

Oh, so you don't want me to bring the cakes and jelly I made?

I hope you're kidding.

I am. Do you have any allergies or anything?

No, I eat anything and everything, which is why I haven't got a stick-thin body.

They're over-rated, in my opinion. They tend to snap under pressure.

There was a pause, and Milo read his last message back, suddenly horrified. What if she thought he was... oh gawd... she wouldn't think that, would she? A few agonising minutes went by before another text pinged onto his phone.

Sorry, Pat called me. I'll see you later, minus jelly. Is 4.15 ok?

Excellent. Are you driving?

No, are you?

Yes, sadly. Apple juice for me today but would you like fizz?

No thanks, apple juice is fine.

Lots to tell you.

Looking forward to it. X

Milo sat back in his chair and re-read all the messages, breathing a sigh of relief that he'd managed not to say the wrong thing. It had been so easy to offend Marianne. His ex-wife had almost made an art form of misunderstanding him. Kate was so relaxing. She wasn't cynical or sarcastic and each time he met her, Milo felt as if he was getting a step closer to knowing her better. Maybe she'd give away more information about her own marriage today, if she was starting to trust him. He set off to work well before seven o'clock with more of a spring in his step than he'd had since Frankie's death, and even enjoyed his trolley dash around the local supermarket in his short lunch break.

Max was away from work, having rung in to say he was taking his wife to the hospital. Checking the office manager, Jenny, was happy to be left in charge, Milo left work in good time to meet Kate, first getting changed into shorts and T-shirt again in the cloakroom. The weather was perfect for sitting by the lake. It was still warm and sunny, but the gentle breeze would keep the two of them from over-heating. Just in case Kate was sensitive to the sun, Milo had packed a large beach umbrella. It took two trips to get everything from the car but at last he was ready to begin his preparations.

Luckily, Frankie's bench was vacant and Milo set out his stall very efficiently. He'd even brought a small folding table which he pulled out of the bag with the air of a conjuror. He covered it with a pale yellow tablecloth in his sister's honour as she'd loved all shades of yellow so much. The cloth was one of the few things he'd insisted on taking from the family house when Marianne was blitzing her way through the drawers and cupboards. Soon a very tempting feast was ready, just as a familiar figure approached.

Milo leapt to his feet, almost upending the table, and went to meet Kate, who was gazing wide-eyed at the scene he'd set.

'You made it,' he said. Well, that's blindingly obvious. Can you not think of something a bit more original, man? He quickly upped his game.

'Come and sit down, I've got lots to tell you,' he said. 'You look absolutely lovely. But then you always do. I like the dress.'

Kate laughed. 'You'd say I looked lovely if I'd come straight from a shift at the coal face,' she said. 'But thanks. My poor battered ego loves your compliments. I've been ditching all my most boring clothes. Anything, black, grey or indigo has gone unless it's really smart and I've ordered some brighter things online. This one's from way back. My mum bought it me. She said the colour was primrose. It even matches your tablecloth.'

Milo nodded approvingly. 'You suit bright colours. You're like a ray of sunshine today. Urgh, that sounded much cheesier out loud than it did in my head.'

Kate laughed. 'Nobody's ever called me that before. Wow, look at this picnic. It's amazing. And you did all this for me?' She fanned her face and swallowed hard, as if overcome by the trouble he'd taken. Her cheeks were glowing. 'All my favourite things to eat are here. Are you psychic, or what?'

'I'd like you to think that,' Milo said, blushing too. This was uncomfortably like being a teenager again, on a first date and desperate to impress. 'But actually I rang your boss at the café this morning to ask her what sort of snack food you like. She said I couldn't go wrong with olives, cheeses, a bit of token salad and some really good crusty bread. Maybe add smoked salmon with some chunks of lemon to squeeze. And don't forget the paper napkins.'

'Ah, Pat knows me so well,' Kate said, sitting down and admiring the spread. 'I'm greedy and messy too. I thought she was being a bit furtive when she answered the phone earlier.' She reached for a paper plate and Milo poured her a glass of fizzy apple juice, well-chilled from the freezer bag.

'So, you said you had something to tell me,' Kate said, taking a grateful sip of her drink and leaning back on the bench.

'Yes, it's not very good news.'

'Go on, I can take it.' Kate's smile was warm and encouraging, and Milo felt the tension of the last weeks lessen a little.

'I'm going to be evicted from my flat.'

Milo waited for Kate to make her excuses and go home, but she patted his arm sympathetically. 'Do you love your flat?'

'Er... no. But it's been somewhere to live when I really needed it. Although now things might be changing. I know my son would really like to come and stay with me for a bit and this flat is a bit grotty and very small so I'd have had to move anyway, I guess.'

'There you go then. It's a new chapter for you both. It's exciting, isn't it? I've got my phone. Shall we both search online for some places for you to view with Luka when we've had the picnic?'

Milo's eyes met Kate's, which were shining as if the whole eviction idea was a big treat. How great to meet someone whose glass was half-full, not half-empty. In addition to that, she was looking at him as though he was the most amazing man in the world. He wanted to kiss her so badly that it hurt.

'The thing is, Kate,' he mumbled, tearing his gaze away from her beautiful eyes with difficulty, 'I'm at a kind of crossroads in my life and I'm guessing you are too. We're probably both still feeling battered. I don't want to push you into anything you're not ready for, if you know what I mean?'

'Well, no, I don't, actually. What were you intending to push me into? So far, you've fished my goddaughter out of the lake, we've texted a bit and chatted in the café and you've made me a picnic. Am I missing something?'

They both looked at the floor. Milo had never fully understood the saying about wishing the ground would open and swallow you up. Now he got it.

'Let's just pretend I didn't spout out all that stuff,' he said eventually, when he couldn't stand the silence any longer. 'It's a lovely day otherwise. Let's eat before the wasps descend.'

Kate didn't argue, and she and Milo made short work of everything on offer. Milo was glad to see that although he'd clearly unsettled Kate, she was determinedly getting on with having a good time, and praising him for making such a perfect picnic. Afterwards, he poured coffee from a flask and opened a packet of chocolate biscuits.

'I love cooking, but I didn't have time to make cakes or cookies,' he said. 'Maybe next time?'

'Absolutely. I'll hold you to that. If there is a next time, of course. I mean, I totally understand what you said, at least, I think I do, but honestly, you're quite safe with me. I wasn't about to drag you into bed, Milo. We can make our own rules up as we go along if we do choose to see each other, can't we?'

The new silence that followed didn't seem as uncomfortable to Milo, but he feared he was about to rock the boat again. Even so, questions needed to be asked if they were ever going to get to know each other properly.

'Kate, when we were at the pub, we started talking about our... current circumstances,' Milo blurted out eventually. 'I wondered what happened when you found out your husband had someone else. Were you devastated? Oh, but don't feel as if you've got to answer if it's too painful.'

Kate looked down at her hands. They were well-shaped, Milo noticed, with long, graceful fingers and neat nails.

'I don't mind talking about it to you,' she said. 'It's not very interesting, though. I found out he'd been seeing a woman at the golf club. She was his partner in the tournaments and she was married. They had a long affair before he finally decided to leave me. It's a bit of a cliché but he'd had a good promotion at work and then a hefty win on the Premium Bonds quite recently. He'd inherited them years ago from his uncle and at the time I'd wanted him to sell them so we could have some exotic holidays but he never would. I guess he was right in the end. They certainly paid off for Howard.'

Milo froze. The club? His golfing partner? It couldn't be... could it? If not, it was a bizarre coincidence. For a long time, Marianne had spent most of her spare time at the club and some months before she left him had mentioned a more experienced partner in the latest run of tournaments. But Marianne's new lover was called Brad. He swallowed hard and told himself not to be ridiculous as Kate continued.

'Howard used the cash to put a deposit on one of the really swanky houses near the clubhouse and he moved his new woman and her son into it. He took all the nicest furniture and said I hadn't got anything to complain about because he was leaving me our place. It's not very big and the mortgage was paid off because we'd been together for years and years.'

Still Milo didn't reply.

'So I stayed put,' Kate said. 'It was the only home I'd known for a long time and I wasn't sure what else to do with myself. Anyway, I love it there and I can see now that my house has got loads of potential to be made more interesting and colourful. But to answer your question, no, I wasn't devastated, exactly. Just angry and embarrassed at being duped for so long, still reeling from losing my dad and sort of... lost for what to do next, if you know what I mean? Is that how you felt?'

Kate looked at Milo properly now and finally noticed the horror on his face.

'Have I upset you?' she asked. 'Was that too much?'

He didn't reply for a moment. Then he said quietly, 'Does your ex go by any other name, Kate?'

'Howard? Why do you want to know that?'

'Oh, hell. Look, does your ex-husband call himself Brad, by any chance?'

'Erm... yes, I think he does, actually. However did you know that? I seem to remember it was what he always put down for the tournaments. Bradley's his middle name. I thought it was a bit posey, to be honest, but he liked it.' She pulled a face. 'At work he had another different one. He was only known by his initials there. HB. He used to make jokes about the lead in his pencil.'

'And do you know the name of the woman he left you for?'

Now Kate was really confused. 'I haven't met her, needless to say. Howard never wanted me to go to the social functions at the club in the later years, for reasons that are obvious now. He only referred to her by name a couple of times. I knew he had a new tournament partner. He called her Annie. She'd got a teenage son who lived with her. Howard said he was a bit surly.'

Kate finally stopped talking, and the silence that followed wasn't a comfortable one this time. She was no fool. The teenage son had finally given it away.

'Her full name is Marianne,' said Milo, through gritted teeth. 'And she is... was... well, still is technically my wife. Howard is Brad. And my son is definitely not surly. Not very, anyway. I guess this changes everything for us, doesn't it?'

'What? That's bizarre. Oh, my life. I'd never even considered we could be linked like that. I suppose it does kind of complicate matters,' Kate said sadly.

'I can't believe you were married to such a git, though.'

'Excuse me?'

'I mean, why did you choose to spend your life with the kind of man who'd treat you like dirt, have a long affair and then dump you?'

Kate's eyes were blazing now. Milo shivered. Angry Kate was scary.

'Are you kidding me, Milo?' Kate said. 'Isn't that a bit rich coming from you?'

'What's that supposed to mean?'

'You married *her*, didn't you? Presumably your life together wasn't perfectly blissful. Aren't you a pathetic chooser too?'

There was a pause while Milo took this in. He blinked at the outrage in Kate's voice but couldn't quite bring himself to apologise for triggering the horrible situation. They glared at each other in furious silence and then Kate stood up.

'I think it's best if I go now, before we say any more hurtful things to each other,' she said.

'But... no, don't leave, Kate. I... I didn't mean...'

'Oh, but I think you did. You made your meaning very clear.' In seconds, she was walking away, head held high.

Milo jumped to his feet, watching her go with despair in his heart. Should he run after her? But why should he be the one to make the peace? Kate had flown off the handle without waiting to see if they could talk things through, just like Marianne used to do.

He sat back down and shook his head in bewilderment. No wonder he'd been so rubbish at being married. If he lived to be a hundred and ten, he'd never understand women. Maybe this way was for the best. His and Kate's relationship hadn't had the chance to get off the ground yet, and now it never would. He began to collect up the picnic gear, sick at heart. What a stupid idea it had been. And yet, she'd loved the picnic part of it, so at least he'd got one thing right. Unfortunately, one thing was never going to be enough.

20

Milo spent the next few days feeling like a complete idiot but not knowing what to do about it. To begin with, he was furious with Kate for leaving so suddenly, but with every hour that passed he became more aware of how spectacularly badly he'd handled all of that conversation and how very much he needed to say sorry. Kate wasn't answering her mobile when he called and his text messages were also being ignored. The next step had got to be turning up at the café but every time he tried to plan what he should say to her, his nerve failed. Being married to someone who'd undervalued him from day one had given Milo no sense at all of his own worth. He couldn't see why Kate would want to see him even if he had plucked up his courage.

On top of this, he'd been madly busy at work. The King's Lynn manager was back so he didn't need to worry about that side of things but in Milo's brief absence, his partner appeared to have taken his eye off the ball and let the staff completely do their own thing. Max had called in at the office once or twice but not stayed long enough to check out what was going on behind the scenes. Milo had always taken a back seat when it came to office management and concentrated on building up their small but previously very efficient business, but working for a control freak for so long had meant that the other three members of staff looked to Max far too much when it came to making big decisions, and when he abruptly stopped telling them what to do every step of the way, they floundered.

Milo debated ringing Max at home to arrange to meet him somewhere for a team talk, even if he wasn't available to come back to work yet. He knew he was being cowardly, putting off discussing the work issues, but it wouldn't be fair on Deirdre to rock the boat just now. Max had left messages on the firm's answering machine early every morning, each one sounding more depressing than the last. His wife was worse than she'd ever been, he said. He was only leaving her in the house if one of their daughters could take over. He promised to pop into the office for a quick catch-up session as soon as he could.

Milo was desperate for a couple of days off to go flat hunting but he didn't feel he could abandon work unless he'd found out what was going wrong and tried to fix it. On the third day after his disastrous picnic with Kate, he was upstairs on the phone when he heard Max enter the main office and shout a greeting to the staff. Ending his call as fast as he decently could, he ran downstairs and followed the older man into the inner sanctum where his partner normally spent his working days.

Max had shrugged off his jacket already, dropped his mobile down in front of him and slumped in his chair before Milo even reached the impressive, marble-topped desk. No expense had been spared over the years with this room. The walls were painted dove grey and the paintwork in a sophisticated shade of charcoal. Even the pictures had been chosen to match, designs in black, white and grey with steel frames. It was all super-smart but also, Milo now realised, very depressing. For himself, he'd always been contented with the upstairs office because it was quieter, had a lovely view of the neighbouring park and was right next to the kitchen for breaks. The others shared an open-plan space, with a couple of small interview booths behind glass partitions for any private business with clients, but his partner liked to make sure that visitors got a proper idea of his importance in the firm.

Max glanced up in what looked like alarm, and Milo was shocked to see that his eyes were bloodshot and his trademark bow tie was askew.

'Something up?' Max asked, rubbing his chin and seeming surprised to find it stubbly. 'I haven't even had any coffee yet. Can't you wait a bit?'

'No, sorry, I can't,' Milo said, sitting down opposite his partner. 'I want to know what's been going wrong in the office.'

'Come again?' Max looked genuinely bewildered. 'You must be stupid if you don't realise Deirdre is the problem and I'm doing my best to cope.'

'Yes, of course I was really sorry to hear she's having a tough time, we all were, but there are other things we need to discuss while you're here. I was away in King's Lynn for a short while and I thought you were holding the fort but everything seems to have gone to pot,' Milo said. 'Jenny says there have been a couple of serious complaints regarding clients having to wait too long for you to get back to them about important business.'

'What? Oh, ignore Jenny, she does like to flap.'

'No, she absolutely doesn't, Max. Lucy's off sick again and I've discovered you've not once followed it up. That's the third time this month. If I'd been here I'd have given her a call to check she was okay, but you just called in a temp and ignored the issue. You need to tell me if you need extra help. I'm not unsympathetic, it must be awful being so worried about Deirdre, but we've got to keep the business afloat.'

Max leant back even further in his chair. The usually neat, silvery waves of hair were dishevelled today and Milo couldn't remember ever seeing him look so rumpled. A waft of alcoholic fumes hit him as his partner sighed heavily. Surely Max hadn't been drinking this early in the morning? He'd always appreciated fine wines and plenty of them, but this smelt suspiciously like whisky.

'Any other grievances?' Max said, lifting one eyebrow. Did he think he was James Bond? Milo started to get angry now, rather than worried.

'Haven't we got enough here?' he said. 'What's going on, Max? It's not just about Deirdre, is it? You definitely look under the weather.'

'I think you need to remember who's in charge here, mate.' Max's face was red now and he'd broken into a sweat. 'I'm the senior partner, if it had slipped your mind. Get yourself out there and chase up why the temp hasn't brought my coffee yet, if you want to do something useful, why don't you?'

Milo got to his feet, more amazed than angry now. Max was always full of bluster but he'd never pulled rank like this before. Even so, Milo's need to sort out his life was stronger than his immediate concern about office politics.

'I *am* going to talk to the staff now, yes,' he said as calmly as he was able. 'I also came to tell you that I'll be out of the office for a couple of days. I've got annual leave coming out of my ears because I never take any. Before I go, I'll sort out any tangles that occurred while I was away in King's Lynn, but you need to make sure no more of them happen... *mate*.'

'But I can't be here. I need to get back to the house and relieve my daughter. Deirdre mustn't be left alone.'

As Max spoke, the intercom on his desk buzzed and Jenny's voice rang out. 'Your wife's on line one for you, Max,' she said. 'Putting her through.'

'But... wait...'

Max's voice was drowned by Deirdre's clear tones, cut-glass accent as sharp as ever.

'Darling, I can't remember what time you said you'd be home from your club but I'm going out for lunch with Prissy, okay? Don't forget we're having dinner tonight with the Hendersons, will you? Oh, and you can tell Milo from me that he should give you a chance to take more holidays like this. You've been working much too hard. See you later, sweetie.'

Deirdre ended the call and Max put his head in his hands without meeting Milo's furious gaze.

'Your club? That poncy place in town with waiters who all look as if they've been sucking lemons? And *holidays*?' Milo asked, keeping his voice even with an effort. 'I've had a feeling that you've been taking the piss for a while now, Max. Well, you can pull your finger out and do some work for a change, because I've got urgent family business to attend to. And when I get back, we're going to have a serious talk.'

Milo strode out of the door, resisting slamming it behind him with difficulty, and took a few calming deep breaths. He set about putting right some of Max's remaining mistakes, soothing the ruffled feelings of the poor girl who was bawled out yesterday by a client who'd been let down and generally troubleshooting for the next hour. Max didn't emerge from his den. Soon, satisfied he'd done everything in his power, Milo left the office and stomped off, muttering under his breath as he walked.

Milo had nearly reached home when he spotted Luka standing in the entrance to the flats, a bulging rucksack by his feet. His son waved and Milo picked up speed.

'Hi, Dad,' Luka said, and Milo was so pleased to hear these two precious words that he risked enfolding the boy in a hug. After a moment, Luka responded and then pulled away.

'I wanted to talk to you some more about the flat-sharing thing,' he said quietly. 'Are you free for a little while?'

'I certainly am,' Milo said, resolutely pushing all thoughts of Max away. Luka deserved his full attention.

'Well, I've ballsed up completely now. I had a massive row with Mum and I walked out. Is it okay if I stay? I'll help you cook, that is if you teach me how, and I'll keep everywhere clean and tidy for you, I...'

Luka broke off and rubbed a hand over his face. Milo's heart felt as if it was being wrung out. 'Of course you can stay. Things have changed, as it happens, and I've got to move out of here soon but we can flat hunt together.'

Milo opened his arms and Luka walked into them again. This time he didn't move away quite so quickly.

'Thanks, Dad. Hey, I'm starving. Got any food?' Luka said, sniffing hard and heading for the kitchen.

'Let's go and eat at the pub, or get fish and chips... I mean veggie burger and chips. We deserve a bit of an easy night tonight.'

Luka punched the air. 'Great! Is it okay if I have a shower if we're going to the pub? Brad hogs all the hot water every morning.'

'Go for it. We've got all the time in the world.'

What a wonderful phrase that was. Milo's heart soared at the prospect of more time with the boy. He hadn't expected this opportunity to bond with Luka after everything that had gone wrong in the past but he was going to make damn sure that nothing came between him and his son ever again.

21

20 MARCH 2013

Kate definitely doesn't want to do anything special for her fortieth birthday later in the year, and Howard readily accepted this when she mentioned her feelings, mainly because the date clashes with one of the main golfing tournaments at his club, but now suddenly, here he is with a big smile on his face and a large manilla envelope in his hand.

'Surprise,' he shouts, doing a little dance. 'I know I'm early but the big birthday looms, come September. This is for my first love. My only love,' he adds hastily. 'Go on then, open it.'

Kate looks down at the envelope. She's getting very bad vibes. Howard has folded his arms now and is looking at her expectantly, eyebrows raised, so she slides her finger under the flap and reaches in to find a glossy A4 booklet.

'Well? What do you think?' Howard says, beaming.

'Think about what?' The brochure is heavy in her hands and she glances down at the front cover. It's a photograph of what looks like a country house, with an extensive gravel sweep in front of it and a background of lush woodland. Gold letters underneath the picture spell out:

Visit Towster Towers for that special occasion: you won't regret a moment. Luxury you can afford.

'Why have you given me this?' Kate asks, already knowing the answer.

'Duh. It's your surprise present. Happy fortieth birthday, Mousey.'

'But we said... I said...'

Howard grins. 'Oh, I know you were banging on about forty just being a number but what good husband would listen to that? We're going to celebrate early. Our wedding anniversary and your early birthday all in one go. This very night, in fact. Pop upstairs and pack a bag, and we'll set off in an hour or so to beat the traffic. It's in Wiltshire, so we can't hang about. I'm *whisking you away*, as they say.'

'Howard, I've got the school Easter Fair tomorrow, I'm helping to man a stall and doing face painting too, I can't let them down.'

'But you'd be happy to let *me* down when I've gone to all the trouble of organising your surprise?' He's pouting now. 'Bloody hell, Kate, just tell the boss you've got a stomach bug or something. They can't argue with that.'

Every part of Kate is fighting against lying to her headteacher and she doesn't even want to go away with Howard, but a sudden thought hits her and she goes upstairs to mull it over, leaving him thinking that she's now in complete agreement with his plan. And perhaps she is. Since the last miscarriage, Howard has taken charge of all contraception on the odd occasions he's graced her with his limited sexual repertoire, apparently not trusting Kate to play fair. He's insistent that they should never try again for a baby because it clearly isn't meant to be.

But after years of monitoring her body's rhythms, Kate is

achingly aware that this weekend she'll be in the middle of her most likely window to get pregnant, and this could be her absolute last chance. She's assuming that on Saturday night Howard will decide it's one of the few times he's interested in her, because by bedtime they'll have exhausted what little conversation they ever had and he'll be bored. If she can just subvert his well-practised condom routine somehow, maybe get him tipsy but not too drunk, or even sabotage one of the horrible rubbery things with a pin, she might, she just might have one more spin of the wheel. Even thinking about such a desperate, shoddy act made Kate shudder. To think she'd come to this. It was unthinkable. No, better to just hide Howard's stash of condoms. Kate would have to hope he'd be carried away in the moment and give up looking before he'd found them.

She can hear Howard coming up the stairs two at a time to get his own bag ready. Quickly, she sends an apologetic text to the school secretary, too ashamed to go to the head who's been a good friend to her. Kate explains that she's been struck by a violent bout of diarrhoea. Thank goodness for spellcheck. Reaching for her smallest case, Kate makes her plans. This time it's going to work. This time she's definitely going to have that elusive baby. Nothing's going to stop her now.

22

Kate's day was going from bad to worse. It had started with a headache that hovered over her eyes and made her feel queasy. Unable to face breakfast, she'd decided to walk to work, thinking that the fresh air would do her good, but had tripped on a tree root going through the country park and fallen flat on her face, scraping both knees and laddering the striped tights she'd bought specially to go with her new red skirt.

At the café, she'd stripped off the tights and gratefully accepted a spare pair from Pat, only to find they were the hideous shade of brown known as American Tan. The last time she'd seen tights this awful was on Mrs Nightingale and that was years ago. Even Mrs N didn't deign to wear them these days.

'I'm sorry, love,' Pat said, when she saw Kate's expression. 'They're the only ones I've got. Someone sold me a job lot when I was going through a brief phase of smart skirts for work and that was the pair I couldn't face wearing.'

The morning passed slowly. It had started to drizzle soon after Kate arrived and business was slack. Kate was relieved when Winnie and Anthea came in, clearly glad to get out of the rain. Anthea went to hang her Burberry up on the coat stand in the corner and Winnie, resplendent in an orange macintosh and a matching orange and jade-green head wrap, waved to Kate.

'Oh, I'm so glad you're here today, honey,' said Winnie. 'I always feel better after a chat with you and one of Pat's fruit scones.' She sat down at the table nearest to the counter and watched approvingly as Kate made them a pot of coffee and began to scoop clotted cream and cherry jam into small dishes. 'Anthea gave me a lift and we're meant to be meeting Beryl here but looking at the weather, I don't reckon she'll turn up.'

Kate busied herself getting their tray ready but just as she finished, the door swung open and in strode Beryl in a flapping magenta raincoat. She turned to shake her umbrella outside before collapsing it with a thump.

'What a blooming awful day,' she said, beginning to unbutton her macintosh, and wincing as her chilly fingers struggled with the wet fabric. 'If I hadn't been planning to see this pair I'd have stayed at home in front of the fire, but then I saw Tim who lives on the other side of me going out to his van and I remembered he said he was going into town today. He dropped me off at the end of the drive.'

'It's a good job you came,' said Anthea. 'I think our friend here needs cheering up, don't you agree, Winifred?'

'Yes, she's got a face like a wet weekend in Skegness today, and that's not like our Kate. Are you going to tell us what's bothering you, dear?'

Kate made more coffee and slid a slice of Beryl's favourite carrot cake onto a plate as the three ladies settled themselves at the nearest table to the counter, shedding their waterproofs and plastic rain hoods. The only other customer was sitting on the sofa. It was Kate's favourite book-loving customer, the dapper elderly man who was today absorbed in doing the crossword in his newspaper. He didn't look up. Pat was in the kitchen icing a chocolate cake and Sam was there too, getting the sandwiches ready just in case there was a sudden influx of lunchtime visitors, which seemed unlikely.

The sky was a sullen grey and the drizzle had now turned to a proper downpour, but the atmosphere inside the café was warm and mellow. Kate had switched a gentle, classical soundtrack on and it played softly in the background. The distant chatter of Pat and Sam as they worked was soothing and Kate began to relax for the first time that day.

'I didn't mean to look grumpy,' she said. 'I've just got a few things on my mind today. Well, one in particular really. Are you sure you want to hear me moaning?'

'Bless you, lovey, we're all ears. It'll take our minds off our rheumatics. This wet weather plays havoc.'

'You speak for yourself,' said Anthea. 'I still play tennis and swim twenty lengths twice a week and if I need to, I can get my leg above my head just as well as Angela Rippon did on *Strictly*.'

'Why would you need to do that, though?' asked Kate, innocently.

Anthea gave a bawdy chuckle and Winnie snorted. 'Best not to ask,' she said, settling herself more comfortably. She poured herself a cup of tea and Beryl and Anthea did similar with their coffee. Then the three ladies turned to face Kate, who wondered where to begin.

'Okay, in a nutshell, here it is. You all know that Howard left me for another woman. I don't miss him, to be honest. I've met a sweet man who seems interested, although he's grieving for his sister who died fairly recently, so I'm worried that he's not in the right place for something new at the moment. He's kind of available though, because his wife has left him too, but it definitely looks as if he's got a few issues of his own to sort out before we can get to know each other better. If we ever do.'

She paused to try to think how to word the rest, and Winnie leaned forward. 'Carry on then. Sounding good so far, apart from the *kind of* bit.'

'Well, the bottom line is this. It turns out that his ex-wife and my ex-husband had been having an affair for ages and they're living together now. We've only just found out they're an item. It's a bizarre coincidence. Of all the people they could pick...'

'I see.' Winnie took a big bite out of her scone and wiped a smear of jam from her chin with a paper napkin. 'So tell me why this is a problem, dear?'

'I would have thought that was obvious. It's claustrophobic and weird. Also, he was really rude about me having chosen to be married to someone who he thinks of as a homewrecker and a bit of a tosser.'

Beryl was leaning forward now, keen to chip in. 'So, is this mystery man still heartbroken about losing his wife as well as his sister?'

Kate shook her head. 'No, I don't think so, unless he's hiding it very efficiently.'

'And are you grieving for your lost lover?' said Winnie, eyes shining.

'You make it sound like a tragic novel. No, absolutely not.'

Winnie demolished the rest of her scone while she gave this some thought. 'In that case, what's the big deal?' she continued eventually. 'No offence, honey, but why are you being so negative? What do you think, girls? Sounds like a storm in a teacup to me.'

Anthea nodded. 'My ex moved his next floozie into our house almost before the removal van had got to the end of the drive with my belongings, but nowadays I couldn't care less who he's sleeping with, even if she is half my age with boobs that still point upwards. The past is... just that, darling. Past. The future could be a lot more fun.'

'I get your point, but I'm angry with Milo – he's the one I was talking about – for belittling my marriage even though his own sounded just as much on the skids,' Kate said.

'No, my love, it strikes me you're sad more than you're angry,' said Winnie. 'Tell us why that is.'

Sam came out of the kitchen just as Kate was thinking how to answer this question without crying. 'You okay?' he asked. 'Hey, I meant to ask, are you still on for having Elsie to sleep at yours tonight? It's fine if you're busy,' he said hastily, seeing Kate's face crumple. 'I don't have to go out. It was just a pub gig.'

Kate tried to answer but her throat seemed to have closed up.

'I don't think it was you that's made this lovely lady cry. It was probably us to blame for digging,' Winnie said. 'We need another cuppa after all that emotion, don't we?'

Kate nodded, glad of a break from all this unexpected soul-searching. As she bent to load the trays with empties, the stones in her engagement ring flashed blue in the light from the wall lamp nearby. Having taken it off her finger when the marriage ended, although she'd never worn it for work anyway, she was still wearing both the engagement ring and her wedding band on a chain around her neck. Really, Kate had no idea why this seemed the right thing to do. She supposed it was due to some long-held belief that they might be stolen if she left them lying around in the house. Howard had often impressed on her how expensive they'd been.

'That's a pretty ring,' Winnie said, peering at the contents of the chain. 'If it was me, I'd flog both of these now. I don't know why you're even still carting them around. Sapphires fetch a lot. You've got three lovely dark blue stones there with two tiny diamonds and that looks like a decent wedding ring too. I told you I used to work for a jeweller,' she added, seeing the puzzlement on Kate's face.

'Oh, yes. But I can't do that... can I?' Kate wondered aloud.

'Why wouldn't you? They're not bringing you happy memories, are they? I'll write my phone number down, and you should give me a call later. We can talk about how you can get a good price for them. I've still got a reliable contact in the trade. His name's Maurice.'

'Ooh, I know Maurice too,' said Anthea. 'He sold most of the contents of my jewellery box for me and took me out to dinner afterwards. He's a smoothie.'

Anthea's smile told Kate there may have been rather more than dinner going on there. It seemed as if everyone was having an interesting social life while she'd initially had to force herself even to go to bingo with The Saga Louts.

'And you and me can chat more later, Katie,' said Beryl, ignoring Anthea's comment. 'Why don't I pop round to yours when Elsie's safely in bed?'

Kate nodded. Talking to Beryl would be a relief. It was time to face up to the fact that it wasn't the Milo situation that was making her feel as if she'd been run over by a truck. Before he dropped the bombshell about his wife's lover, he'd made her feel optimistic and bubbly and it was wonderful to see such naked desire in a man's eyes after so long, even though he soon qualified it with the warning about his overwhelming sadness. Kate was aware that Milo had nearly kissed her the other day, and she had wanted him to, so much that she'd almost grabbed him and taken charge herself, right there and then on his sister's memorial bench, which felt tacky, to say the least.

But the whole thing was much more complicated than the Milo situation. Changing her life wasn't as simple as turfing out the dull clothes from her wardrobe. It was going to take a lot of effort to turn into the person Kate had always dreamed of being. A confident one, with her life sorted. A woman who both knew her own mind and made other people's lives better for knowing her. She still felt crushed by the weight of her failed relationship with Howard. At what point had it all gone wrong?

'I know Anthea's got a more jaundiced view of marriage,' Kate said, turning to Beryl and Winnie. 'But you two have had it sussed in the past, haven't you?' she said. 'Happily married to kind-hearted men for years. You must miss them.'

Suddenly feeling parched from all this emotion, Kate reached for her bottle of water and took a large swig, but almost choked as Winnie said, 'Well, to be honest, I mostly miss the sex.'

'What?'

Beryl let out a cackle. 'Look at her face, bless her. They think our generation never had any hanky-panky. Len and me knew how to raise the roof when we wanted to. Mind you, I liked that bit afterwards just as much.'

Winnie nodded. 'Yes, I know what you mean. Once he'd put his pyjamas back on, my Ron used to fetch me a nice cup of tea and an iced fancy. Then I'd read my *Woman's Own* and he'd have a look at one of his car manuals. It was the most peaceful part of the day.'

'I'd always go for a couple of rounds of toast with my cuppa,' said Beryl. 'If it'd been a particularly good night there'd be raspberry jam on it.'

Anthea laughed. 'Oh, now you come to mention the afterwards part, my various experiences of married life weren't always bad, if I'm honest. Even Justin used to appreciate me at one time. He was my first. It was always champagne afterwards for us, though, and a dish of olives and nuts.'

Kate took a moment to let this information settle. 'You... you got rewarded for sleeping with your husbands?'

'No, no. Not rewarded, dear, don't be silly,' said Beryl. 'It was just a bit of companionship. And then lights out and a cuddle. That's marriage for you, isn't it, Winnie?'

'Absolutely. You need the good, quiet times, the closeness... there's plenty to stress about if you don't keep a balance and a marriage can fall apart while you're not looking. Take Sylvia Nightingale at the shop, for instance. She always kept her husband short.'

Kate was lost now, still thinking about toast and iced fancies. 'Short?'

'You know what I mean.' Winnie sniffed. 'Anyway, her bloke went off with a barmaid from Meadowthorpe. I warned her, but she'd never take any notice of me. Not after...'

Beryl completed the sentence. '...after the bow tie incident.'

All three doubled up with laughter and the gentleman in the corner glanced across with a smile. None of them noticed this. Kate folded her arms. 'Come on, tell me more.'

'Well, it was one Saturday night in November. Ron had been over to The Fox and Fiddle for a few pints and he brought some beer back for me in a jug. That was the thing at the time. Women tended not to go into the bar and the lounge was a grim place before they did it up. Anyway, we were both a bit tiddly by bedtime and he told me to wait downstairs because he'd got a surprise for me.'

Beryl snorted with laughter. 'It *was* quite a surprise, wasn't it, dear? When Winnie went upstairs, Ron was standing in the bedroom window wearing nothing but a bow tie.'

'And what a sight that was. He was a fine figure of a man, was my Ron. Gorgeous. People used to say he reminded them of

Sidney Poitier but these days they'd probably pick that other one. I always forget his name. Iris somebody, isn't it?'

'Do you mean Idris Elba?' asked Kate. 'Wow. You were one lucky lady, Winnie.'

'Yes indeed. It was a pity he hadn't thought to close the curtains first, though,' Winnie said. 'Sylvia was just passing by with that silly little dog of hers. I heard her shriek and by the time I got to the window she was running up the road. After that, the atmosphere in the corner shop was a bit frosty, to say the least. It took months for her to thaw and be friends again.'

Kate was laughing so much now she could hardly breathe. As she tried to get control of herself, she heard a shuffling movement by the sofa and the elderly gentleman cleared his throat.

'That was most entertaining, ladies. Thank you for brightening my day. Oh, and if any of you ever need a little cosseting, I'd just like to say I've got a cupboard full of iced fancies and I make a splendid cup of tea. Goodbye for now.'

The others watched him fasten the belt of his gabardine mac, put his trilby hat on and go out into the light drizzle that had replaced the downpour. Kate had to giggle at the sight of all three of them with their mouths hanging open. 'I didn't think he was listening,' she said.

Beryl rallied first. 'Ah, don't worry about it. He enjoyed hearing us reminisce. But Kate, you need to remember that if you do decide to go for another man… or woman for that matter, I'm not biased… make sure they know how to do the quiet times as well as the rumbustious ones. Now we must get a move on. The rain's almost stopped, thank goodness. Come on, girls, shake a leg.'

'Thanks for brightening my day too, all of you. I'll give you a call tomorrow when I've thought more about selling my jewellery, Winnie,' Kate said. 'And I promise I'll ring *you* later when Elsie's asleep,' she told Beryl. 'If you've got the time to listen, I've got a lot to tell you.'

23

20 MARCH 2014

It's time to do the deed. Kate's been psyching herself up to do this job for a whole year, ever since she and Howard got back from that terrible weekend in Wiltshire, but there's never seemed to be a moment when she's felt brave enough. Now, *East-enders* has finished and the rest of the evening stretches away endlessly. Howard won't be home from the club for hours and it's too soon to try to sleep, although Kate's eyelids are already drooping. She's helped to run a lively follow-up activity to World Book Day today with lots of drama and art, and although everyone's had a great time, it's left her feeling emptier than ever.

Climbing the stairs, step by exhausting step, Kate wonders if this is what her life is going to be like now. She's only forty and yet tonight she feels as old as the hills, because she's had a busy day. Or is that really why she's so tired? Maybe it's the fact of it being her wedding anniversary yet again, and the thought of that only brings a kind of resignation instead of any kind of romance.

Romance was almost what she'd thought Howard had in mind this time last year when he'd presented her with the brochure for the fancy hotel. She'd even started to look forward to the break as they'd driven through pretty countryside chatting about what they might choose for dinner. It was just like being a happily married couple who were celebrating the day when they'd made their promises, instead of two people with very little in common trying to avoid awkward silences.

Howard had parked the car and taken Kate's case and his overnight bag out of the boot. It was only then that she'd spotted the full set of golf clubs that had been hidden beneath the other things.

'You forgot to take your clubs out of the boot,' she said. 'You don't usually like to leave them in there overnight.'

The shifty look that Howard often adopted when golf was mentioned appeared on his face. 'Oh, didn't I tell you?' he said. 'This place has got a deal with the local club, and part of the package for the weekend is a day on the green. A couple of the guys and their wives are joining us. We'll meet them in the bar when we've checked in. You like Billie, don't you? She says she's looking forward to seeing you again.'

Kate opens her mouth to speak but there are no words. She can't believe she's fallen for this trick yet again. Not only is she going to be spending her wedding anniversary and birthday celebrations without a husband by her side, she's also going to be stuck with the woman she always thinks of as Botox Billie, who's had so much work done that it's impossible to tell what she's thinking. Or if she's thinking at all, for that matter. Her forehead never moves.

Kate follows Howard into the hotel, which in happier circumstances she would have found impressive, with its Agatha Christie-style furnishings and thick carpets. What a waste of a lovely venue.

'Mr and Mrs Howard Brown, here for a weekend of luxury,' her smiling husband says to the receptionist. She bats her eyelashes at him, and Kate realises with a shock that Howard is looking his best tonight, with a new, shorter haircut and a definite spring in his step. Well, why wouldn't he be bouncing with vitality? He's going to have a few beers, eat a huge dinner with plenty of excellent wine. Tomorrow, untouched by any kind of hangover, because he's always been able to avoid them for some strange reason, he'll be out on the golf course, bright eyed and bursting with enthusiasm.

On the other hand, Kate will be forced to spend the entire day listening to Botox Billie droning on about what procedure she's planning next and her recent holiday in Marbella or Florida or one of the many other places where she loves to swan about, giving her husband's gold card a battering. Frantically, Kate thinks of different ways she could escape from this hell. Could she fake an emergency phone call? One of her family could have been taken ill, perhaps. But Howard knows her parents are away on a cruise and she's never been particularly close to her brother. In any case, this hotel is miles from anywhere, so she'd need a taxi and a train station to break away. No, she'll just have to brazen it out, because there's still a slim chance that tonight could be The One. If she can keep Howard this side of legless, she might just be able to get him into bed and suitably inflamed before he crashes out for the night.

To begin with, Kate's plan seems to be going well. The other two men in the party are on some sort of health kick and they're taking their drinking slowly, although their wives are making up for it by necking enough Prosecco to float a boat. Kate bides her time, joining in the conversation as best she can and keeping her own drinking to a bare minimum. The dinner goes as well as can be expected, and Kate is almost at the point of suggesting that she and Howard call it a night when disaster happens. Layton

Armitage, a big cheese at Howard's club, arrives in a flurry of apologies with his smug wife by his side.

'Gutted to miss the first part of the festivities,' he booms. 'But I told Gabriella it was better to get here late tonight than miss the start of play in the morning. No, don't ask them if they can give us supper, we ate on the way down, but I'm more than ready to see if this place has got a decent malt behind the bar. How about you, fellas?'

Kate holds her breath. She even slips her hand into Howard's to try and give him the message that she's more than ready to go upstairs, but he pulls away and rushes over to clap Layton on the back.

'You'll find a sad lack of drinking buddies here,' Howard says. 'These two have been lightweights tonight, but if you're up for a whisky or two, I'm your man.'

'Excellent news, and you can fill me in on how young Jamie's getting on at the same time. Wonderful job you did, coaching that boy, Howard, old chap. He's probably a better player than you are by now.'

Kate has to smile at the look on her husband's face. It's blatantly obvious that he can't decide whether to be flattered or offended. Mind you, it's true Jamie has done extremely well for himself since Howard took him in hand. He's even talking about making a move across the Channel, now he's got a steady girlfriend and the prospect of relocation from work.

'Haha, you're probably right, Layton, but why are we wasting time talking about the lad?' Howard says, through gritted teeth. 'The bar's this way.'

'I'll see you in our room, darling,' says Gabriella. 'I'll get a herbal tea sent up and do my evening yoga. Are you going with them?' she asks Kate.

Kate shakes her head. It's probably game over, as far as she's concerned. Leaving the others making plans for the morning, she makes her way up to their room. The covers are neatly turned back and there's a chocolate on each pillow. Kate eats them both before undressing and getting into her prettiest nightie. It's not exactly sexy but at least it's not flannelette. Maybe, just maybe Howard will escape after only a couple of drams. Just in case, she hides his condoms under the mattress. Never give in, that's her motto this evening, even though the digital clock on the bedside table is now telling her that tomorrow is here already.

An hour later, there's a scrabbling at the door and Howard at last manages to make his key card work. Kate, who's been dozing, sits bolt upright and smiles at him hopefully but instead of speaking to her, Howard hurtles towards the bathroom and she hears the sound of him being violently and copiously sick. Talk about recreating the mood of our wedding night for the anniversary celebrations, thinks Kate, bitterly. She reaches for the fluffy towelling robe provided by the hotel and opens her book.

Eventually, Howard staggers back into the bedroom, peels off his clothes and, after dropping them on the floor, crashes into bed next to Kate. He groans and gestures for her to put the light off. 'Must be something I ate,' he mumbles. 'I'll be fine in the morning.'

But it turns out that he isn't fine at all. Kate's fictitious stomach bug has become reality, but in a strange twist of fate, not for her. Howard spends the weekend moaning piteously and sleeping in between bouts of vomiting, whilst Kate dodges the other ladies by taking as many massages and spa treatments as she can wangle. They leave on Sunday afternoon with Kate at the wheel and a pale and fractious Howard by her side, chewing indigestion tablets and sipping from a bottle of spring water. Kate's skin is glowing and the tension in her shoulders has more or less gone, thanks to all the massaging, but her spirits are at rock bottom. When she gets home, she'll make a start on packing away all the lovely baby paraphernalia that she's collected over the years. This endless round of hoping and being disappointed can't go on.

Now, a full twelve months later, as she enters the smallest bedroom, Kate is resigned to the inevitable. It's time to give in at last.

24

Elsie arrived at Kate's house late that afternoon with a bulging backpack and a bag full of her favourite books, but her face was streaked with tears.

'What on earth's the matter?' asked Kate as the little girl flung her arms around her waist and sobbed.

'Elsie's lost Horny,' said Sam. This was clearly a major disaster because the name didn't raise even the glimmer of a smile today. 'She took him to school and somehow he didn't come home with her. By the time we realised and went back, everyone had gone.'

'She's going to be so lonely,' Elsie wailed. 'It'll be dark soon and she'll be very frightened in the classroom all on her own.'

'Oh, I don't think she will,' Kate said briskly. 'And there's a very good reason why.'

'Is there?' A note of hope crept into Elsie's voice, so Kate pressed on.

'Yes, of course there is. It's well known that unicorns have magic powers. When they're all alone, their horns light up and the ones with silver horns are the most magical of all. I bet Horny's even playing music.'

Sam grinned at Kate. 'You seem to be having a competition with yourself to see how many times you can say the word *Horn* in one sentence.'

'Is it true, Daddy?' Elsie said, ignoring his comment. 'Is Horny magic?'

'Absolutely. I bet she's playing her music to the tropical fish right now. There's no need to worry. We can fetch her back tomorrow.'

'But it's Saturday tomorrow.' The tears were back now, and Elsie's bottom lip was wobbling again.

'I bet Aunty Kate's got a cuddly toy you can borrow, haven't you?' Sam said hopefully. 'Everyone's got a teddy... or something...'

'She's got Alfred the tatty rabbit,' said Elsie. 'But he belongs on her bed. I need one just for me.'

Kate bit her lip. She knew exactly where to find a brand-new cuddly toy, but could she bring herself to do it? Sam's anxious face helped her to make the decision. 'It's fine, I've got the very thing,' she said. 'Now say night-night to Daddy, Elsie, and we'll go and look.'

Sam beat a retreat with relief, pulling the bobble from his long blond hair as he went, and shaking it loose as if he was starring in a shampoo advertisement. Kate smiled as she and Elsie set off up the stairs hand in hand. Sam was clearly off the lead tonight, as her dad used to describe the feeling when he set off for a bowls or Morris dancing night.

'First we'll find something to cuddle, then tackle the spellings,' Kate said.

'What are we looking for?' asked Elsie, all tears forgotten.

'You'll see. We need to go into the little bedroom.'

Kate led Elsie along the landing and into the boxroom. It wasn't much more than a large cupboard but it would have been plenty big enough for a cot and the pretty chest of drawers that Kate had planned to buy for it. In the event, the room had only been used for storage, and the rows of plastic crates almost filled one wall.

'Wow, you've got a lot of stuff,' said Elsie. 'What's inside all those?'

'Oh, all sorts of things. At least three of them are full of pictures and photographs in frames.'

'Why don't you put them on the wall then? We've got lots on ours. Daddy paints them for us. And there's photos of me all over the place.'

'I know. Your dad is very clever. Well, I took mine down when we decorated. Then Howard... you remember Howard?' Elsie nodded without much enthusiasm and Kate carried on. 'He said he liked the walls with nothing on them. He said they looked cluttered before.'

'He talked out of his bum then,' said Elsie.

'What? Where did you hear that?' Kate tried not to snigger but it wasn't easy.

'I heard Daddy say it about the man next door when he told him our music was too loud. It wasn't that bad, and we were dancing,' she said.

'Well, anyway, it's a bit rude and I shouldn't let anyone else hear you say it.'

'Okay. So, where's the cuddly thing?'

Kate looked around rather desperately. There were boxes full of books stacked next to the pictures and several that held spare bedding. Finally her eyes came to rest on the one she was looking for but dreaded finding. It was smaller than the others and was tied round with a thick silver cord. She reached up and fetched it down.

'Let's go in my bedroom to open this,' she said. Elsie skipped after Kate, humming a tune. At least Horny seemed to be forgotten for now.

Once in Kate's room, she put the plastic crate on the bed, steeled herself and untied the cord.

'This is nice,' said Elsie, running the cord through her fingers. 'It's like Horny's horn. Is it magic?'

'Maybe,' said Kate. 'It's looked after some treasures for me for a long time.' She opened the lid of the box, revealing a cloud of tissue paper, also silver.

'Can I look inside?' breathed Elsie.

Kate sat back to let the little girl get closer and Elsie carefully lifted the delicate layers of paper to reveal the contents. Her eyes were wide as she fetched out the tiny garments.

'Whose clothes are these?' she asked, still whispering.

'Nobody's, really,' said Kate, swallowing the lump in her throat with difficulty.

'Why have you got them then?'

'Oh, because at one time I thought... I kind of hoped I'd have a baby boy or girl to wear them, but in the end I didn't.'

'That's sad, but you've got me now, haven't you? Dad said you share me with him.'

Kate couldn't speak for a moment. Eventually she managed to croak, 'Keep on looking. You're nearly there.'

Elsie lifted out a couple of white woolly cardigans and then a tissue-wrapped bundle. 'Is this it?'

'Yes. Open it.'

When the silver tissue paper was removed, Elsie gasped. A

beautifully soft, snowy-white sheep lay on her lap, its boot-black eyes seeming to gleam with interest.

'Oh, he's lovely. Is he yours?'

'No, he hasn't got an owner. Or he didn't have until now. He's yours if you want him.'

'*Yes, please*. I love him. I bet he was really fed up being packed away in a box for ages. What's his name?'

'He hasn't got one yet. You can decide.'

Elsie held the bundle of white strands in both hands and looked into the sheep's eyes. 'I'm going to call him Shaggy,' she said. 'He can be a friend for Horny.'

'Excellent choice,' said Kate, stifling a giggle. 'Now we need to use my enchanted formula to get ready for your spelling test on Monday.'

Downstairs again, Kate rummaged in the dresser for a large tin decorated all over with flowers.

'Biscuits?' said Elsie hopefully. 'Oh, no, that's the felt-tip tin. Why do we need those?'

'Because this tin holds the special magic. Spellings are always more fun in colour.'

'Spellings aren't fun.'

'They can be. Bright colours make everything better, you'll see. I'm trying to make my whole life more colourful, Elsie.'

They sat down at Kate's small dining table, fortunately rejected by Howard because it was 'much too small for entertaining and anyway, it's tatty.'

'Shall we do the spellings now?' said Elsie. 'The book's in my backpack.'

Relieved, Kate watched as Elsie reached for her spelling diary and opened it at the right page.

Kate lifted the lid of the felt-tip tin and they both peered in. Elsie rummaged and brought out a handful of multi-coloured pens, spreading them out on the table, and Kate set about writing out the list of spellings in a variety of shades.

'Why do you want to get more colourful?' Elsie said, watching the list grow.

It was a good question. Kate pondered for a moment. 'I suppose it's because I haven't felt very happy lately,' she said, deciding it was best to be honest. 'We all get sad sometimes, don't we?'

Elsie didn't answer this. 'I wish you were my mummy,' she said instead. 'Mine doesn't come over to see me very often. She's quite busy.'

These were deep waters. Kate had no idea how to handle this one. 'I expect she misses you, though,' she said eventually.

'No, she doesn't. I don't think she likes little girls much.' Her voice tailed off, and she looked up at Kate hopefully. 'Can I do it? Get all the spellings right, I mean?'

'Of course you can,' said Kate, with more conviction than she felt. 'And after that you can draw a picture.'

'We could give it to Dad then, couldn't we?' she said. 'He likes me better than Mummy does.'

Kate couldn't think of a reply to this that didn't involve expletives. Her blood boiled when she thought of Lara Shaughnessy and her total disregard for her beautiful daughter's feelings. What a waste of a chance of being a mum. Thank goodness Sam was willing to share. To be chosen as Elsie's godmother was an honour and a joy.

It occurred to Kate for the first time that you didn't need to actually be a mother to be properly motherly. It was a stirring thought. She'd already learned through her work at the school that you didn't have to be related by blood to someone before you could make them feel loved and treasured, but this was taking it to a whole new level. Could the true knack of mothering be developed by anyone, at any time, with anybody at all? Actually, at the moment, the three Saga Louts were being more maternal towards Kate than her own mum was. She yawned and shelved this interesting idea to be pondered on later. Mum or not, it was extremely tiring entertaining a six-year-old, however much you loved them.

The rest of the evening passed peacefully. When numerous stories had been read and Elsie was safely tucked up in the spare bedroom with Shaggy under one arm, Kate tiptoed downstairs and made a mug of peppermint tea. Once she was convinced Elsie was really asleep and not doing her pretend snoring trick, Kate lit a few candles, reached for her phone and pressed Beryl's number to tell her the coast was clear.

'Hello, pet. I hoped you'd call,' she said. 'On my way in five minutes.'

Beryl's five minutes stretched into double that but she was soon knocking on the door carrying a small footstool that she'd apparently brought round for a gift.

'That was why I was a bit late,' Beryl said, pointing to the stool. 'I noticed you hadn't got one when I was here last time and everyone needs to put their feet up, don't they?'

Kate looked at the new addition to her living room. It would certainly be a talking point, with its velvet buttoned padding and ornate carved legs.

'Thanks, Beryl. What an unusual shade of green. Are you sure you don't need it?' she asked hopefully. 'I'd hate to deprive you of your own comforts.'

'Not at all, dear. I've always hated it,' said Beryl. 'Hang on, I've got another present for you. Just got to pop back home.'

Within a couple more minutes, Beryl was back bearing a huge carrier bag. 'I saw these on the market and thought of you,' she said. 'Now you've got the stool, we can go for a colour theme.'

Kate's eyes opened wide as Beryl rummaged in the bag and produced four cushions, patterned in zigzags of lime green and purple. She arranged them along the sofa and stood back in admiration.

'There you go, pet,' she said. 'Nobody could call this room dull now. A nice fire, some candle ambience, as Anthea likes to call it, and Bob's your uncle.' She wriggled herself into the cushions, rested her feet on the stool and prepared for a chat. 'Look, before we get to the more serious stuff,' she said, 'let me pass on the number of Winnie's friend Maurice. She gave it to me so I could remind you to call him. Have you got a pen handy? Maurice will tell you how to sell those rings if you do decide it's time. You might as well have the cash. You could treat yourself to something fun.'

Kate found a pen and added Maurice's phone number to the list in her notebook. She took a large gulp of tea and waited for Beryl to get down to business.

'So, let's get on to the important things,' said Beryl.

'And what are they?' Kate braced herself for the reply. She wasn't used to baring her soul. It was much easier listening to other people's problems than airing her own.

'Firstly, you were telling us about meeting someone who might turn out to be important to you but I'm not convinced you're ready yet. You were very easily put off by the first hiccup.'

Kate could feel herself bristling. 'You can hardly call his ex and mine shacking up together a hiccup,' she said. 'It was pretty shattering news.'

'It must have been a surprise, love.' Beryl's voice is gentler now. 'But it's not the end of the world. The way you reacted tells me you've got a lot of healing to do before you jump into something new. You're hurting badly, I can tell.'

This was not what Kate wanted to hear. Renewed outrage

that Beryl had stuck up for Howard filled her mind. 'He wasn't that great a husband, whatever you think,' she snapped. 'I stayed with him for more than one reason but I wasn't sorry to see him go in the end.'

'I'm not talking about Howard.' Beryl closed her eyes and leaned her head back, waiting.

The pause that followed this statement went on and on, making Kate wonder if Beryl had nodded off, but she couldn't bring herself to break the silence. Eventually, she whispered, 'Tell me what you mean.'

'Your heart's full of sadness, I see it in your eyes all the time,' said Beryl, opening her own eyes again and blinking. 'You smile at us all and you give out that lovely warm radiance that makes everyone want to unload their worries onto you in the café, but you're carrying round a big weight of unhappiness. Do you want to talk about it?'

Kate bit her lip. Did she want to? Long-buried pain was already starting to surface with these questions. Could she bear it? But if she wasn't able to share some of the hurt, it might never go away. She cleared her throat.

'Okay. My biggest regret is that I never had children. I lost four babies over the years,' Kate said at last. 'Each time I was pregnant for a bit longer than the last so I kept hoping that this would be the one to make it, but it never was. I only let myself tell people I was pregnant the last time because before then, we never got past the three-month mark.'

'Oh, Kate, that's so sad. I knew about the one you're talking about but you didn't seem to want anyone to mention it at the time, so I took the coward's way out and avoided the subject.'

'Don't feel bad. That was how I wanted to play it at the time. Later on, I stayed in the marriage even though Howard wasn't really interested in me because it was the easier option and we jogged along quite nicely, but then everything seemed to get worse between us when my dad died. I never got the chance to say goodbye.'

'I know. What a lovely man he was, and a fine doctor. It was a terrible shock to the whole community, but of course much worse for you and the family.'

Kate thought about the condolence cards that had arrived in what seemed like their hundreds, all with messages of heartfelt sympathy. She'd almost found herself resenting the fact that her dad had been loved by so many outsiders. They couldn't possibly understand the pain she and her mum and her brother were feeling. She pressed on.

'And then Howard left. Looking back, I think he was ready to go a lot sooner but just as he was plucking up his courage to tell me, my dad had his heart attack so he stayed a bit longer.'

'To support you.'

'Maybe. I assumed he just didn't want to look bad to everyone else by jumping ship when I was in such a mess but I know you saw a different kind of man.'

Adjusting her mind to this slightly kinder version of Howard was hard and Kate decided to shelve it for another time. 'So anyway, once the dust had settled and I was used to the idea of living on my own, I began to think I could come out of the other end of my sadness, but the flashbacks of my dad's death just wouldn't go away. They would hit me at all sorts of random times. It was especially difficult if I was at work.'

'Go on,' Beryl said quietly. 'You're doing really well.'

Another sip of tea. Deep breaths.

'I don't know if you remember the details, Beryl. My mum was out, so someone at the club rang me instead to see if I knew where he was. It was a Saturday so I was at home. I went round to their house first but he wasn't there. He always used the same shortcut to the bowls club and I ran all the way because by then I had a feeling something was badly wrong. My dad hated to be late for anything. By the time I got to him I could hardly breathe.'

Kate thought back to the crushing sensation, as if the air was being squeezed out of her lungs, breath by laboured breath. The faster she ran, the harder it was not to pant. In the end, she'd seen him lying in the grass on his stomach and fallen to her knees, gasping.

'The ambulance came quickly but it was already too late. I rolled him over and tried to do CPR, I really did. I've had all that training with the dummy but it's much harder with a real person, especially when you... when you love them. The paramedics said I couldn't have brought him back, though. He must have died instantly. I knew that really.'

Beryl waited while Kate steadied herself again and then said, 'So on top of your marriage ending and you trying to get to grips with all your past grief about the babies, you lost someone very special. And did you have any kind of counselling at the time?'

'No. I didn't want to blurt it all out to a stranger. My mum went down that route, though, and she seemed to pick herself up quite quickly. I couldn't believe how well she was doing. She was very sad, but she was coping. Then my brother persuaded her to go and live near him in France, as you know, so I lost her too. The house sold fast. Mum was brutal about getting rid of pretty much everything and there was no time to think about what we should keep. It was as if she wanted a clean sweep. New life, new start.'

Kate let the peace of the room enfold her again for a few moments. The ticking of the clock on the wall and the act of unburdening herself was making her feel unusually calm. She tucked her legs up underneath her on the sofa. It was really very comfortable even if it was a bit too purple. Her eyes started to close.

'Are you with me, dear?' Beryl's voice cut into the peace of the living room and Kate put her mug down just in time.

'Sorry. I almost dozed off then.'

The old lady chuckled. 'Yes, I have this uncanny knack of sending people to sleep. Myself included. We're doing it in shifts tonight.'

'I didn't mean...'

'I know you didn't. Look, it's very brave of you to tell me all this but I think you probably do need to speak to someone more professional now you've got over the first hurdle. How do you feel about that?'

Kate pondered. 'I might. I could ring my doctor. He offered to refer me after Dad... but I said no.'

'I think that'd be a very good step to take. And the other thing I want to suggest is that you get away from here for a few days. Is there any chance of you having some time off work?'

Kate thought back to the item on her list that said she should branch out and go somewhere alone. 'I suppose so. Pat's been nagging me to take the leave I'm owed and she said her ex-girlfriend was always willing to come and help out if we're short staffed. But where would I go? I haven't been on holiday for a very long time and it'd be weird to go off travelling on my own, wouldn't it?'

'Not weird, but maybe not a good plan for your first adventure. There's definitely someone you could ask to go with you. A friend who cares about you very much.'

'Yes, of course there is. I know Sophie would be glad for me to go and stay with her and then maybe we could go off and have an adventure together. Although she's only just got back from the last jaunt with Paul.'

'Perfect,' Beryl said. 'I happen to know that Sophie's winding down her hairdressing round because she hates cancelling appointments when Paul wants her to travel with him. She's just keeping a few of her oldest customers.'

'Really? I thought she loved her job.'

'She does, but she loves her husband more, and they don't need the extra money she brings in these days. Her hairdressing rates are rock bottom because she can never face telling us oldies she's raising her prices.'

Kate considered this. If Sophie was going to have more spare time it might be worth asking her if she'd come on some sort of trip. Just a short one to begin with.

'Now, I'm almost ready to go home and pour myself a nightcap before I head for my bed. I do like a nice glass of Baileys at this time of night, but there's one more thing I want to talk to you about. I think you know what that is.'

Kate's hands started to tremble and she clasped them together in her lap. She'd dreaded this moment. It had been bound to come at some point.

'The baby. The one I... took?'

'Absolutely. You're still dragging around a whole load of guilt about that, aren't you? And much as I liked Howard... well, most of the time, anyway... I think he could have helped you to work your way through it, instead of burying what happened and pretending it never happened. Am I right?'

'But I'm bound to feel guilty,' Kate said. 'It was an evil thing to do. And I never even got to say sorry.'

'Evil's a very strong word, love. You were distressed and not really in your right mind at the time. Nobody was hurt, nobody was any the wiser and the family moved away soon afterwards so you didn't have to see them around. It's time to let go of all that guilt. It's not benefitting anyone and it's preventing you from moving forward with your life.'

Kate sat for a moment, trying to let these comforting words penetrate the icy ball of horror that was still keeping her awake in the small hours, even now. Gradually, the warmth of the room and Beryl's soft, wrinkled hand on hers began to do their work. Her tense shoulders relaxed and she yawned widely. It was only the beginning of the thaw, but a flicker of hope like a tiny candle flame was at last coming to life inside her.

'Now, you're exhausted and so am I,' said Beryl. 'But I suggest you get in touch with our Sophie right now, before you go off the boil. Goodnight, lovey, sleep tight. I'm off.'

'Thank you so much, you've been...' Kate began, but Beryl was already up and heading for the door. Kate stretched her arms above her head and yawned again. She flicked through her contacts and found Sophie's number in her phone. Might as well try now, before she chickened out.

Hi Soph. Did you really mean it about me coming to stay?

The reply came almost instantly.

You bet I did. When can you come? Name the day, the sooner the better.

Kate thought for a moment.

Let me just talk to my boss tomorrow, and I'll be back in touch asap. The other thing is, have you got time to take a bit of a trip with me? Not sure where yet. Nowhere very far away.

Wow! This is so great. I've been ringing round earlier telling people I'm semi-retiring soon so I can be free next week if that's any good? We'll have a fantastic time. More soon, we'll make a cunning plan when you've fixed your leave, okay? Just don't bring anything navy. Or indigo xx

Sophie's answering message made Kate laugh out loud. She got to her feet and crept upstairs, peeping at Elsie as she passed the spare bedroom. The duvet was rucked but Shaggy was still held firmly under her arm. Kate tiptoed in and straightened the bedding, looking down at her goddaughter with a tenderness that held very little of the sweet melancholy that usually accompanied the sight of the sleeping child. She went back out onto the landing and into the boxroom. There, behind a row of boxes, was what she was looking for. A glossy burgundy suitcase, top of the range, as all Howard's birthday gifts had tended to be.

She lifted it out. The shiny surface was hardly marked. They'd been on a weekend break to Majorca after one of Kate's miscarriages. Still fuddled with disappointment and grief, she'd naively thought that Howard had only arranged it to cheer her up and actually, he sort of had, but when they arrived she found that several of his golfing buddies were already ensconced in the hotel and, as usual, her days were to be spent with their wives. The holiday had dragged. Shopping and sunbathing had never been on Kate's list of favourite activities. When the next golfing weekend was arranged, Kate had opted out, enjoying having the house to herself for a change, and that had become the pattern in the years that followed.

Now, she took the case into her bedroom and opened it on the ottoman. A faint aroma of coconut suntan lotion was released, and an old swimsuit lay in the bottom. Kate smiled. It was navy. She took it out and dropped it into the waste bin by the bed.

'Okay, Beryl, I'm really going to do this,' she whispered. 'It's high time I climbed out of my comfort zone and I really want to have at least as much fun as The Saga Louts do. Why am I so nervous?'

Closing the case again, Kate left it ready for packing. Nerves or no nerves, she was going to talk to Pat and get this show on the road.

'First adventure for ages, here I come,' she said aloud. Even in the empty room, the words sounded good.

25

The following morning, Kate buttonholed Pat as soon as she got to work and got the go-ahead to take some time off the very next week. She texted Sophie with the news, expecting the planning of their trip would take a while, but her friend was obviously worried that Kate would lose her nerve if they didn't make some firm arrangements quickly.

> I'm going into town shortly but I'll call in at the café on my way back. Do you get a lunch break?

Kate checked with Pat and when Sophie arrived on the dot of one o'clock, she was ready with a plate of sandwiches for them both and a large pot of Sophie's favourite Earl Grey tea.

'Hi, love,' Sophie said breathlessly, giving Kate a hug. 'I can't believe this is happening and we're really going on a jolly. There are just a couple of hiccups, though.'

Kate paused in her pouring of the tea. 'Oh, no, what's gone wrong?' she asked, half relieved and half disappointed that the scary plans might need to be shelved for now.

'Don't look so worried. I've fixed everything. Just needed to check, have you got an up-to-date passport?'

Kate frowned. 'Yes, I have, but we won't need that, will we? I was thinking of somewhere in this country, not too far away.'

'I've got a plan for a day out and you might want it for ID. It'll be an adventure. Trust me. Now stop panicking,' she said, seeing Kate's expression. 'It'll be fine. I'll tell you which station to come to and meet you there. We'll have a night in the cottage first and then some fun. No arguments. It's by the sea, we often go there. Paul's already sorted it this time because he's working in the area. It's an Airbnb but we go so many times a year that the owners let us book direct now. You'll love it.'

'Won't he mind me hijacking your break?'

'Paul wouldn't have been bothered at all but as it happens he won't even be there when we arrive. He's had to go to another job further along the coast. We might see him before we come home, if he's finished in time.'

Kate could feel the butterflies starting in her tummy. She opened her mouth to argue and say that all she'd wanted was a peaceful break and to overcome the challenge of travelling alone but the look on her friend's face told her any resistance would be pointless. In any case, this would give her the chance to add two ticks to her list – going on a journey alone and having a holiday too. It was time to put her worries on one side about the possibility of one of Sophie's crazy adventures and take a leap into the unknown. Then a sudden awful thought struck Kate. Maybe this was going to be a real leap rather than a virtual one. What sort of lunacy would you need ID for, to prove your age? Bungee jumping? Paragliding? Or even, perish the thought... a parachute jump? She'd put nothing past her friend when she got an idea in her head.

The days seemed to drag one minute and whizz by the next

as Kate waited for the adventure to begin, but barely a week after her conversation with Sophie, she was on the train south, heading for a holiday cottage in a little seaside town that she'd never heard of before, called Periwinkle Bay. The burgundy case was stowed in the luggage rack and her large handbag contained a pack of cheese and pickle sandwiches made by Pat at the close of the day before, along with two buttered scones and a slab of ginger cake.

'You don't want to have an energy crisis,' Pat said, when Kate refused any more food. 'It's a long way to the seaside, and train food's not always very nice in my opinion.'

'I reckon I'll be okay with all this,' said Kate. 'If you gave me any more I might have to start selling it on to hungry commuters. Which reminds me, talking of selling, Winnie's friend Maurice is going to value my rings for me and help me to get a decent price for them. He thinks I'll make enough to get a new TV. I need a decent dining table and I want to do some decorating but I think the telly should come first.'

The motion of the train was giving Kate a relaxed feeling, even though her stomach had been full of butterflies when she woke up this morning. It felt like a very big mission, this trip to Periwinkle Bay. Sophie had messaged photographs to show her that the place she'd be staying had a view of the salt marshes and was fairly close to the cobbled streets of the little town. Resolutely ignoring the thought of the passport in her bag and the possibilities it held, Kate made herself focus on the moment instead of panicking about what else might lie ahead.

As she gazed out of the window at the passing scenery, Kate wondered what Milo was doing today. His messages had dried up when she hadn't replied to the last three but she still found herself checking her phone several times a day just to see if he'd tried again. Nothing. Suddenly feeling churlish for ignoring him,

Kate decided to get in touch but to keep it brief. As Winnie pointed out, there was work to be done on her life before anyone else got a look in. Maybe she never would get to know him better. Having a man around would certainly complicate things. Being alone was peaceful since Howard moved out, and being without his alarmingly pungent socks was a huge bonus, but there was no harm in having a friend.

Hi Milo,

I've made a snap decision to have a break and I'm on the way to stay on the south coast. Time for a blast of sea air. Travelling light so I've packed my toothbrush but not much else. Hoping all's well with you.

Kate

There, that'd do. No kiss this time but sociable enough. He could make of it what he would. There was no need to go into details. Putting all thoughts of Milo firmly out of her mind, Kate concentrated on checking the details of her trip on her phone for what felt like the hundredth time. The journey to Periwinkle Bay was complicated but she managed the changes of train easily, and by the time she reached the station at Rye where Sophie planned to meet her, she was acting like a seasoned traveller. Only crumbs remained from Pat's pack-up and Kate had done a crossword and also read most of a book on her Kindle. This was the life. Another tick on the list and it had been quite painless. She lifted her suitcase from the carriage and looked around, but there was no sign of her friend.

In seconds, all of the newly acquired confidence seemed to trickle away and Kate felt like a child whose parent had forgotten to do the school run, abandoned at the end of the day with no prospect of rescue. She turned full circle to view the activity on the station platform. Everyone else seemed to know what they were doing. Some were hugging the people who'd come to collect them, others bustling towards the exit. A gang of teenagers had gathered round a bench on the opposite platform, waiting for the next train to Hastings. Where was Sophie? What if she never came? Waves of panic washed over Kate and she made herself take a few deep breaths. As she tried to work out what to do next, her phone pinged.

> So sorry, had a problem with the car but on the way now, with you in ten. Grab a coffee at the café and I'll see you soon. S x

The relief was intense. Kate took hold of her case and wheeled it towards the tables set out in front of a little coffee shop just outside the station. She went inside and ordered a mug of tea and then came back out to sit where she'd be able to see Sophie approaching. There was plenty of action to keep her occupied. A couple at a nearby table were having a hissed argument, something to do with a faulty lawnmower. This didn't seem very inspiring, so Kate leaned slightly to the other side and began to eavesdrop on two young girls, one of whom appeared to be on the verge of tears.

'He ain't worth it, chick,' said the darker-haired girl, who was drinking Coke and flicking glances at a sporty-looking man jogging past. 'He's done the dirty on you before. He'll do it again. Cancel him right now, and I will too. Or I will after the party anyway. We don't want to get uninvited, do we?'

Kate was just getting interested when she heard a shout and turned to see Sophie rushing towards her from the car park.

'Oh, my life, I'm so sorry,' she gasped, reaching out to hug Kate. 'I told them in Meadowthorpe Motors when my new car had its MOT that there was still a clanking noise afterwards but they just brushed me off. I hate garages. Anyway, I'm here now. You must have thought I'd forgotten to get you.'

'I knew you'd be here soon,' Kate said, returning the bear hug. And she had, really, it was only for those first few seconds that she'd wished she'd stayed at home.

'We're going to have a great time. We can have a look at the sea first and then settle in and watch a cheesy film tonight. We'll put our dressing gowns on and have dinner on our knees.'

'Bliss,' said Kate, breathing a huge sigh of relief that she'd actually made it out of the village at long last.

By this time they were at the car, a nippy little jeep in a zingy shade of green. It had colourful creepers and flowers painted down each side and a long strand of fake white blossoms along the dashboard.

'This is my latest present to myself. I call it The Jungle Bunny,' said Sophie. 'It always cheers me up. Well, it does when it goes properly, anyway.'

'Do you need cheering up then?' asked Kate. She'd always assumed Sophie's life was a bundle of laughs from dawn to dusk.

'Only when one of my clients is sad,' said Sophie. 'It's part of the job. I listen. I'm winding down to have more time with Paul and Ralph just now but my business has been a big part of my life. It's so much more than just doing people's hair. They don't want my advice. I just lend a friendly ear, like you need too, I'm guessing. You've got a lot to talk to me about.'

'Have I?'

Sophie didn't answer, having turned down a particularly winding lane and met a tractor head on. She reversed, shuffled the car back and forth and finally negotiated the manoeuvre skilfully before following a sign that pointed to Periwinkle Bay.

'We'll drop your things off at the holiday cottage, have a

quick cuppa and then we're heading for the beach with Ralph, okay?'

'Forget the tea, I just need to find my trainers and you're on,' said Kate, suddenly bursting with energy. 'I can't wait to see the sea. It's been much too long.'

'And whose fault's that? There's an amazing beach not a million miles from Willowbrook. I know, I know, things have been tough but this is a different coast and a whole new ball game. Literally, as far as Ralph's concerned. I hope you like it.'

Kate looked around as Sophie pulled onto the tiny concreted area across the lane from their destination. The cottage was right on the edge of the salt marshes, one of a pair that nestled between trees that had been bent and shaped by the sea breezes. As she stepped down from the jeep, the salty air was clear and enervating.

'Oh, Soph, this is wonderful,' she breathed.

Sophie took charge of Kate's suitcase and headed for the passage that led round the side of the cottage. 'The owners told us to never use the front door,' she said. 'It's sunk so much you can hardly open it, and anyway they've put a dresser in front of it now so we couldn't even if we tried. They have to use all the space they've got because the place is tiny, but it's plenty big enough for us. Paul always books it when he needs to work in the area.'

Kate followed Sophie round the outside of the cottage along a flagstoned path lined with the bluey-purple starry flowers that must be like the ones that gave the little town its name, and in through the back door, tearing her eyes away from the stunning view across the marshes with difficulty. The kitchen floor was uneven, paved with ancient tiles that must have been shaped by the footfall of years. The pale green Aga that almost filled one wall was sending out a comforting warmth. In front of it, a creature that looked vaguely like a cocker spaniel snored gently in a tartan dog bed. As they walked in, it opened one eye, curled its lip and went back to sleep.

'Here's our Ralph,' said Sophie. 'I can't believe you haven't met him before but I tend to leave him with Aunty Beryl rather than carting him from place to place when I'm in Willowbrook. It was tricky when we first adopted him because he'd had a hard time before that but he's been with us a while now and it's going well. He's about ten years old, the vet reckons, and he thinks he's an elder statesman or something equally grand.'

'What breed is he?'

Sophie laughed. 'Now there's a question. The jury's still out. Part spaniel, we think, with a bit of collie and maybe a light touch of beagle. He looks dopey at the moment but he'll perk up when we're ready to go out.'

'I don't blame him for wanting to stay in front of the Aga, though. This is a lovely snug room.'

'It gets chilly out there on the marshes in the evening when the wind gets up,' said Sophie. 'This is the cosiest place in the house but I'll light a fire in the sitting room later and we can settle in for the night. We'll put our dressing gowns on before dinner and be slobs.'

'Sounds wonderful,' said Kate. She was shown her room under the eaves, and found herself looking longingly at the double bed that almost filled the floor space.

'Are you tired?' asked Sophie. 'You do look knackered, to be honest. We don't have to go out if you'd rather chill here?'

Kate yawned, but then glanced out of the window and shivered with delight. 'I can see the sea,' she said. 'Come on, let's go and explore. I'll just change my shoes and I'll be ready.'

The way through the marshes was fringed with unusual plants and the occasional sturdy flower. Ralph, having stirred himself into action when a lead was produced, gambolled happily ahead, long ears flapping in the breeze. He even got interested enough to chase a seagull.

'I only use his lead if there are other dogs around,' Sophie said.

'Why, does he fight?' Kate looked around in alarm.

'No, he's much too lazy for scrapping, but he's got a nasty habit of following other people home. I think he assumes their food's better than ours and he's still not got the hang of knowing he'll be fed without scrounging. He was so skinny when we got him. I could cry just thinking about it. Anyway, enough of the bad memories, we just need to go through this clump of trees and then... here we are. Now Ralph might have a paddle. I'll throw his ball a few times to get him going.'

Here we are signified the edge of a beach that rolled away for what seemed like miles. The tide was out and gulls wheeled and swooped, their cries mingling with the sound of Ralph yapping at a bunch of seaweed. He grabbed it in his teeth and careered towards the water's edge, ignoring the ancient tennis ball that Sophie had thrown. Kate and Sophie followed him more slowly, stopping every now and again to pick up shells. Kate tasted salt on her lips. She'd made it, at last.

Reaching a rock pool, Kate glanced down at her reflection in the water. She was feeling good about her choice of clothes; a faded denim skirt that she'd loved years ago teamed with a red and white checked shirt and a cherry-red sweater. They'd been languishing in the back of her wardrobe for years, but getting them out and trying them on had made her feel much younger. Sophie hadn't mentioned the lack of indigo but had given her an approving nod.

'This sort of place makes you feel guilty for having worries,' said Kate, breathing in the sea air in great gulps and bending to unlace her new glittery baseball boots, bought with a total image revamp in mind.

'So tell me what they are?' Sophie was busying herself taking off her trainers and rolling up her jeans ready to paddle.

'Maybe worries is the wrong word. It's more a case of baggage, I think. Look, Soph, tell me to mind my own business if I'm being nosy, and I know we talked about this before, but did you and Paul honestly never want to have a family?'

Sophie led the way down to where the waves were gently lapping against the shore. She still hadn't answered when they were both ankle deep in water. Kate was just deciding that she should apologise and change the subject when Sophie said, 'I didn't tell you the whole story. Paul can't have children.'

'Oh.' The stark words could have been forbidding but Sophie's voice didn't sound unhappy, so Kate pressed on.

'Did you know that when you moved in together?'

'Yes, it was one of the first things he told me. A really bad case of mumps as a child, he said. We met at a speed-dating thing at the village hall. It was a fund raiser for the church roof. As chat-up lines go, it was a bit of a conversation stopper.'

'I bet. What did you say to that?'

Sophie giggled. 'I asked him if that was a crafty way of telling me it was quite safe to sleep with him. He said no, he just didn't want to give me any false hopes because he'd decided as soon as he saw me that I was the woman for him.'

'That's actually really romantic, in a crazy way. What did you do next?'

'I told him I'd never had any desire to have a baby and I couldn't see that ever changing. We left the speed-dating halfway through, called at the pub and then I took him home to bed. He never really moved out after that.'

Ralph now spotted a couple of Alsatians over towards the

marshes and left the water at a brisk trot, so Sophie had to follow. She galloped up the beach, caught him just in time before he was out of range and clipped on his lead.

'Come on, Katie and Ralph. Home time. We can carry on this conversation when we've got a roaring fire going and a glass of wine in our hands, okay?'

Kate nodded. She already had a feeling that the evening ahead was going to involve quite a lot of soul-searching on her part, but the thought didn't make her feel panicked, but rather as if she was going to a very informal therapy session with a person who cared very much about her.

'Shall I make dinner tonight?' she offered. 'What have you got in the fridge?'

'No, no, no. You're the guest. I should look after you.'

Kate raised her eyebrows. One thing she'd always known about her friend was that this was a person who hated cooking. Sophie grinned.

'I was going to ring for a takeaway actually,' she said. 'But Paul had planned to rustle up some sort of pasta dish with cream and mushrooms and chicken before he was called away, so all the stuff's there. You don't want to be bothered tonight, though, do you?'

'If the wine's provided, I'll do the rest,' said Kate. 'You can just about manage to make a salad to go with it, I suppose?'

'My salads are the best known to mankind,' said Sophie grandly. 'Paul's trained me well in that area at least.'

They ambled back towards the cottage with Ralph trailing at their heels. He clearly didn't approve of the lead or the decision to leave the beach but Sophie dug in her pocket for a couple of dog treats and, mollified, he allowed himself to be persuaded to hurry up.

'I'm really glad you decided to do this trip, and you're

trusting me with a mystery adventure too,' said Sophie. 'Old friends are the absolute best, don't you agree? Here's to the next bit.'

Kate didn't answer because she couldn't get the words out. She bent to pat the dog and he licked her hand, looking up at her with liquid brown eyes. Both Sophie and Ralph seemed to understand. There was no need to say a word. Although the phrase *next bit* was starting to sound a little ominous.

26

Back in the kitchen, Kate rummaged in the fridge to find everything she needed for dinner, while Sophie set about getting paper, kindling and logs together to create a cheerful blaze in the living-room grate. The air outside was cooler now, but the Aga was giving out its usual comforting warmth. Kate had switched on the radio in the corner and found it already tuned into a station playing old hits.

Ralph settled himself in his bed, curled into a ball and let out a contented sigh as the mellow sound of one of Kate's all-time favourite songs filled the room. She sat down for a moment to listen, overcome by a wave of nostalgia. It was an old Dire Straits hit, 'Why Worry?' The lyrics had always meant a lot to her, because it was one of the few CDs that Howard had bought for Kate, and this track was the reason he'd given it to her.

At the time, they had been reeling from the loss of their second baby. As the introduction played, Kate allowed herself for once to remember one of the times, albeit bittersweet, when she and her husband had been on the same wavelength. He'd come home from work to find Kate slumped on the sofa in her pyjamas, still un-showered and with matted hair. Without a word, Howard slid the new CD into the machine and found the track he wanted. Then he'd sat down and put his arms around Kate as she sobbed.

The mention of the words *red* and *gold* as the song played had filled Kate's mind with a luxurious Christmassy kind of feeling and she'd been distracted from her grief for a little while. Howard had gone upstairs to run her a bath and then, while she soaked away a little more of her pain, had nipped along to the fish and chip shop. Later, they'd eaten their dinner on trays in front of the TV, watching a re-run of *Fawlty Towers*. It had been one of the best nights of their marriage, Kate remembered.

The song ended and before Kate could collect her thoughts, the opening bars of a much more dynamic The Who track jolted Kate back to the night at the pub with Milo, as she remembered commenting on his favourite T-shirt. A pang of regret went through her as she checked her phone. The fledgling relationship was over before it had really begun, because now Milo was the one not answering texts. Kate got to her feet and busied herself chopping mushrooms as Sophie entered the room.

'You should have this as your theme song,' she said, gesturing to the radio. '"Won't Get Fooled Again". That's you, isn't it? No more Howards.'

Kate smiled but didn't reply. The memory of a kinder, softer-edged version of Howard was still too fresh to relate. Sophie was doing her own search of the fridge now, fetching out a bag of leaves, tomatoes, spring onions and a few other items that Kate was pleased to see would feature in the salad.

'Black olives and feta? Artichoke hearts? Have you and Paul gone all posh?' she said.

'Definitely. There's a brilliant deli in the town,' Sophie said.

'Paul can't walk past it without going in and spending a fortune. I don't try and stop him.'

They worked together happily, while Madonna sang about a holiday. 'See, even Madge thinks you were right to take a break,' Sophie said, pouring them both a cola. 'We're not going to hit the wine just yet, and we'll need to be sensible with it because... well, anyway, this first. It's not the diet version because I can't stand the stuff.'

'Why?'

'Why what?' said Sophie, suddenly very busy chopping tomatoes.

'You're suggesting we need a clear head tomorrow morning.'

'Am I? Well, you'll just have to accept that's the case, okay? Cheers!'

Sophie held up her tumbler of cola, complete with ice and a slice of lemon. Clinking glasses with Sophie seemed to flick a kind of switch in Kate's brain. She took a sip and the effect of the cool, fizzy drink had almost as big an effect as champagne. The sugar rush kicked in just as the background music changed to a track that had been on her wedding disco playlist, and it didn't make her sad, just full of wild energy. Sophie grabbed her by the hand and they began to dance, using all the available space around the table to show off their best moves.

'You can't beat a bit of Wham! for getting the evening started,' gasped Sophie. '"Wake Me Up Before You Go Go" was always the best one.'

They came to a halt as the track ended, both breathless. 'Right, now for dinner,' said Kate. 'That's made me ravenously hungry.'

An hour later, they were sitting in front of a crackling log fire at either end of the sofa with trays balanced on their knees. Sophie had persuaded Kate that they should get changed while the pasta cooked and had lent her the biggest, fluffiest dressing gown she'd ever seen. It was the colour of Cornish clotted cream. The thin robe Kate had packed was instantly relegated as she put on her pyjamas and snuggled into its warmth.

'Ralph isn't allowed on the furniture,' said Sophie. 'Don't let those puppy-dog eyes tell you otherwise.' With a disapproving bark, the dog jumped up between them and settled down with his nose on his paws.

'Unfortunately, he's against regulations of any kind, though,' she continued. 'He says they're an infringement of his rights.'

Kate laughed. 'My cat had rules of his own too,' she said. 'I miss Barnaby every day, even though it's been ages since he had to be put to sleep.'

'Why didn't you adopt another one after he died? You've always loved cats.'

She shrugged. 'I might do now. A rescue cat, maybe. The feline version of Ralph.' The thought was immensely cheering. She could already see herself visiting the centre where all the unwanted moggies ended up. She ought to have done it as soon as Howard left.

They began to eat, both making happy murmurs of enjoyment as the creamy texture and subtle flavours of Kate's pasta bake mingled with the crisp sharpness of Sophie's salad dressing.

'Paul taught you well,' said Kate. 'This is great.'

Sophie didn't answer because she was fiddling with the TV controls. 'I'm a very bad hostess. I was so caught up with thinking about food I forgot to get a film ready for us. What do you fancy?'

'Oh, anything cheesy and easy,' said Kate. 'I'm not in the mood for high drama tonight.'

'How about *Bridget Jones's Diary*? I haven't watched that for years.'

'Perfect.'

The familiar introduction took Kate back to going to see the film at the cinema. 'Colin Firth's a lot like Milo,' she breathed, as the story unfolded. 'If he had a beard and was taller, that is. And Milo's also weirdly like that man who used to be on *Pointless*.'

'Not Alexander Armstrong? He's my secret celeb crush.'

'No, Richard Osman. The crime novel one. He's big and a bit bumbling but pretty huggable.'

'So who's this Milo guy?'

'Oh, just someone I met fairly recently.'

'Kate, come on. Don't leave me hanging. You've met someone who's a dead ringer for Mark Darcy and RO?'

She shook her head. 'Milo's not a dead ringer for either of them by any means, it's just that he's really tall, probably about six feet six, I'd guess. And broad shouldered, kind of rugged looking but sensitive too…' Kate's voice tailed off. Sophie had stopped eating with her fork halfway to her mouth.

'Don't stop there,' she said. 'Tell all.'

'Let's watch the film and carry on eating. I promise I'll fill you in later,' said Kate. 'Although there isn't much to tell. It was over before it started. I'm not going to waste time stressing about him.'

They finished their meal and Sophie paused the film. 'Right, I'm going to fetch the wine and we'll have a break from *Bridget* while you reveal all. I want to know what made you finally decide to visit after all this time. No, don't get up, you've already worked harder than a guest should be allowed to.'

Kate sat back on the sofa stroking Ralph's silky fur as Sophie cleared their trays away. He nuzzled her hand and wriggled closer. Even though she was preparing herself to talk about personal things, never her favourite activity, Kate felt incredibly relaxed. She really should have come here sooner. The sea air, the welcoming cottage and Sophie's open-hearted friendship were more healing than anything else she could imagine.

Sophie came back into the room carrying a bottle beaded with condensation. 'We'll definitely need a glass of this if I'm going to get you to bare your soul,' she said, pouring the wine carefully. 'So, off you go. First, tell me about your new man.'

Kate took a gulp of her drink and tried to get her thoughts in order. 'Okay, he's definitely not mine, and probably never will be now, but I met Milo at Willowbrook Park. His sister Frankie died late last year and he was visiting her memorial bench. She was only in her mid-thirties. He's fifty-one,' she said, in answer to Sophie's unspoken question.

'The ideal age for you,' said Sophie. 'Big gap for them, though. Go on.'

'To cut a very long story short, Milo's wife left him around the same time as Howard dumped me. We didn't put two and two together when we first talked about it but it turns out the two of them had been having an affair with each other for months and they're now all loved-up together in a big grand house next to the golf club.'

'No way! And you really had no idea who the git had left you for?'

'He wouldn't tell me what she was called, and then later only let slip that her name was Annie. I think at first he thought I'd storm the golf club and punch her, but it turned out I didn't care that much and anyway, I'd never met anyone at the club with that name. I decided that whoever she was, she was welcome to him.'

Sophie seemed to be struggling to get her head round all this information. 'But didn't Milo even get the name of the bloke who was living with his ex? This is all very odd, you've got to admit. You couldn't write it, could you?'

'Well, Milo only knew him as Brad. Howard calls himself that now.'

'Poser,' said Sophie, taking a big swig of Prosecco.

'Yep. And as Howard only ever referred to his new woman that once as Annie, I didn't know that her name's actually Marianne Clifford, estranged wife of Milo.'

Sophie got up to add more logs to the fire and refill their glasses, which seemed to be emptying very quickly. 'Right, I'm with you so far. Awkward.'

'Very. And then we insulted each other really badly about our choices of dodgy partners, which kind of threw cold water over anything that might have developed.'

'Kate, are you kidding me? You met someone who you obviously fancied the pants off and you let him go just because of some stupid little squabble about exes? Are you insane?'

Kate sighed. Put like that, it did sound ridiculous.

'But I'm not sure if I need a man in my life at all,' she said. 'Beryl was the one who persuaded me to have a break and come and see you...'

'Sensible woman.'

'Yes. Anyway, her view is that I've got a lot of baggage to unload and sort out before I even think about relationships, if I ever do.'

'Aha. Now we're getting somewhere. Look, we can watch the rest of *Bridget* any time. I'm turning off the TV and you're going to tell me more about the baggage. We're warm and comfy and there's ice cream in the freezer for later. Go on, Kate. Let's have it.'

27

Kate settled herself more comfortably at her end of the sofa. Seeming to sense her tension, Ralph wriggled along and put his head in her lap again. She stroked his ears and immediately felt less anxious about digging into the past. 'I don't know where to start.'

Sophie reached out and patted her arm. 'Why don't you give me a whistle-stop tour of being married to Howard and where it went wrong along the way? Would that help?'

'The thing is, was it ever right?' Kate tried to get her thoughts in order. 'I guess I wanted to start a family so badly I pushed any doubts I had under the carpet. Alarm bells should have rung when Howard persuaded me not to train to be a teacher when he knew how much I was looking forward to uni.'

Sophie nodded. 'But to be fair, you let yourself be persuaded too easily. Just being devil's advocate here,' she added hastily when she saw Kate's expression.

'Okay. So then I threw myself into my new job as a TA and I loved every minute. I still wanted to teach but as time went on I was asked to step in more to help with the children who needed extra support and I went on every course I could wangle. In the end I was the most highly qualified TA in the school and I didn't have all the teachers' responsibilities of the planning and marking at home.'

'Bonus.' Sophie got up and threw another couple of logs into the grate and sparks flew, causing Ralph to rumble in his sleep. 'Keep going.'

Kate's head was starting to swim now. She blinked to clear the misty feeling caused by alcohol and memories and the warmth of the room. It was almost too much effort to speak but she forced herself to carry on.

'By now Howard was really getting well in at the golf club and he was also being promoted at work. We could have afforded for me to step back and retrain at that point but at last I got pregnant. I lost the first baby pretty quickly but I was determined to try again. The doctor said there was no reason why that should happen next time, so I put a brave face on it and kept going.'

Sophie listened as Kate poured out the story of the following three almost-babies. She looked close to tears by the time Kate skated over the incident with her neighbour's little boy.

'Did I hear you right? You actually abducted a baby? A real live baby?' she breathed, hand to her mouth.

'That's a harsh word, Soph. I only meant to soothe him. I was pretty deranged around that time.'

'But... but...'

'I know, it could have been a completely different story if Howard hadn't got him back home so quickly. You know the layout of our cottages, we've got long back gardens with gates at the bottom that open onto an alley, and that leads to the car park at the back of the flats and Mrs Nightingale's shop. I'd come home that way and Howard dashed back with the pram along there.'

'So nobody saw him. Phew.'

'No, but Beryl knew.'

'At the time? And she didn't tell the others in her coven?'

'No, not a word. Howard spoke about it to her just afterwards so it seems as if she began to keep an eye on me, but very discreetly. We were incredibly lucky that nobody was out and about to see what I did. I had to stay with Howard after that. I felt as if I owed him for covering it up.'

'And you honestly never had any counselling or anything? Kate, you were ill.'

'Not really ill, just sad.'

'You can be sick with grief, you know? Well, you didn't get professional help so I suppose you just went back to work?'

'Yes, and work was always my saving grace. The parents of the kids gradually found out what had happened with the final baby. The others hadn't been announced because they happened earlier. The first was lost after only eight weeks and after that I was cautious about getting my hopes up. I'd been four months pregnant the last time so people had started to notice my bump. Everyone was really kind.'

'And that was it? You didn't see a doctor to try and find out why it kept happening?'

Kate thought about that time. Howard had been absolutely adamant that they shouldn't try again and the only GP she'd seen when the bleeding carried on for far too long afterwards was brusque with her when she said she wasn't having any investigations.

'There was no point in finding out more if we wouldn't be going through with another attempt,' she said. 'The miscarriages were spread out over a few years so it wasn't as if I was always off sick and it was never the same doctor I saw afterwards. I didn't get pregnant easily but that might have been because Howard actually wasn't very interested in sex. Or not with me, anyway.'

'But what about your dad? Couldn't he have helped? There's no point in having a doctor in the family if you don't pick their brains.'

'We didn't want to involve Dad. He was always a bit weird about family ailments and Howard thought it wasn't fair to ask him for advice. We'd have needed a specialist by the point when we realised it wasn't likely to happen and... well... we just didn't go there, that's all.'

There was a long silence while Sophie took this in. 'It all sounds awful,' she said, eventually.

'Telling it like this doesn't fill in the gaps. Mostly I was really happy at work and there were all the godchildren to get to know. That was fun. I just accepted we led separate lives for a lot of the time. Until Howard met Milo's wife, that is. She was the catalyst that finally ended the marriage but it had been dead in the water for years.'

'And all this with Milo's wife happened after your poor dad had his heart attack, and worse still it was you that found him. I remember you telling me about it at the time and I couldn't believe how shocking it must have been for you.'

'It was so horrible, Soph.' Kate couldn't hold back the tears now. 'I saw his jacket first. Lovat-green tweed. Dad loved that jacket. He was lying face down on a grassy bank halfway through the wood.'

Sophie moved closer to Kate, ignoring Ralph's protesting growl. She put her arms around her friend and let her cry and cry. All the months of bottling up the grief took some unloading. At last, Kate felt as if she had no more tears left inside her.

'I think it's time for rocky road ice cream,' said Sophie.

'You've done really well getting all this off your chest. It's a great start to feeling better, but now we need a sugar rush, okay? I bet Ralph's ready for his supper too.'

Sophie got to her feet and Ralph opened one eye. He yawned noisily and clambered down to join her. The room seemed very quiet after they'd gone to the kitchen, and exhaustion threatened to overwhelm Kate but it was a peaceful kind of tiredness.

'I think I might sleep for a week after this,' she said, when Sophie presented her with a huge bowl of ice cream.

'That's fine by me. It's time for bed right after you polish this off, and tomorrow... well. That will take care of itself. No, don't ask questions. Just relax, get ready for a great night's sleep and leave the rest to me.'

28

The next morning, Kate woke early to see sunshine already streaming through the gap in her curtains. Through the open window, she could hear birds singing lustily in the garden and up the stairs drifted the sounds of her friend clattering around in the kitchen.

Kate stretched and yawned. It was years since she'd slept so heavily. The months of middle-of-the-night wakefulness that had followed her father's death and then Howard's departure had taken their toll but this morning she felt ready for anything. It was partly the after-effects of Beryl's comforting advice about moving on and also the fact that Sophie now knew her secret too. Neither of them seemed to think badly of her. Perhaps it really was time to make a fresh start. Today should be about the birth of a new Kate – someone who made concerted decisions about what was going to happen to her in the future rather than just letting everything float along. She'd already made changes since Howard left by taking the new job at Pat's Place, and now she'd taken the trip south, but these moves and the wardrobe revamp were only the tip of the iceberg.

As Kate pondered her next steps, Sophie knocked on the door and came in without waiting for an answer. 'Tea,' she said. 'And then you can have a shower before I make you a bacon butty. After that, we're off.'

'I thought you said I could sleep for a week,' Kate said, grinning as she sat up to take her tea.

'That was a silly idea. We've got too much to do to waste time sleeping. It's seven o'clock. I've already pegged out a load of washing, fed Ralph, had a shower and done the breakfast prep. I was about to get some saucepan lids out and play a rousing tattoo outside your door if you didn't respond to tea therapy.'

Barely an hour later, Kate and Sophie were in The Jungle Bunny, heading along the lane that led out of the town and along the coast. Sophie had insisted on vetting the clothes her friend planned to wear and was happy that Kate had chosen rust-coloured jeans with a lovat-green T-shirt. 'For Dad,' Kate said, but there were no tears this morning, only a feeling of delight that she was finally here with one of her best and oldest friends at the seaside with nothing to do but have a great time.

'But where are we going?' Kate asked.

'You'll see. You did bring your passport, didn't you? I reminded you on the phone before you came.'

'It's in my bag. But why do I need...?'

'No questions. All will be revealed in good time.'

They wove their way along the coast, picking up speed as the road became wider.

'Katie, I can't stop thinking about what you told me last night. That baby. You must have been so scared afterwards and you've been beating yourself up ever since. But look, no harm was done. You've served your time with the guilt and you've given so much love to lots of other kids.'

Hearing this echo of Beryl's opinion eased Kate a few more

paces towards forgiving herself. It wouldn't happen overnight, but it seemed as if it really was time to put the past firmly behind her now and look to the future. Today was going to be an even bigger adventure than yesterday and suddenly a wild sense of freedom filled her soul.

'I suppose that's France over there,' said Kate with a shiver, pointing across the wide expanse of sea stretching out to their left. 'Funny that it's so near. I hadn't thought about that.'

'You're right about being very close to France. Great, isn't it?' Sophie said. 'Shall we go?'

'What? Go where?'

'Normandy, of course. It's high time you visited your mum and your brother. How long is it since you've seen them?'

Kate frowned. 'They don't come and see me, though,' she muttered. 'They didn't have to take themselves off halfway across the world.'

'It's the Channel, Kate, not the world. People swim across it, it's so narrow.'

Kate looked at Sophie, unsure if she was joking. 'You mean it, don't you?'

'Absolutely. Why do you think I told you to bring your passport?'

'Erm... I thought we might be doing some sort of extreme sport where we'd need to prove we were over eighteen.'

Sophie laughed. 'I know we both look super-young and gorgeous, darl, but I don't think anyone would doubt we were of age, do you?'

'So, what are you suggesting? We can't go to France, I haven't even got any luggage.'

'Ah. I nipped up and quickly packed you a bag while you were taking Ralph out for a wee. Hope you don't mind. We're almost at the ferry port now. Your mum only lives twenty miles or so inland from Dieppe and the boat from Newhaven goes there.'

'But I can't just take off to France. I thought you wanted us to have fun… I mean…'

An awkward silence fell. Sophie waited, eyes on the road ahead.

Eventually, Kate blurted out, 'I came to see you, and maybe have an adventure, not to visit the runaways.'

'Is that how you see them?'

Sophie's question hung between them. At last, Kate nodded. 'I suppose so. They didn't want to hang around Willowbrook. Jamie was off as soon as he could afford to have his big lifestyle change. His kids are at the nearest village school now and they all speak French and love living out in the sticks. Davina bakes bread and helps out with village events. As for Mum…'

'And that's the elephant in the room, isn't it? You feel as if she heartlessly abandoned you after your dad died. You're grieving for the loss of both of them and for the end of your marriage even though Howard was an idiot, and then there are all the babies too. It's no wonder you're coming a bit unstuck.'

'Am I?'

'You know you are, my lovely, or you were. I'm here to rescue you, or at least start the ball rolling towards a happier you. We've talked about all the lost babies and the… other one… now let's get on with having a great time, eh? The ferry crossings are booked and we'll be at the port very soon. I didn't prewarn your family in case I couldn't persuade you to come with me, but your mum and Jamie and co will be delighted to see you.'

'Are you quite sure about that?'

'I planned for you to ring Caroline as soon as we board. We won't land ourselves on them, just book into a local B&B, or whatever they have in Normandy, and dip in and out of their homes for a couple of days. Are you in, or shall I turn round and go back?'

Part of Kate yearned to put this reunion off for another few weeks, or even months... however long it took to stop being so angry and sad, but then a vision of her mum swam into her mind, with that wide smile, newly blonde hair shining in the sun, arms open and waiting for a hug. She'd missed her so much.

'I'm in,' she said.

29

Many years had passed since Kate had been on a passenger ferry and the last time she'd disgraced herself by being very sick on her dad's shoes. Her stomach was already jittery so, before they reached the port, she reached for her bottle of water and took the precaution of dosing herself up with some of Paul's travel sickness tablets that Sophie still had in her bag from their last jaunt over the water. 'He even goes green on a pedalo,' she said. 'We don't take any chances nowadays. I always make him take a couple just as insurance.'

The waiting time to board was short and the queue of vehicles were soon trundling up the ramp. By now, Kate couldn't decide whether she was more terrified or excited. She was quivering with both emotions, the hairs on the back of her neck standing on end as the passenger ferry got ready to sail out of Newhaven on a mercifully calm sea.

'Coffee?' asked Sophie, after re-settling Ralph in the jeep with his water, his comfy bed and some dog biscuits.

'We can't just leave him in the car!' Kate hadn't realised this was the rule, and felt far more outraged than Ralph did, by the look of him. He was already curled up with his nose on his paws and merely rolled an eye at her when she patted him consolingly.

'We're not allowed to take him on deck or inside the boat. He's fine. We do this fairly often because we've got friends who live in an old farmhouse not far from Dieppe. They've got a gite too, and we go and stay whenever we can. Paul loves it there. Ralph'll sleep most of the way. I think the motion of the boat and the noise of the engine acts like a lullaby for him. He's a seasoned traveller, which is more than you are. Calm down.'

As they clanged their way up the metal staircase to the passenger decks Kate began to picture her mum, still glamorous at seventy, in the home Jamie had made. Always keen on her own space, Caroline must surely have part of the house to herself, and she'd definitely need a kitchen. She'd probably be making one of her lemon drizzle cakes right now if she knew they were on the way. Her mum had sent her numerous photographs of the surrounding countryside and villages when she first arrived in Normandy, many showing market stalls overflowing with fresh vegetables and fruit and baguettes and strings of garlic. Lately, she'd given up on trying to convince Kate that she'd made the right decision.

'Mum's kind of washed her hands of me,' Kate said to Sophie, her mouth dry at the thought of the phone call she needed to make, and soon. 'This is a mad thing we're doing. She's not even going to want to talk to me.'

'Don't be ridiculous. Off you go and ring her, and don't forget to tell her we've got Ralph with us. I'm sure she won't mind, though, he's no bother. I'll get the coffee and croissants in. Chop, chop. I'm starving.'

Kate was back within five minutes. She joined Sophie at a

table by the window of the café and reached for the steaming mug of coffee that her friend had provided.

'I can't believe we're doing this. It's so exciting. Tell me what your mum's reaction was when you rang her,' said Sophie. 'I bet she's in the kitchen already making one of her special cakes for you.'

Kate sighed. She was glad in a way that Sophie was fizzing with delight because she was finding it hard to muster much joy herself. This whole situation felt out of her control.

'Mum was thrilled to hear about our plan and she said of course we must stay with her. She's got a twin-bedded spare bedroom and it's ours for however long we want it. Jamie and his gang are away on a camping trip, though. Mum said he'll be devastated to have missed us.'

Even to herself, Kate's voice sounded doubtful. Her relationship with her younger brother had never been particularly close and why would her mother be so pleased to be dropped on like this? The row they'd had before she left for France remained etched in Kate's mind. Both still reeling from her father's death, neither had held back from hurling bitter accusations. Kate had shouted that her mum wasn't facing up to her grief by running away and the reply had been that Kate was burying her head in the sand by refusing to see that a new start was just what all of them needed.

'I hate surprises,' Kate said. 'I can't imagine why Mum would be so happy to have unexpected guests, especially when one of them yelled at her in a big way the last time they were together.'

Sophie laughed. 'Look, Kate, some people don't object to acting on impulse. I've sorted out this trip really fast. I didn't need three weeks' warning. It was unexpected, of course, because I know you of old and you don't make snap decisions as a rule. You hang on to what you know, even when it isn't working.'

The journey passed peacefully. Although the morning air was chilly, Kate and Sophie were warmly wrapped up so they settled on the front viewing deck with more coffee as they sailed towards the coast of France, watching the sunshine turn the sea into a blanket of green, turquoise and gentian blue streaks with diamond-tipped ripples. Kate's heart seemed to beat a little faster whenever she thought of her mum, but the fresh sea breeze and the soothing hum of the ferry's engines were doubly relaxing.

A phone bleeped as she daydreamed, bringing Kate sharply back to reality. 'Was that yours?' she asked Sophie, but her friend was dozing now, chest covered in biscuit crumbs, leaning on Kate's shoulder and snoring gently. With difficulty, Kate managed to wriggle her phone out of her pocket, only to find three unread messages. The first was from Pat, who she'd contacted to warn her of the new plans, in case there was a hold-up anywhere.

> Have a great break, honey, and take more time if you need it. An extra two days is no prob. Don't stay away too long though. Michelle makes a mean scone but the regulars are missing your trademark crispy bacon rolls xx

Kate messaged back brief thanks and, stifling a sudden longing for a bacon butty with extra tomato sauce, opened the next one.

> Elsie says don't forget her present. Sam x

Smiling, she finally clicked on the text that was making her heart do a strange dance. It had been a while since she'd had a WhatsApp from Milo, and Kate had almost stopped checking her phone for them. Almost but not quite.

> Hi Kate
>
> Hope you have a great time by the sea. Just to say that I'm spending a couple of days with Luka. It turns out he's left his mum's house and wants to stay with me right away, so I need to sort us some accommodation before I'm on the street. We're just organising the emptying of this place. It's a bit of a whirlwind decision but you were right, a new start is what we both need. Hope to see you soon, it's not too late to have that theatre trip if you're up for it. M x

Kate re-read Milo's message twice. It was hard to know how to answer it. She'd never been good at letting go of anger and she was still sore when she thought back to how scathing Milo had been about her marriage to Howard when actually he was standing on very shaky ground himself and also how he'd appeared to be warning her off getting close to him, as if she was some sort of predatory female in desperate need of a man. If the loathsome Marianne hadn't lured Howard away, she'd still be in her safe bubble. A small voice in her head told Kate that she'd given at least as good as she got in that last exchange of insults and anyway, why would she want to be living with Howard again when the single life was so much more peaceful? She'd given in to impulse when she'd messaged him about visiting the coast, which wasn't her style at all, but encouraging Milo now might be jumping from the frying pan into the fire, as Sophie would no doubt say.

Kate thought of Winnie's wise words. Did this renewed suggestion of the theatre trip mean he'd had a change of heart about dating or was she over-thinking everything, as usual? If Milo did want to backtrack and start again, there was a lot of healing to do before she could even think about another possible relationship. One word kept coming into her mind since she'd had the heart-to-heart with Sophie. Forgiveness. This trip was about starting to forgive her mum and brother for whatever misdeeds she'd laid, rightly or wrongly, at their door. It was the first step on the road to getting to know herself again. It took a while to formulate the right message but in the end she was reasonably happy with the one she typed.

Hello again, Milo

That's fabulous news for you both. Best of luck with the reorganisation,

Kate x

She dithered for a moment about the kiss and then deleted it and pressed *send*. That would have to do. No need to tell him about France, and going to the theatre with him was a step too far at the moment as far as Kate could see. The boat lurched slightly and so did Kate's stomach. The calm sea of the start of their journey was a thing of the past. Sophie began to stir as Kate wriggled with anxiety.

'You okay, pet?' she asked. 'Not feeling yucky, are you? I think I might have nodded off there.' She yawned. 'Let's go for a walk round the boat, shall we? I need a top-up of caffeine and a sticky bun before we get to Dieppe.'

'Good idea.'

'You look a bit down,' Sophie said, linking arms with Kate as they swayed along the deck toward the restaurant. 'Are you still worried about meeting your mum?'

Kate shrugged. She was beginning to feel more and more like

the spotty teenage girl who had sighed and scowled her way through adolescence. Life seemed to be getting unnecessarily complicated.

'I wish I'd stayed at home,' she burst out, when Sophie nudged her for a reply.

'No, you don't, not really,' said Sophie as they reached the busy café, guiding Kate towards an empty table. 'Sit down here and I'll fetch snacks. Doing nothing's a cop out. We're making things happen. The best is yet to come, as they say. Tea or coffee?'

Sophie bustled away, her white-blonde hair and red dungarees standing out from the crowd. Kate wished she had half her friend's enthusiasm and confidence. The nearer they sailed to France, the less she felt like confronting her skittish mother. Looking out at the undulating waves, Kate sighed. Sophie was right. Making things happen was the only way to get over this hump in her life. She just wished they didn't have to roll up and down on a choppy sea to do it.

30

20 MARCH 2020

Leaning over the edge of the narrowboat, Kate peers down into the murky depths of the canal. They've only been travelling for a couple of hours but already both her nephews are bored. They're too little to help with the steering but too big to be happy inside the boat for long. If only it wasn't raining so torrentially she could entertain them better on the small seating area at the front, but for now, all three of them are wrapped up in waterproofs and counting ducks.

'Can we go in now, Aunty Kate?' says Ben. 'I'm really wet, and I'm hungry.'

'Is it lunchtime yet?' his little brother whines, tugging on Kate's coat. 'I need a wee.'

Kate sighs and takes them inside again. A family holiday had seemed like such a great idea when her dad had suggested it. 'Jamie and Davina, Ben and Charlie, you and Howard and me and your ma,' he'd said happily. 'It'll be fun. You used to love sailing down the canals when you were little.'

The memories that spring to mind of those times mainly involve feeling queasy and being mildly terrified of the deep locks but Kate and Howard haven't been away anywhere together since the awful Wiltshire weekend so she pulls out all the stops to persuade her husband that they both need a break.

'I've never been on a narrowboat before,' he says now, joining Kate and the boys inside the main cabin. 'Is there any cake? I'm starving.'

'Me too,' says Charlie. 'Can we have chips for lunch?'

'Not really. I can't make enough chips for all of us in this tiny oven,' says Kate. 'Howard, what have you been doing all this time, and where's Davina?'

'She's having a lie-down,' Howard says, ignoring the first question. 'That poor girl. She really does suffer with morning sickness, doesn't she? Your mum's keeping her company so she doesn't get lonely.'

Kate seethes. Not only does her devastatingly pretty sister-in-law get pregnant just by glancing at Jamie, it seems, she also gets sympathy for the entire nine months and then produces endearing offspring with very little effort. Not for Davina the endless yearning for a baby. She can have as many as she likes. Also, she gets to have a nap on her bunk in the middle of the morning.

'So, what's happened to Jamie and Dad? They surely don't both need to steer?'

'You're sounding a bit waspish, Kate. You need to watch that sharp tongue. You don't want to get a reputation for being the crabby old aunt,' says Howard, winking at the boys.

'Crabby Aunty Kate, Crabby Aunty Kate,' sings Ben, and Charlie is joining in within seconds.

'Thanks so much for that, Howard. How about you doing something useful and making some sandwiches instead of inciting the troops to mock their elders?'

Howard pulls what he must imagine is a regretful face.

'Sorry, love. I'm getting off at the next lock. I've got to meet a couple of the staff for an update. We're meeting at the pub just along the cut. Ah, Ted's slowing down, we must be nearly there. Where's my cagoule?'

'An update? But you've barely been out of the office for half a day and you've already taken two long phone calls,' Kate shouts, as he disappears through the engine room, presumably en route to execute a daring leap from the back of the boat.

'Big deals don't crack themselves,' Howard yells back. 'I'll drop back on board at the next lock. Or possibly the one after, it depends how soon I can wrap this thing up. Ciao.'

Both boys are now jumping up and down on the spot, still chanting *Crabby Aunty Kate*. She wonders how she's going to bear a whole week of this so-called fun. Maybe being childfree isn't such a bad thing after all.

'Come on, lads, let's make my speciality,' she says wearily.

'What's your speshulality, Aunty Kate?' asks Ben.

'Crispy bacon rolls,' says Kate. 'You'll find they make everyone a lot happier.'

'Even Mummy? She doesn't like bread much.'

'Even Mummy. As soon as she smells that bacon frying, she'll be in here, you just see.'

And Kate's quite right, as it happens. The rain stops, a watery sun tries to come out, Ted moors up fairly soon and Kate's mum and Davina appear, ready to set up the folding chairs and table on the tow path. Jamie makes tea, slices the rolls and finds plates and tomato ketchup. Soon, a riotous picnic is in full swing, and when they set off again, both boys are more than ready to take a nap. Kate settles down on the front deck with her book as they drift along between meadows and woods. She keeps an eye out for Howard as they pass each lock, but he doesn't join them until they've moored again for the night, and then it's only to say that he's staying nearby at a village inn tonight so he can *tie up a few loose ends.*

'Yeah, right,' says Jamie, exchanging glances with his mother, but Kate doesn't argue, because actually, this holiday is so much more relaxing without Howard in it.

At seven o'clock, Charlie, looking even cuter than usual in his giraffe-patterned pyjamas, brings his favourite story and climbs onto Kate's knee. 'Don't you wish you had a little boy like me to play with all the time, Aunty Kate?' he asks sleepily as she finishes reading.

'I'm very lucky that I get to share you and Ben, and lots of other children at home too,' says Kate. 'I'm much too lazy to have kids of my own.'

It's her stock answer to the question, and actually, this time she really means it. Her bunk beckons, and tonight she'll actually be able to turn over without bumping heads with Howard. If the boys wake in the night it won't be her job to soothe them and, in the morning, she'll be free to get up early and go for a walk along the towpath, completely alone. This warm feeling of contentment might not last, but for now, life is suddenly and absolutely the way it should be.

31

The drive to the hamlet where Caroline Baxter and Jamie and his family now lived took Sophie and Kate through some of the prettiest scenery either of them had seen for a long time. Once they were free of the built-up areas around Dieppe, it was easy to find quiet routes away from the main roads. Sophie was clearly used to driving on what Kate still thought of as the wrong side of the road, and she was full of admiration for the cool way her friend negotiated the traffic at the start of their journey.

Soon, Sophie's sassy little jeep was taking the two of them far away from the ferry queues and they were singing along to her Abba CD. 'Do you see yourself as an Agnetha or a Frida?' Kate asked. 'I always wanted to be the blonde one but now I think the brunette is classier.'

'Oh, blonde every time for me,' Sophie answered, as she skilfully overtook a tractor. 'And I'm sure your mum would agree. Look at how she's revamped her image. I really respect how she's changed her life around since your dad died.'

Kate's response was to stare out of the window. With every second they were drawing nearer to the moment when she'd have to face up to her resentment at Caroline's swift departure to this admittedly beautiful part of the world. She bit her lip, wondering how to approach the meeting. Her gut feeling was to make an effort and start afresh but it was hard to tamp down the burning rage she felt every time she thought of those agonising days after the family house was sold and plans were made for a new life in the French countryside.

When they finally wove their way through a stunningly pretty village square and out the other side, Kate said, 'Aren't you tempted to stop at one of those pavement cafés for a coffee? There was a baker's shop and the church looks worth a visit. You must be shattered.'

'Ha, nice try, Katie. No, we're here now and we're going through with it. You know I've got your back. It's time to put things right with your mum.'

Kate fell silent as Sophie listened to the final Sat Nav instructions, which took them sharp right down an overgrown lane between high hedges until the tarmac blended into rough grass and the hedges were replaced by low shrubs. They both gazed open-mouthed as Sophie brought the jeep to a standstill and turned off the engine. In front of them, the ground dropped away to reveal a stunning view. A grey stone house sat to one side of them, looking as if it had been there since time began, and beyond it lay a heavily wooded valley. In the distance, another village nestled on the upper slopes of a hill. The sound of church bells drifted across the intervening landscape, and somewhere nearby, a sheep bleated a shrill greeting to its companions.

The noise of the jeep approaching must have alerted Kate's mother, because she came hurrying around the side of the house almost before the car had stopped. Caroline was carrying a large oval trug that looked as if it contained vegetables, and she was dressed as if for a day's gardening. Kate did a double take. Was this the woman who used to put make-up on just to answer the door? The person who never went out in non-matching clothes and was a big fan of the twinset and pearls vibe? Kate and Sophie climbed stiffly out of the jeep and released Ralph, who immediately scuttled over to the nearest bush and cocked his leg happily.

'Kate, Sophie and a beautiful dog too,' said Caroline. 'I'm so glad you could bring Ralph and that you finally made it. People often get lost after the village. We're a bit remote here. The lanes are so narrow and the entrance to the drive gets obscured when the trees...' Caroline seemed to realise she was rambling, and stopped talking abruptly. She and Kate looked at each other, both unsure of who should make the first move. Eventually, Caroline made the decision. She put the basket down, opened her arms and after only a moment's hesitation, Kate moved forward into the familiar embrace, the one she'd longed for but had been much too angry to accept before this moment.

'Oh, my Katie, I've missed you so much,' Caroline murmured. She smelt of fresh air, lavender and... Mum.

'You went away,' Kate croaked, trying her hardest not to cry.

Sophie had clearly had enough of this waiting around. 'Look, guys, all this hugging is great but unlike Ralph, I can't use the shrubbery. I really need a loo and a cup of tea in that order, and anything heavy can wait till we open the wine. I'm presuming this outdoorsy life hasn't made you go all teetotal, Caroline?'

Kate's mum laughed and released her daughter. 'I'm so sorry, you must both be ready for a comfort break. Come on in and I'll show you your room. It's got its own little bathroom so you'll be private. I don't have guests very often but Jamie and Davina do, so we share the use of the spare bedroom. Where will Ralph sleep? You're welcome to have him in with you if that's best.'

'No, he'll be fine downstairs,' said Sophie, pulling Ralph's dog bed and his bag out of the car along with her own rucksack and water bottle. She reached for Ralph's bowl to refill it and he drank noisily.

Ralph's thirst satisfied, Kate and Sophie followed Caroline inside with the dog trotting along behind them, his tongue hanging out. She led them through a cool, stone-flagged hallway and up a staircase that took them to a long corridor. 'This place is bigger than it looks from the outside,' said Sophie. 'It's lovely. You must be very glad you made the move.'

Kate opened her mouth to say something but Sophie quelled her with a look.

'Yes, it was a good decision but obviously there's a downside. Leaving you was very hard,' Caroline said, turning as she reached the last doorway and facing Kate. Their eyes met.

'It didn't strike me as all that hard, to be honest,' said Kate, unable to keep the bitterness out of her voice, even though Sophie's face was still saying *shut up*.

'Oh, Kate, it was more difficult than anything I've ever done,' Caroline said. 'I was expecting you to want to thrash all this out later but now's as good a time as any. Why don't you both freshen up, and then I can give Sophie her tea on the terrace with Ralph and you and I can take ourselves off to my sitting room to do this in private. I don't think it's fair to make Sophie listen to us bickering, is it?'

'Are we going to bicker?' Suddenly Kate knew for certain that arguing with the gentle-faced woman who'd given her such a happy childhood wasn't the way forward.

'Up to you, darling.' Caroline opened a door to reveal a long room with two windows that looked out over the valley. The late-afternoon sun made everything seem golden. The walls were painted in the palest yellow and the bare boards were varnished in a shade that seemed to create warmth and cosiness. Two beds were covered in lemon and cornflower-blue patterned duvets and huge vase of flowers on the chest of drawers echoed the colours.

'There you go, make yourselves at home,' Caroline said. 'I'll go and make the tea and see you downstairs. There's no rush.'

Watching her mother disappear along the corridor, Kate found her hands were trembling and her mouth was dry, but Sophie was already through the door and into the bathroom with a cry of relief. This was no time to panic about the coming confrontation, it was much too late for that, so Kate concentrated on unpacking her bag and hanging up the summer dress Sophie had packed for her to change into this evening, although now she was thinking that her mother's attitude to clothes had changed so much that this might not be necessary. The dusty calf-length jeans and loose cotton top that Caroline was wearing were nothing like the smart outfits that had once filled her wardrobe.

'This place is heavenly,' Sophie sighed, coming out of the bathroom looking much refreshed. 'We're never going to want to leave.'

'I wouldn't bank on that,' said Kate. 'A lot depends on how this next part goes. We might end up doing a runner and booking into that little hotel in the village if I can't see eye to eye with Mum.'

'For goodness' sake, Kate.' Sophie's exasperation was no longer hidden now Caroline had left them alone. Her arms were folded and an unusually severe expression transformed her face. 'You need to make this work. We've come a long way to see your mum and if you mess this up, the rift between you two will just get wider all the time. Get a grip and get over yourself. It's not just about you. I'll see you downstairs.'

With this, she stalked off, Ralph at her heels. Kate could hear

Sophie stomping down the corridor and the click of Ralph's claws as he followed her. The shock of the forthright words made Kate stand still for several seconds until the call of the bathroom forced her to move. The plumbing clanked alarmingly as she flushed the toilet and the water gurgled out of the taps in the basin as if it was travelling from the depths of the earth. Kate splashed her face with blissfully cold water, dried herself on the fluffiest of hand towels and used the lemon-verbena scented hand cream that their hostess had provided. Much restored, she made her way down the stairs, noticing how the solid oak had been worn away in the centre of each tread by what must have been generations of residents.

In the kitchen, Sophie and Caroline were viewing the contents of the fridge and Ralph had settled himself in his bed next to the cooking range. 'Shall we have dinner about half past six?' asked Caroline. 'I've made a quiche, and the bread was only baked this lunchtime. I was just collecting the makings of a salad when you arrived.'

'Sounds perfect,' Sophie said, as Caroline took a pottery jug full of milk from the fridge and added it to the tea tray set out ready on the table. 'I've got a good book and I'll take my tea outside, so don't feel like you've got to hurry your chat.'

She shot another warning glance at Kate as Caroline poured large mugs of tea and handed them round. 'There are biscuits here too, I baked them this morning, help yourself,' Caroline said, leading Kate through another door that took them to a large annexe.

'This is mine,' she said. 'We give each other a lot of space. The kids are a bit boisterous sometimes, especially Charlie, and I like to be peaceful. Anyway, Jamie and Davina don't want me breathing down their necks all the time.'

Kate sank down gratefully onto the large, fat sofa that almost filled one wall of the room. The view was the same as the one from the guest bedroom and both windows were open to let in the scent of the old-fashioned roses that grew in a long flower bed outside.

'I've got this living room, a bedroom, small bathroom and tiny kitchen,' Caroline said, sitting down next to Kate but leaving a gap between them. 'It's plenty for me. That big house was getting me down. Your father loved it but it was never my choice.'

'Really?' Why hadn't Kate known this? She'd always assumed Caroline liked living in detached splendour with a beautifully manicured lawn that sloped right down to the riverbank. It had been a stylish setting and Caroline had dressed accordingly. She looked at her mother properly for the first time since their arrival. The short honey-blonde hair seemed to be Caroline's only concession to elegance nowadays. Her face was bare of make-up and lightly tanned, with only the faintest tracing of lines around the eyes and mouth. Her clothes looked as if they'd been washed many times, and on her feet she wore battered sandals that had definitely seen better days.

'You look... so different...' Kate said.

'Better, or worse?' Caroline's smile was unsure.

Kate considered this question carefully before answering. 'Much more natural, very pretty and... happier in your own skin?' she suggested tentatively.

The smile grew broader and Caroline reached out as if to touch her daughter's hand, only to withdraw quickly. 'Thank you. That sums up how I feel. Not sure about the *pretty* part. Otherwise... yes, much happier all round.'

'But you miss Dad.' It was a statement, not a question this time.

'Of course I do, that goes without saying. But life goes on, doesn't it? I had to do something for myself, Katie. Coming here... well, it's been a game-changer. I know you felt as if it was too soon or maybe just the wrong choice altogether, but please try and understand that if I'd stayed rattling around in that place, I'd just have mouldered. Either that or gone completely mad.'

'But you had friends.' *And you had me.* The unspoken second part of that sentence hung between them like a black cloud.

'A lot of them were your dad's Morris dancing and bowls club friends rather than mine, though. I think you know what that feels like.'

Kate bit her lip. The friends that she and Howard had shared turned out to be mostly his too. 'I didn't realise it was like that for you,' she said. 'You seemed happy with Dad.'

'Oh, we were fine on the whole,' Caroline said, stretching her legs out and kicking off her sandals. 'Drink your tea, darling, it's going cold.'

'Don't change the subject, Mum. Did you and Dad have problems that I was never told about? Did... did Jamie know?' Resentment flickered again and Kate picked up her mug, pretending to be absorbed in her drink.

'Jamie always used to joke that your father and I had a bacon sandwich type of marriage.'

'Erm...' Kate was lost now.

'You know the sort of thing. When one of you says, "Hey, I really fancy a bacon sandwich this morning," and the other says, "I was just about to put the pan on." Neither of you should insist on wholemeal bread or mention calories and nobody should say they prefer fruit and yoghurt that day.'

'I don't get it. Explain.'

Caroline took her time answering. At last, she turned to face Kate. 'It's just a flippant example of how people in long relationships grow together and have similar aims, even about the simple things in life I suppose. Don't forget that very few marriages are how they seem from the outside. I always thought yours was reasonably civilised, and look what happened there. Jamie and his family moved in with us for a while when they were waiting for this house to be ready. He saw how things were between us.'

'In what way?' Kate wasn't sure if she wanted to hear any more, but somehow she had to ask.

'Well, much as we all loved him, your dad could be... short-tempered. Oh, he was good with his patients and his bowls cronies and the Morris guys only saw his genial side, but at home, he wasn't always... very relaxed. You always saw a different version of him because you were his favourite. No, don't argue, you know it's true. He doted on you, to an unhealthy level, in my view. He stifled you. Also, living with Ted was getting more difficult. I'd been trying to persuade him to see a specialist because he was really getting obsessive about a few areas.'

'Like what?'

Caroline was silent for a moment. Then she sighed and said, 'The only doctor he'd agree to see was Jim Buckley. You remember him?'

Kate pulled a face. 'The ancient one who smelt of pipe tobacco and whisky and always wanted me to sit on his knee?'

'That's him. Well, Jim lived in the dark ages, as far as I could see, but he loved your dad. He wanted him to take a whole raft of tablets to get his heart back on track but Ted... he got it into his head that I was trying to poison him. It was one of his funny ideas.'

'Funny ideas? You mean, he was getting...'

There was a silence. Then Caroline nodded. 'He was showing a lot of signs of dementia. There was nothing I could do, love. He wouldn't go and see anyone but Dr Jim, and Jim was worse than he was. He just palmed him off by saying everyone gets forgetful as they get older.'

'But... but...'

Kate floundered and Caroline came to her rescue. 'You're wondering why you didn't notice. He was very good at covering up for his little... wobbles, he called them, and you know he'd always had a reputation for being absent-minded. I suppose I didn't help by going along with it, but the rows were so traumatic if I called him out in the hope of getting some sort of diagnosis and treatment.'

An awful thought struck Kate. 'Jamie knew about this, didn't he?'

She could see by her mother's expression that she'd hit on a very unwelcome truth. Her shoulders sagged.

'You both noticed all these things about him and you didn't tell me.'

Caroline reached out a hand. Kate ignored it. She let this new idea wash over her, but in all honesty, she couldn't keep the anger going, because in her heart of hearts, she'd known too. Several times she'd almost tackled her father about his forgetfulness but had held back. Why hadn't she been more open with him? Was it out of some misguided idea of respecting your parents? Or more likely, had she just been scared? Terrified that the man she adored was slipping away from her. Longing to keep everything normal in this part of her life, because everything else was increasingly sad and hopeless.

'But now I can't even ask him how he felt about all this. How he must have worried and why he couldn't talk to us about it.' The words burst from Kate as a wave of grief plunged her back into the dark place that claimed her whenever she let herself think of the way her father had left them.

'I know. When somebody dies suddenly, there are always lots

of things unsaid and puzzles that'll never be answered,' Caroline said. 'We all have to live with that. Maybe I can help with a few of your questions, though, if you let me.' Now she reached for Kate's hand again, and when her mum linked fingers with her, Kate didn't recoil. The feeling of the soft skin brought back countless memories of walking hand in hand, on the way to school or heading off somewhere for a treat.

'Can we talk more later?' Kate asked. 'I feel as if I'm on overload just now. I need to think.'

'Absolutely. Go and have a little nap on your bed. You'll feel better after a sleep.'

Her mum had said these same words to Kate many times over the years, and she was usually right too. There would be time for questions later.

32

Later that day, when the sun was setting over the trees behind the house, Kate, Sophie and Caroline sat on the terrace with large, chilled glasses of Sauvignon Blanc and Ralph asleep at their feet. Kate and her mother, by unspoken agreement, had shelved the serious talk and concentrated on eating the delicious dinner that Caroline had prepared.

'That salad was legendary, Sophie,' said Caroline. 'I normally hate anyone taking over in my kitchen but you can visit any time. And Kate... when did you learn to make such brilliant crepes?'

Kate smiled. 'I always make them for Elsie when she's with me for breakfast but we don't drizzle Cointreau over them and then smother them in double cream.'

The three women sat in silence, drinking in the peace of the evening and watching the bats wheeling over the nearby forest. Kate couldn't bear the thought of spoiling this hiatus with harsh words but the dreaded conversation was looming now. Sophie stretched her arms out wide and yawned theatrically.

'I know it's early but it's been a long day. I'm going to take Ralph for a quick stroll down the lane and then turn in and have a read in bed. Don't worry about creeping about when you come up, Kate, once I'm asleep nothing on earth will wake me.'

Kate watched her friend disappear into the semi-darkness, closely followed by Ralph.

'Should I go with her? Will she be okay on her own?' she said.

'She'll be fine. She's got her dog, and nothing ever happens round here anyway. It's the quietest place I've ever been to.'

Kate waited for what must come next. The burning resentment was less now but she knew there was still plenty of ground to cover.

'So, let's cut to the chase, shall we?' Caroline said, standing up and moving to the edge of the terrace. She had her back to Kate now and the tension in her shoulders was plain to see. 'In a nutshell, you seem to think I've let both you and your dad's memory down by making a new life in France, is that right?'

'Well...'

'I know you do. But don't forget, I wanted you to come too. I honestly hoped it would be a fresh start for us all. Howard had acted true to form and finally made his own selfish choice, and you'd left your job. I really thought we could all begin again. Jamie was looking into holiday lets and he and Davina already had planning permission for an annexe and for a separate single-storey home next to it. In the end, they just had my part built, but he's always said he'd be happy to add on one for you.'

Kate's mind whirled. In the weeks after her dad's death she'd been floundering in such a sea of misery that none of these suggestions had made sense. She vaguely remembered an evening when Jamie was over from France helping her mum with the house clearance and sale. They'd talked, but even a family discussion had been too much for her at that time.

'I was in a very bad place,' Kate said eventually. 'It made me so bloody angry that you and Jamie were able to do all those normal things like see solicitors and send Dad's clothes to the charity shop when all I seemed to be able to do was weep.'

'You didn't listen properly to what Jamie was suggesting. I realise that now. I was reeling too, but somehow when he floated their idea, my brain felt completely clear. It had been years since I'd felt I had real choices. It was a kind of luxury to be able to plan my own future and not to have to worry about what was going to happen with your dad if he carried on refusing to accept his problems.'

'A future without your life partner, though.'

'Which is what you've done, but in a different way.'

Kate was on her feet too now. An owl hooted somewhere in the trees and she vaguely heard Sophie letting herself into the house, talking softly to Ralph.

'Mum, I had no option but to make changes with work and so on. You said you had choices, so you could have bought somewhere nearby. Maybe moved to a smaller place? I needed you so badly after Dad died.'

They were both crying now but the short distance between them felt too big to breach.

'I know you felt I let you down, Katie, but I was grieving too. My marriage was by no means perfect but I loved your dad, more than you'll ever know. We'd been together for so many years and we'd had you and Jamie, and then the grandchildren. I was as angry as you were, though. He left me in the lurch with no chance of reminding him about all the hopes and dreams I'd put on one side to be a good wife.'

'You make yourself sound like nothing but a doormat.'

'I think we both had quite a few elements of doormatishness, didn't we?'

'Is that even a word?'

Suddenly, they were both giggling, the tears of sadness and anger turning to mild hysteria as they looked at each other. As they had when her daughter first arrived at the house, Caroline's arms reached out, and Kate walked into the most loving embrace she'd ever known. It was like coming home.

'Let's finish our wine and go to bed,' her mum murmured. She stepped back but kept hold of Kate's shoulders. 'When you got out of the car, I wanted to say how beautiful you looked. You seem... I don't know... lighter somehow, and you've got rid of the sad clothes. It's great to see you letting the colours back in. You always used to wear such a rainbow of shades when you were younger but over the years, it's just been navy, black and grey. Was that Howard's influence?'

'Indigo, not navy,' Kate corrected absently, but even so her mum's words warmed her. 'He didn't like me wearing loud colours, he thought they were tacky. But anyway, losing all the babies made me feel less colourful each time. It wasn't just Howard.'

'You shut me out when you were mourning your babies, Kate. I wanted us to draw closer so I could help you through the pain, but I couldn't seem to get near enough.'

Kate thought back to those sad times, and managed to recall the brief abduction of the other baby almost without flinching. 'I'm sorry, Mum. I did want to talk to you, but you always seemed more interested in what Jamie was up to, and Dad would have got too stressed and protective if I'd unburdened myself. He was great with his patients in distress, but with us... not so much.'

She broke off and Caroline nodded sadly.

'And now I think what we have to accept is that our hopes and dreams are different,' Kate said.

'Yes, I can see that. We should talk more, whenever we can.

I... I don't suppose you'd ever think about changing your mind and joining us here?'

This was a tricky one to answer without hurting her mum's feelings. The new-found closeness was too fragile to risk damaging. 'What you've got is wonderful,' she said. 'I can absolutely see why you wanted to be near your grandchildren too, but I love my new job at the café and walking through the country park seeing the seasons change and being in touch with all my lovely godchildren.'

Caroline smiled and reached out for another hug. 'In that case, my love, we've both made the right choices in the end. And tomorrow morning I'm going to take you both into the nearest town and buy you the brightest red dress I can find to celebrate. It's the ideal opportunity for you to shine even more than you do already. We're not going to waste any more precious time.'

33

With so much on his mind at the moment, Milo decided that he needed to have a serious talk with his son, and the best place to do it would be away from the flat. Everything they planned to take to their next place was now in boxes and Milo had booked them into a budget hotel at the far end of the country park while they found a new place to rent. Once the two of them had ferried Milo's remaining possessions to a small storage unit nearby, they got back into the car and set off for their temporary home.

The hotel was large and impersonal, standing on the edge of the woodland that bordered Willowbrook Country Park. Milo thought Luka would hate it, but their room was large, with a single bed at either end and a view of the distant lake, and Luka swiftly chose the one nearest to the TV, flinging his rucksack down with what sounded like a relieved sigh. Milo went over to the window and opened it as wide as the security lock would allow.

'Well, this is home for a little while,' he said. 'Flat hunting again tomorrow, but this'll do for now, won't it? We can eat out or have picnics in here. There's a fridge and a kettle.'

'Luxury,' said Luka, grinning. 'And anyway, I'd be happy in a damp basement with cockroaches if it meant getting away from Brad. Dad... do you think we could get a dog when we're settled? I've always wanted one. Or a cat?' he added as an afterthought, when Milo didn't answer immediately.

'I suppose it depends on the landlord, wherever we end up. And we'd have to make sure there was somebody to look after a dog in the daytime. Let's wait and see.'

Luka seemed to accept this answer. They unpacked the few bags they'd brought with them and then turned to each other with the same idea in mind. 'Walk?' Luka asked.

'You bet,' Milo replied.

The path from the car park led directly to a way through the woods. The sky was a brilliant blue today with only a few puffy clouds to break up the azure expanse. Milo could smell loamy soil and pine needles as they tramped along the track beneath towering trees. The occasional scuffles of small creatures in the undergrowth were the only sounds apart from their footsteps. It seemed a shame to break into this atmosphere of peace, but it had to be done. As they strolled and Luka chattered about this and that, Milo tried to think of a subtle way to bring the conversation around to his main preoccupation, but in the end, he decided to jump in in at the deep end.

'I've been doing some thinking,' he said. 'All this talk of finding a new home has made me realise that I was more than ready for big changes. The last place was just a jumping-off point but now it's the real decision time. I want to really enjoy what's left of my life.'

Luka turned to look at him, alarm clear on his face. 'What's left of it? You're not sick, are you, Dad?'

Milo shook his head. 'No, no – sorry if that sounded over-dramatic. I mean I'm over fifty now and I've not been very happy for a long time.'

'You didn't have to stay with Mum all that time, did you?' The voice was defensive now, and Milo reminded himself to be tactful. Luka, annoyed as he obviously felt with Marianne for putting him in a very uncomfortable situation, was still a loving son underneath, and that had got to be good.

'We jogged along quite well for a long time,' Milo said, choosing his words more carefully now. 'That might be what a lot of marriages are like after a while.'

'Sounds depressing to me. I'm never getting married. At least... Dad, I wanted to talk to you...'

Milo missed this cue to listen because all of a sudden he knew exactly what he wanted to say. 'I think our timing is exactly right when it comes to this flat-hunting business. A fresh place to live and a new routine is what we both need. You're nearly ready to spread your wings but you'll want a base to come home to in the holidays if you're not jetting off having adventures. My next step is to talk to Max about the way we work. It's time for us both to make some big changes. What I'd really like is for us to sell up completely and then I can work from home, but I'll have to get Max's okay as we're joint partners.'

'Right. So... was that all you wanted to talk to me about? I mean, it's enough, to be fair, but you still look worried, Dad.'

Milo took a deep breath. No point in putting this off. 'Luka, did you ever meet the lady who works in the café at Willowbrook Park?' he asked.

Luka stared at him. 'That's a bit random. I... I don't think I ever went into the café. Why do you want to know?'

'Oh, I was just wondering. I kind of made friends with her and she's... nice.'

'Nice? That's a bit of a limp word. Do you mean you fancied her? You do, don't you? Dad, are you on the pull?'

Milo's face was burning now and he couldn't meet his son's eyes. The sound of Luka's infectious chuckle was making him deeply uncomfortable but at least the boy didn't seem to be incensed at the idea of his dad being interested in someone who wasn't his mum.

'It's not like that,' he said, trying not to sound defensive. 'She's just a friend. Or she was until I offended her, anyway. Now I'm not so sure. We're texting again but it all feels a bit chilly.'

'What did you do? Did you come on too strong? Do I need to give you some dating advice? Not that I've been a big success in that area, to be fair. Dad, actually I wanted to talk to you about...'

But Milo still wasn't listening. 'I more or less told Kate she was a lousy picker of men,' he said. 'And then she bounced back with a similar comment to me about choices. We'd just found out something really weird and we were both still gobsmacked. Kate used to be married to your mum's new bloke. He called himself Howard then but he's Brad now, isn't he?'

Luka stopped walking so suddenly that a small boy walking an even smaller dog who had been trying to dodge past him ran straight into the back of his legs. When Milo had finished untangling the lead and sent the boy on his way, Luka put his hands in his pockets and turned to face his father. 'I think you and me have got a few things to discuss, haven't we?' he said, reminding Milo so strongly of similar conversations with his own dad in the past that he had to grin.

'It's not funny, Dad,' Luka said, eyes blazing. 'You can't hook up with Brad's ex. It's... it's...'

'It's what?' Milo asked, dreading the reply.

'It's tacky. It's... well, it's bordering on gross, actually. I can't believe you're even thinking about it. What sort of woman would choose *him*?'

'Your mother?'

'Well, yes, but she's got lousy taste.'

'Thanks, son.'

Now Luka was the one who was red in the face. 'I didn't mean you. I don't think you were ever really her type. Mum stayed around because you gave her a comfortable house and you didn't bother too much what she got up to. And don't look at me like that. I heard her telling Brad about it.'

They were walking again now, approaching the nearest lake.

'Look, it's a beautiful day,' Milo said, putting a hand on his son's arm. 'Let's put all the serious stuff off until later. We can talk tonight. There's a pub near our hotel or we can get a take-out. Maybe a few beers... or... whatever seventeen-year-olds drink?'

'Cider,' said Luka. 'Okay, it's a deal. But I'm not letting this one drop, Dad. We've got a lot to talk about, you and me both. You need to really think about this. You'd be making a permanent link with the most annoying man in the entire universe. I know you're pissed off with Mum but she's bound to want us all to be in touch in the future. We'll be stuck with him.'

They carried on making their way towards the path that skirted the lake, both lost in their own thoughts. Milo couldn't help thinking that however awkward tonight turned out to be, at least his son was actually communicating again. After years of mumbled half-conversations and monosyllabic responses, that had got to be progress.

34

Later that night, finally settled at a corner table in the pub next door to the hotel, Milo wondered if there was any way of retrieving the closeness he'd started to find with his son before he'd dropped the bombshell about Kate. This place was definitely lacking in any sort of cosiness, being here mainly for the convenience of travellers stopping off for a night or two and needing cheap, fast food before retreating to their air-conditioned boxes.

'This place is a dump,' said Luka, carving a large chunk out of his vegetable lasagne, which was resisting his knife in a rather bendy way.

'It's not so bad,' Milo answered, peering at his own dinner with a distinct lack of enthusiasm. The menu had shown a glorious photograph of golden thick-cut chips, a juicy steak and a crisp, healthy-looking salad. What he'd got, slapped down on the table by a disinterested boy with a fine collection of blackheads, was a handful of pale French fries, a lump of greyish meat that looked as if it had been dead for far longer than necessary, and a limp piece of lettuce flanked by half an insipid tomato.

'So, what did you think of those last two flats?' he asked, deciding that complaining would only delay the inevitable, and he was very hungry.

'Awful,' said Luka, through a mouthful of food. 'Like this lasagne.'

That did it. 'Right, we're not eating this stuff. Let's go,' Milo said. 'There's a curry house just up the road. Come on.'

'But you've paid for it,' Luka said, getting to his feet. Milo was pleased to see his son was looking at him admiringly.

'Yes, and with a bonus night on the loo thrown in if we eat it.'

Milo led Luka past the bar where their waiter and a dejected-looking girl were manning the beer pumps. 'That is the worst meal I have ever tried to eat,' said Milo loudly, causing the only other three customers to look up from their own efforts to eat their meals. 'My steak was less appetising than a piece of fried shoe and the lasagne could have doubled as a frisbee. I shall be complaining to the management and demanding a full refund.'

Milo and Luka stalked out of the pub, heads held high, and managed not to splutter with laughter until they were safely out of earshot.

'That was brilliant, Dad,' said Luka. 'A piece of fried shoe,' he repeated grandly, giggling uncontrollably. 'I've got to text my mates about this. I wish I'd recorded you.'

'Let's get a curry. Funnily enough, I'm still hungry,' Milo said, grinning at his son.

After a five-minute walk, they found the place that Milo had Googled. The atmosphere in here was buzzing and a delicious waft of garlic-scented air greeted them as they were ushered to the last remaining table.

'Order whatever you like,' said Milo, passing Luka a menu. The next hour was spent in a happy haze of warm naan bread, sizzling Balti and several tongue-tingling vegetarian side-dishes.

'Oh, wow, that was immense,' Luka said eventually, leaning back in his seat and patting his stomach. 'Thanks, Dad.'

'You're very welcome,' said Milo. 'We should have just done this in the first place. Ah, well, at least we never need to go into that pub again. Shall we get back to our room and watch something mindless on the TV?'

'Yes, in a minute. There... there's something I wanted to talk to you about first. I'd rather get it over with here, really.'

Milo sat up straighter and looked at his son with alarm. 'What's up? *You're* not ill, are you, after me waffling on about my stuff? I didn't even ask you if you were feeling okay.'

'No, it's not that.' Luka lowered his voice. 'Look, there's no easy way of saying this. I... think I'm gay. No, that's not right, I know I am. I like boys, Dad. I've tried to... with a girl... but I just couldn't...'

He broke off and drank some of his water. Milo did the same. He was lost. This was the sort of conversation both parents should be having with their child. Silently, he cursed Marianne for leaving him to try to deal with this tactfully and gently on his own. He cleared his throat.

'Have you... I mean, do you...?' Milo couldn't think how to finish the sentence without being intrusive but Luka shook his head.

'I've never had a relationship with a boy,' he said quietly. 'There was a kiss once... but it never went further and I was ashamed. There is something else, though. I lied to you, Dad. I should have been honest.'

Milo's spirits plummeted. He'd thought they'd been getting somewhere in their relationship, at least until he'd messed up with his news about Kate. What fresh hell was this? He waited, holding his breath.

'When you were talking about your friend Kate, I said I

hadn't been in the café. It wasn't true. I went there once but I was too busy staring at the boy... I mean the man who works there. He's got the most fantastic long blond hair, although it was tied back so I couldn't see it properly but I bet it looks epic when he lets it flow loose. He's called Sam, I overheard the woman in charge shouting his name. He's amazing. I didn't see your Kate at all, that bit was true.'

Relief flooded Milo's mind. If this was the worst lie his son ever told him, they wouldn't go far wrong.

'For goodness' sake, Luka, that doesn't matter. I thought you were going to make some awful confession,' he said.

'I'm sorry. I promise to tell you the truth in future. I suppose I've got used to being a bit too secretive these last few years.'

Milo reached for his son's hand and grasped it hard. 'Luka, I don't give a toss what you do with your life so long as it makes you happy. I've messed my marriage up and I'm bloody glad you're realising what you need, so you don't do something similar.'

'Really?'

'Absolutely. We can talk about this more when we get back to the room. There's not much privacy here.' Milo glanced across at the couple on the next table who had fallen silent and were now shamelessly eavesdropping. 'Don't you agree?' he asked them, raising his eyebrows.

They had the grace to look away as Milo and Luka made their second exit of the evening, once again trying not to laugh.

Milo slung an arm around his son's shoulders as they retraced their steps, once again marvelling at how tall Luka had become. 'We've been living in our separate boxes, and that's all changed now,' he said. 'But tomorrow?'

Milo left the question open, and Luke laughed, suddenly carefree. 'Tomorrow we'll find somewhere that isn't the pub to eat a massive breakfast and then you can go into work and talk to your mate Max and I'll go and find Mum and tell her I'm definitely not coming back. It's just us two now, and we've got this.'

'Just us two,' repeated Milo. At one time those words would have filled his heart with uncomplicated joy. The bubble of happiness was still there, but... oh, Kate. Never to have the chance to see if they had something worth trying again for. Never to have their first kiss. Never to hold her close in the night and wake up with her in the morning. Too late, Milo understood how much he'd had riding on the thought of all these possible delights to come. But Luka needed him now. He followed his son up the stairs to their hotel bedroom with seesawing emotions battling for pole position. Sleep was going to be a long time coming tonight.

35

Kate started the next day early by eating copious slices of warm baguette loaded with fresh farm butter and Caroline's home-made apricot jam and then had a long walk through the shady forest trails with Sophie and Ralph. When they returned, foot-sore and thirsty, Caroline provided chilled lemonade (also home-made, which boggled Kate's mind somewhat as her mum had never been into spending hours preparing anything except baked goods and had employed caterers for any entertaining she and Ted had done).

After a brief rest, they settled Ralph in the kitchen where he went straight to sleep, and with Caroline at the wheel they were soon off in Jamie's beaten-up old Land Rover to the nearest town. This wasn't as daunting as Kate had expected. Caroline was familiar with the twisty roads and their destination turned out to be more like a large village than a town, with plenty of places to park the bulky vehicle. There was an attractive market square where business was booming and around its four sides were the usual boulangerie, charcutier and cafés with the addition of Madame Claire's Boutique, a pretty little shop with a green and white striped awning, tucked in between a bistro and a café, both serving delicious-smelling coffee. Caroline saw Sophie homing in on one of the pavement tables and nodded.

'We'll go in and see my friend while you have your caffeine fix,' she said. 'This won't take long. Claire always knows what's right for her customers. My beautiful daughter-in-law is the fussiest person ever when it comes to clothes shopping but Claire can home in on the ideal choice and have her fixed up before she's even had time to get her purse out.'

Doubtful that this would be the case today, Kate followed her mum into the rather gloomy interior of the boutique. As soon as they were inside, a tiny woman dressed almost totally in black emerged from behind the counter and came forward with her arms outstretched.

'Caroline, so lovely to see you, and today you have brought another pretty lady for me to dress, I see. How charming she is.'

Kate smiled doubtfully, unused to being addressed like this. Claire was definitely the pretty one, as far as she could see in this semi-lit little room, but as she considered this new acquaintance, the older woman flicked a switch and the shop was illuminated. Now Kate could tell that Claire was almost her mother's contemporary, with artfully styled silvery hair and an elegant figure. Her only splash of colour was a turquoise silk scarf twisted artfully around her neck. The walls of the shop were lined with mirrors that made it look a lot bigger than it actually was, but there were very few garments displayed on the rails and only one outfit in the window. Kate wondered how Caroline could expect her to find a suitable dress here. The ones on show all looked like size tens or smaller.

'So tell me what occasion you are shopping for, my dears,' said Claire, coming forward to look at Kate more closely.

'It's not exactly an occasion, more a dress to celebrate my

daughter moving into a new part of her life. Something glorious and colourful without being brash. Kate has played safe with her clothes for far too long. I'm thinking red?'

Kate wriggled with embarrassment as both women walked around her, considering every angle. 'I'm a sixteen usually,' she blurted out, trying to forestall the agonising moment when she'd be squeezing into something much too tight.

Claire made a sound that was between 'Poof' and 'Ha'. 'You will fit nicely into the perfect little frock that I provide,' she predicted. 'I have the very thing for you. Wait here.'

Kate tried to protest, but Claire had already bustled away into the back room. It seemed like only seconds later that she returned with her arms full of a dress that was swathed in a silky cover. When she pulled this off with a flourish, Kate and Caroline both gasped. The ruby red of the material seemed to glow in the now brightly lit shop and the braided trim around the neckline sparkled with the tiniest of glass beads.

'It's gorgeous,' breathed Caroline. 'Try it on, I can't wait to see you in it.'

Relieved she was wearing decent if unglamorous underwear, Kate took the dress and went into a cubicle in the corner. As she drew the curtain around her, she steeled herself for the moment when they would all have to accept that the dress was much too small, but to her surprise when she slipped it over her head, the folds settled around her as if it was custom made.

'Do you need me to zip you up?' Caroline called.

'No, I can do it. I'm coming out now.' Kate pulled back the curtain, feeling as nervous as if she was going on stage, and as she stepped forward, saw the faces of the other two women light up in delight.

'Oh, Claire, you've done it again. This is the absolute perfect dress for Kate. We'll take it,' said Caroline. 'That's if you like it, darling?'

Kate walked a couple of paces to the centre of the shop and gazed at herself in the mirrors. The material of the dress was the prettiest shade of crimson she'd ever seen. 'It's wonderful,' she said, her voice not much more than a whisper. 'But you haven't even asked the price yet.'

Caroline clapped her hands. 'I don't care how much it is, this frock was meant to be yours. Now, take it off and we'll go next door and treat Sophie to a celebratory strawberry tart to match the dress.'

Smiling her approval, Claire watched as Kate returned to the cubicle. Soon, the deal was done and with a flurry of kisses on both cheeks, Kate and Caroline left the shop. Looking at her watch, Kate realised that the whole experience had not taken much more than half an hour.

'That was super-speedy,' said Sophie, looking up from her book. 'I thought I'd be on at least my third coffee by the time you emerged, and look at that fancy packaging. I'm guessing that was a successful mission.'

Kate held up the green and white candy-striped bag and nodded. 'That was the most fun I've ever had buying clothes,' she said.

'Well, to be fair you hadn't set the bar very high,' said Sophie. 'Getting all that boring navy stuff off eBay or Amazon can't have given you much of a thrill.'

'Indigo,' Kate corrected automatically, but she couldn't resist a peep into the bag. There it was, nestling in its apple-green tissue paper, the dress of her dreams. 'I don't know when I'm going to wear it, though,' she said.

Sophie grinned. 'I'm certain there'll be just the right

moment. Now, are we having a cake, or what? It seems a long time since breakfast.'

While Caroline and Sophie went inside the café to look at the array of confectionary, Kate reached into her bag to check her phone and, to her surprise, found a message from Milo.

Hi Kate,

It seems ages since I saw you and it would be great to make some sort of arrangement to meet up. Let me know when you're free? I'm enjoying catching up with Luka at the moment and we're still flat hunting together, which is pretty time-consuming and without much luck yet.

Hope to see you soon,

Milo x

Kate's spirits took an unexpected dive. Milo did seem keen to see her, which was cheering, but now the situation with his son was probably going to make life even more complicated. Also, she'd promised herself that before she even considered any kind of relationship with Milo or anyone else, she'd try to come to terms with all the emotions that had been battling away inside her for years. There was a lot more unravelling to work on yet. Learning that her parents' marriage had been less than blissful had been an eye-opener and she was already re-thinking her own privileged relationship with her father. For the first time, Kate wished that her brother wasn't off camping in some remote part of France. The two of them had never discussed their respective relationships with their parents. She mentally added *talk to Jamie* to her list of ways of coming to terms with the past. Hearing Caroline and Sophie coming back, she quickly typed her reply.

Hi Milo,

Lovely to hear from you. Why don't I text you when I'm back and have finished a few important things that I need to attend to? We can see how we both feel then about meeting up. Hoping you're enjoying the time with Luka.

Kate

There, that would have to do. Once more, Kate went back and deleted the automatic kiss she'd added, then pressed send with confused feelings. There was no point in over-thinking all this, Milo's situation might have moved on by the time she returned to Willowbrook and her own too. Happy to be distracted, she looked up to see what her mum and Sophie's foraging mission had produced. A waiter was following them with a loaded tray. Kate could see a selection of the small fruit-filled flans that always made her mouth water, plus a coffee pot, a plate of crispy Langues de Chat biscuits, three glossy blue cups and a jug of hot milk.

'We chose for you,' said Sophie. 'Which wasn't hard as I know there's no cake that you don't like.'

Kate laughed. 'We'd better take Ralph for an even longer walk when we get back,' she said, reaching for a raspberry tart. 'I need to make sure I can still zip up my dress when we go home tomorrow.'

'Couldn't you stay for a couple more days?' Caroline asked, her shoulders visibly drooping at the mention of home. 'It was a really long way to come for only two nights.'

'Not that far at all,' said Sophie. 'I can always drop Kate off the next time I come over to see my friends who live near Dieppe. This is only her first visit of many, I'm sure.'

Kate nodded, her mouth full to say anything. When she

could speak again, she turned to Caroline. 'We've still got a lot of catching up to do and I want to see Jamie and his gang. I'll be back as soon as I can. I'm not sure if my old banger's reliable enough to get me here, I only use it to go to and from work when the weather's bad or for shopping and I've never driven on the right-hand side, but whenever Sophie's available and happy to come over, I can combine a visit to see her and then one here too.'

The thought of all these future trips filled Kate with a restless energy, and as soon as the others had finished eating she was on her feet. 'Let's go and explore a bit more of that lovely forest,' she said. 'And tonight, I'm cooking for you two. We'll call at the butchers on the way to the car and then I'll make my new signature dish. It's beef bourguignon.'

'Really? I didn't know you were into French recipes,' said Caroline.

'I'm not. I've never made it before, but it's definitely going to be my new signature dish,' said Kate. 'Come on, we can't hang around here all day eating cake. Dogs to walk, cordon bleu meals to prepare.'

'Has she had some sort of personality transplant?' Caroline said to Sophie in a stage whisper. 'She never used to be this jolly.'

'How rude.' Kate grinned at her mum and led the way to the other side of the market square, waving to Claire, who was peering out of her window. Regardless of Milo's understandable preoccupation with his son and her own insecurities, so far this had to be one of the best mini-breaks ever, and it wasn't over yet.

36

Back in Willowbrook, Kate tried to decide if or when she should contact Milo. She'd had a brief text that just said:

Are you back home yet? M x

She had replied with a thumbs-up emoji, but since then, she'd put off the moment when she would have to either follow this up with a suggestion to meet or put him off until she felt as if she'd sorted her own life out properly. Kate had mulled over their situation endlessly, still torn between a strong desire to see Milo and lingering irritation at the sweeping way he'd talked about her choice of partner. One thing had become painfully clear since she'd talked to both Beryl and Sophie about that awful day when she'd taken the baby home. Kate knew in her heart that even if she and Milo, or anyone else for that matter, did get closer, she would have to come clean about it too. It was too big an incident to hide and she'd already blurted it out by mistake once but got away with it. Might it be better to step back now from a closer friendship with Milo before the moment came when they would be bound to tell each other more about their past lives?

In the end, work and Elsie helped to distract Kate from brooding on the situation. Pat seemed preoccupied when Kate returned from Sophie's house, and Sam was even worse.

'Could Elsie come for a sleepover again one night this week?' he said one morning, during a pre-lunch lull in the café. 'I need a bit of time to myself to think.'

Kate glanced at him in alarm. Like Pat, Sam had been very quiet ever since she'd been back at work, and now she was looking at him properly she could see that he was paler than usual. His usually bright brown eyes had dark shadows beneath them and his face, always thin, looked gaunt.

'Are you eating properly?' she asked, realising too late that she sounded like a clucky mother hen. Sam shrugged.

'I don't get very hungry at the moment.'

'Do you want to talk about it? I can see something's really bothering you.'

Sam looked around the café. Beryl was sitting at a corner table with Winnie and Anthea but they were absorbed in their chat and were making enough noise to cover Sam and Kate's conversation. He waited for a few moments, giving both himself and Kate the chance to eavesdrop shamelessly.

'So, are you really going to let Maurice take you out again?' Winnie asked Anthea. 'He's a bit of a lad, you know?'

Anthea raised her eyebrows. 'As opposed to what? Make yourself clear, darling. Are you warning me off? I suspect you've got your eye on Maurice for yourself. He's got a lovely place near the coast and he's made a pretty penny with his jewellery business. Are you fortune hunting? He's quite a catch.'

'Don't be ridiculous. It'd take a better man than old Maurice to take me away from my lovely bungalow and my friends in The

Close. It's *you* who's fishing for a chap, if you ask me. Are you running out of cash for your posh frocks and champagne at last?'

Kate and Sam exchanged glances. The three sparky women were the best of friends most of the time but every now and again there was a flashpoint and a mediator was required to calm the waters.

'Should I go over?' Sam asked. 'I don't want to get my head bitten off.'

Kate put a hand on his arm. 'Leave it for a moment,' she said. 'They might sort themselves out if we're lucky.'

Sure enough, Beryl was on the case now. 'Would you two listen to yourselves,' she said, grinning. 'Bickering over a man. We don't need this sort of hassle. If Anthea wants to have a fancy dinner with Maurice it's none of our business, and if she decides to drag him home to ravish him, all she needs to worry about is if his poor old ticker will stand the strain. A dead octogenarian in your bed's no fun at all, I'm guessing. It's never happened to me, obviously. I prefer my men alive and kicking.'

There was a moment when matters could have gone either way and then the other two started to giggle.

'Phew,' breathed Kate. 'That was a close one. Right, say what you wanted to say quickly before we get disturbed.' The ladies were talking more quietly now and Pat was busy in the kitchen getting a tray of pasties out of the oven. Sam cleared his throat.

'I've had a call from Lara,' Sam said, lowering his voice. 'She wants to see more of Elsie. She's saying I'm not a fit person to be a full-time dad. I know she's much too preoccupied with her own life to try for custody but she can still make lots of trouble if she wants to.'

'But you've looked after Elsie ever since she was tiny and you're making a brilliant job of it,' Kate hissed, trying not to let the outrage in her voice alert the elderly ladies, who always had an ear for any unrest in the camp.

'Yeah, and I thought I was doing okay. I know the flat's tiny but we were lucky to get it, and Elsie's doing really well at school. She always looks happy and she tells me she loves me every morning as soon as she wakes up and just before she goes to sleep.'

'So, what's the problem?'

Sam glanced at The Saga Louts again. He lowered his voice even more. 'Lara says she's heard rumours about what I do when I go out now and again.'

'You mean the odd nights you have with your friends? Surely she doesn't object to that?'

'I... well, I might as well tell you, Kate, I don't actually go out with the lads these days. I go to a gay bar on the far side of Meadowthorpe. I've been discreet, I have, honestly.'

Kate reached out to Sam in relief. At last he'd told her what she'd suspected for years. 'Look, sweetie, you don't need to feel bad about anything. You're a wonderful person and we all love you very much. Lara's opinion doesn't matter a bit.'

Sam's eyes welled up. 'Thanks, Kate, I love you loads too, and I knew you wouldn't judge me, but Lara and her family are...'

He stopped talking and Kate mentally filled in the rest of the sentence. Both Lara and Sam had attended the primary school where she'd worked and so she'd known the score with the Shaughnessy clan, who'd made trouble on several memorable occasions. They made no secret of their racist and often homophobic views and loved a battle if anyone challenged them. Lara's mother, in particular, had never tried to hide her extreme opinions and there had been trouble on several occasions when her strident tones had been overheard by other parents who objected to her venom.

On one never-to-be-forgotten afternoon, there had actually been a fist fight between Ma Shaughnessy and another mother. Hair had been pulled out in chunks and the unfortunate parent who'd poked the wasp's nest of Shaughnessy anger had lost half a tooth in the battle before the police could arrive.

The café was starting to fill up now as visitors to the park noticed the tempting scent of Pat's Cornish pasties drifting through the air so Sam and Kate couldn't take this conversation further, but Kate thought of little else for the rest of the day, and offered to have Elsie to stay over that night. She arranged for him to drop Elsie off as soon as he was organised and then to come back after she was safely in bed for a chat.

Half an hour after her shift ended, Kate was home and getting changed when she heard the doorbell ring.

'Aunty Kate, we're here,' called Elsie, letting herself in. 'Dad's going straight off, can I come up?'

'See you soon, Kate,' shouted Sam. 'And thanks. Thanks so much.'

Kate thought he sounded slightly more cheerful, which was encouraging, but the look on his face had frightened her earlier. She turned as Elsie bounded through the bedroom door and leapt into her arms.

'Dad's going for a walk now. What are we going to do? Can we make cakes? It's your birthday soon so we need to...'

Elsie stopped talking abruptly and put a hand up to her mouth.

'We need to... what?' Kate asked, distracted by trying to decide if her new T-shirt was too bright.

'Nothing. I like your top. You'll match the sofa,' said Elsie, hopping up and down on one leg.

'Hmm. It is very purple, isn't it?' Kate looked across at the mirror and winced.

'Violet,' said Elsie. 'Or maybe dark mauve. We've been doing about colours in art. Can we make something? It doesn't have to be cakes.'

They went downstairs hand in hand and surveyed the basket of baking equipment that Kate had prepared some months ago when Elsie had become really keen on cooking.

'Let's put our aprons on and make something we can have for tea,' Elsie said. 'We could do pancakes now instead of for breakfast. They're nice and quick. I'm really hungry. It was aubergine casserole for dinner today at school. The chicken nuggets had all gone by the time I got in the queue. I didn't eat it.'

Kate remembered that there had been a big push lately on vegetarian and vegan dishes in the school kitchen. 'Didn't you even try it?' she said, knowing that the cooks were doing their best with the new instructions.

'Yeah, but it was all grey, Aunty Kate, and it tasted of slime.'

'What does slime taste like?' Kate asked, with interest. 'Do you often have slime at home?'

'No, that'd be yucky. But Dad hasn't cooked much lately. He's sad. We had takeaway pizza again last night but he didn't eat much of it. I did, though.'

Kate's misgivings about Sam's state of mind expanded again. She really needed to talk to him, and soon. Maybe if they made enough batter she could keep some back and tempt him to eat later.

With Elsie's own pancake mountain eaten and her bath and stories finished, Kate tucked her goddaughter up in bed and sat down to sing a lullaby, something Elsie had insisted on since she was old enough to make such demands.

'Do "Train Whistle Blowing",' Elsie said, snuggling down.

Kate remembered her dad singing the old Seekers hit 'Morning Town Ride' to her when she would have been about

Elsie's age. Jamie was just a baby when Kate turned six years old, and even when he was bigger he had never been much of a child for lullabies, so this had been their time alone. Kate began to sing, ignoring the lump in her throat. Her father had always taken charge of stories with her if he was home from work in time, but when she thought back, that probably wasn't as often as her memory suggested.

'My dad used to sing this one when I was little,' Kate told Elsie. 'He knew all the verses. One time I felt poorly part-way through and he stopped but I cried because I wanted him to carry on.'

'What happened then?' said Elsie, who always loved stories about Kate's childhood.

'I said I had a really bad tummy ache and my mum came in to see what the moaning was about. She'd been reading my brother a story. She gave me a cuddle but she told my dad I was making a fuss about nothing and it was probably because I'd had too much cake for pudding.'

'Then what?'

'My dad said I wasn't making it up and he got me out of bed and took me straight to the hospital. It turned out I'd got appendicitis.'

'Oooh. My friend Dottie had that. It really hurts.'

Kate nodded. It had been horribly painful, but now she thought back, the worst part had been seeing the agony on her dad's face as he sat by her bed waiting for the diagnosis. He'd been very pale and at one point he'd had to rush away to the cloakroom. It was the one and only time she could remember Ted getting involved with his family's health issues.

Kate pushed the unsettling thoughts away. It was hard to accept that she and her dad probably had an even closer bond than she'd realised but it was her relationship with her mum that she should focus on now. Had Caroline resented the way he'd swooped in and taken over when she'd done all the tea-and-bath type of hard work? If so, she hadn't made it obvious. Jamie had always wanted his mum at bedtime so she'd still not had a break and then she'd gone straight down and cooked the grown-ups' dinner. Kate kissed Elsie, made sure she was comfortable and stood up to leave the room when she'd finished singing but Elsie reached out and grabbed her hand.

'Is my daddy coming back soon?' she asked in a small voice.

'Yes, he is, my love. Why, do you want to see him?' This was unusual. Elsie had never been a problem to settle before.

'No, but I want him to see *you*, because he needs one of your cuddles, I think. He's very sad. Everyone likes to talk to you when they're sad, Aunty Kate.'

'Who told you that?'

'I just know. It's your superpower, isn't it, like Wonder Woman's got them, and Spiderman? You make people feel better.'

Kate was about to reply when she saw that Elsie had gone suddenly to sleep, as she always did. One moment you could be having a perfectly good conversation with her and the next she'd be out for the count. Going quietly downstairs, Kate pondered on Elsie's words. It made her heart swell with pride to think that this might be the image that others saw. To be able to make people feel better was a great thing. All she needed to do now was to do the same for herself.

Ten minutes later, Sam arrived bearing a bottle of red wine. Kate gave him the biggest hug she could muster. 'Does claret go with pancakes?' she asked.

'That's a silly question. Everything goes with pancakes, and claret goes with everything,' he said. 'And I'm actually hungry tonight. It was such a relief telling you about Lara getting in touch that I ate two bags of cheese and onion crisps on the way home. I don't think that's part of my five-a-day, though. Have you got oranges or lemons?'

'I've got both,' Kate said happily, and proceeded to feed Sam the biggest pancake stack he could eat. When he'd finished, she poured them both a glass of wine and they sat down on the sofa.

'Be careful, Kate, you kind of blend in wearing that T-shirt,' Sam said, smiling properly for the first time since she'd seen him that morning. 'Is purple the new black?'

Kate threw a cushion at him and he caught it neatly. 'It wasn't an insult,' he said. 'It's great to see you in different colours at last. You always looked as if you were in mourning for something.'

There was a silence as Kate wondered how to tell him that that was how she'd felt. This was meant to be Sam's time, when he'd get all his worries off his chest, but he was looking at her expectantly now, having belatedly realised he'd said the wrong thing.

'Oh, shit, I forgot about your dad,' he muttered, blushing. 'You really were in mourning, weren't you? Still are, I bet.'

'It's okay, but yes, I am. And it's not just for Dad.'

Sam sipped his wine as Kate began to tell him the story of the lost babies. His horrified expression told her how moving he was finding it all, but he didn't speak until she'd finished. Then he put his glass down and reached for her hand.

'So, here you are, having lost all those little ones, and your marriage, and your dad, and you're still managing to make everyone around you feel more positive,' he said. 'How do you do it, Kate?'

'I'm only just realising I might be doing anything at all,' Kate said. 'Elsie was talking about this earlier. And talking of your daughter, she's very worried about you, Sam.'

'Yes, well, we'll get onto that next, but you're my priority now.

How can you get some sort of... oh, sod it, I can never remember that word. Begins with c...'

'Closure?'

'That's the one. A bit poncy but you know what I mean. Is there something we can do to make you feel as if... I dunno... as if you've paid some sort of tribute to the babies? I know we've got the benches in the park but they cost quite a lot to commission.'

Kate thought about this. An idea was buzzing around in the back of her brain. 'Hey, didn't I hear Pat say something about a Plant-a-Tree Scheme that the management were starting up? Over by the top pond? It's for recent bereavements mainly, I guess, but if I could plant something to remind me of all those little ones who never got to be born, it might help. I could visit there and think of them all, but not in a depressing way.'

'That's ace, it's a great idea.'

They drank their wine in silence for a while, both lost in their thoughts. Eventually, Sam said, 'I'm guessing you knew all along that I was gay?'

Kate smiled at him. 'Yes, I think I've always known, ever since you were quite little. I was amazed when you started seeing Lara after you moved up to high school. She always thought she was way out of most of the boys' league, even the alpha males.'

'I know. I was still in denial at that point and I think I just got carried away because the others were all dead jealous. And she was really forceful. You didn't argue with Lara in those days or you got a black eye.'

'Even some of the teachers were scared of her,' Kate agreed. 'But Sam, how...' She was too embarrassed to carry on with what she wanted to ask, but he guessed the rest.

'How did she get me into bed when I was such an obvious player for the other team?' He laughed. 'I was quite drunk. We only did it the once, and oops... there was Elsie on the way. As soon as she knew she was pregnant, she tried to get an abortion but her mum and dad and the whole shebang of them are Catholics and they wouldn't allow it. So that was lucky.'

'You're an amazing dad. I'm sure she won't really want to see Elsie more. It's just one of her power games. Lara's probably between boyfriends and kicking her heels for something new to do. She's living quite a long way away now, isn't she? Just the travelling should put her off. And Elsie won't want to go anywhere with her so she'll be... uncooperative.'

They both grinned. Elsie in a stroppy mood could put a damper on any burgeoning maternal urges, and she'd recently developed a skill for having sudden stomach aches that caused her to writhe around wailing. These had been very convenient to begin with if she needed a day off school or wanted to avoid anything that she considered tiresome but Sam had swiftly become wise to it and wasn't fooled any more. Lara wouldn't have the same intuition.

'I hope you're right,' said Sam. 'But anyway, you've made me feel as if it's not the end of the world. I was on a right downer earlier. Thanks, Kate. For everything. Hey, did you hear about the school summer fair being cancelled? They've already had to postpone it from last term.'

For a moment, Kate couldn't decide if she was relieved or disappointed. 'No, they didn't let me know about the latest changes,' she said, reaching for her phone. 'Although... yes, there is a message here, I must have been putting Elsie to bed when it came through. Richard says there have been a few problems with the existing committee and they've decided to shelve the arrangements for now and try and find a new fund-raising organiser. What a shame. I was kind of looking forward to the face painting, actually.'

'I heard there's been a lot of in-fighting. The woman in charge at the moment is a relation of Lara's so...'

They looked at each other and grinned.

'You could do that job, Kate,' Sam said. 'You've had a long enough break from school events. Why don't you offer to take over? They'd jump at having you back, and now you don't work there, you could escape whenever the committee got irritating.'

Kate's initial reaction to this idea was to run in the opposite direction very quickly, but it really was a pity that the new headteacher hadn't got a decent fund-raising organisation. Maybe she could...

'Think about it, anyway,' said Sam, watching her face. 'It might be just what you need. Being fifty is going to be the start of a whole new you. Actually, you've begun the metamorphosis already, haven't you?'

'How do you mean?'

'Oh, you know. Different clothes, getting in touch with the school when you weren't sure if you could do it, going off with Sophie for an adventure, getting chatted up by a gorgeous bloke... This is going to be your year, and you haven't even had the big birthday yet.'

Kate gazed at him in amazement. 'I didn't think you noticed things like that, Sam.'

'I notice lots of things, actually, and I'm really proud of you,' he said, standing up to leave.

Kate put Sam's comments on one side to think about later as she looked him up and down. 'You're still way too thin, even with all those pancakes inside you,' she said. 'I'm going to make sure Pat gives you all the leftover pasties and cakes in future. You need a bit of feeding up.'

'Look, don't ruin my lost and hungry appeal,' he said. 'It's all I've got going for me on Grindr.'

Kate waved goodbye and went back indoors, deep in thought. As she made her way to the kitchen to tidy up, she glanced at the calendar on the wall. Only two days until her birthday and she still hadn't made the effort to plan anything, even dinner with her old friends from the school. Until now she'd put off the idea of arranging a celebration because even with the way her life was changing, turning fifty was a definite milestone event and just a few drinks and a meal in a pub seemed a bit limp. She'd felt that doing nothing at all might be better than being half-hearted about the birthday but Sam's words were making Kate think again. Perhaps The Saga Louts would have some ideas about how she should mark the occasion even at this late stage. Kate made a mental note to speak to Beryl the very next day. If anyone could make the day go with a swing, it would be those three.

37

The morning of Kate's fiftieth birthday started early. It was Saturday, and she'd planned a leisurely start, with a huge mug of tea and three slices of hot buttered toast in bed. The phone call to Beryl had resulted in the older lady making the excuse that her gang had already committed themselves to a party with old friends, something that had been booked for a long time. Beryl had been very apologetic but said there was no way they could get out of the event.

Kate told herself it didn't matter. She had a new crime thriller, sent by Jamie and his wife, and she'd been saving it for just this occasion. In the event, a pigeon crashing into her bedroom window at half past five had broken a beautiful dream where she'd been paddling in the sea on some Caribbean beach, and she'd leapt out of bed, stubbing her toe in the process. By the time she'd hopped to the window, the bird had flown away, leaving a sad imprint on the glass and a little heap of grey feathers.

'Happy birthday to me,' Kate muttered as she headed downstairs to put the kettle on. While she waited for the toaster to do its work, she fetched butter and marmalade from the fridge, wondering what it would be like to have a partner who would do all this for her and bring it all upstairs on a tray with a dainty linen cloth and a single small flower in a bud vase. The thought made her grimace. In all their married life, Howard had never brought her breakfast in bed. She doubted he even knew where the trays were kept.

Back under the duvet, Kate flicked the radio on and consoled herself with the thought that she'd got a day off from the café because she rarely worked Saturdays. Pat had insisted her birthday should be no exception, and so she could do whatever she liked. She sipped her tea and decided to postpone opening the new book until her buttery fingers were clean again. The mellow sound of The Carpenters filled the room, and Kate closed her eyes, letting the music fill her mind. At first, only the words registered. Karen Carpenter was singing about it being yesterday once more. Her deep, gentle voice made Kate vaguely nostalgic but she couldn't work out for what. Not for her marriage, that was for sure. Her childhood? That had been generally fun, without any real hiccups.

Would visiting yesterday once more ever be a good idea? Kate pondered on this as she relaxed into her pillows. The schooldays had been okay in the main, but Kate had no desire to go to reunions or catch up with any random schoolmates on Facebook. People who banged on about those days being the happiest of their lives were deluded, in her view.

When it came to the crunch, Kate decided that her time working at St Jude's had been the best so far when it came to friendships. Her godchildren were very dear to her and she expected that, as usual, they'd all be round here today at some point with cards, some of them home-made and still sticky with glue and glitter. Also, the warmth of Pat's friendship had been a beacon since Howard left, and reconnecting properly with Sophie lately was joyful. Beryl and her gang were like surrogate grandmas.

Relaxing, Kate allowed her thoughts to drift back to that awful day when, overwhelmed by a desperate need to hold a baby in her arms, she had momentarily thought it was acceptable to help herself to the nearest available one. What had she been thinking? Had she even been thinking at all? It was hard to imagine herself at such a low ebb that stealing someone else's baby would seem the next logical step to being a mother.

Since talking to Beryl and Sophie about what happened, Kate had taken a few more opportunities to dig deeper into the harrowing incident with each of them. Every time she managed to discuss that day, the weight of guilt lifted a little. She'd put herself on the waiting list for counselling at last, realising that this issue and her flashbacks to Ted's death were only the tip of the iceberg. There was a lot of baggage to unpack with her relationships with her parents and brother and also her marriage. It wouldn't be a fast fix but at least she'd made a start on the road to understanding herself. It was a good feeling.

Then, also on the plus side, there was the prospect of more holidays with her mum and talking to her properly at last about her dad, and hopefully with Jamie and his family around next time, there would be the chance to reconnect with the whole lot of them. *Fifty* was going to be a word that signified movement and progress and positive thinking.

'I'm very lucky,' Kate told herself aloud as she had a long, leisurely bath. 'I've got a safe place to live, lots of friends and a great family, if I make more effort to see them. That's quite enough for now. I definitely don't need a full-time partner. Not now, not ever. And it's actually really good to spend some peaceful time here by myself, although the more I think about it, some no-strings outings with Milo might be fun. Just as friends, obviously.'

Kate pushed away the unwelcome memories of how she'd felt in the pub garden when Milo held her hand, and resolutely banished all thoughts of the other times they'd been together. There was no need to torture herself like this. She was only human, and it seemed she was still not immune to his charms but while they got back on track with their own lives, Milo was now firmly in the *friends* section of her small world, rather than his brief sojourn into *potential lovers*. The important thing was to stand alone and be a strong, independent woman.

By mid-morning, the feeling of self-sufficiency was wearing off. The sky was full of heavy grey clouds that seemed to be getting darker by the minute. Nobody had phoned or visited and it was beginning to rain, a dismal, sleety kind of downpour that put paid to Kate's plan to go for a walk by the river and then have lunch outside at her favourite bistro watching the world go by. At eleven o'clock, the sound of the doorbell broke into her rather gloomy musings that everyone had forgotten her birthday.

'Hiya,' called Sophie, coming into the living room where Kate was sitting on the sofa, idly flipping through the channels to find something that wasn't about moving house or having a makeover. 'Happy birthday to you,' her friend sang tunelessly, handing over a wicker basket bulging with gifts wrapped in shiny cherry-red paper.

'Thank goodness,' said Kate. 'I was beginning to think nobody cared. Not that I want to make a big deal of it, being fifty. It's just another day, even if it does feel like a new beginning in a lot of ways, thanks to you, and The Saga Louts, and... stuff.'

'Yeah, yeah, yeah,' said Sophie, giving Kate a hug. 'Just another day. I need a cup of tea, because it's a bit early for fizz.'

She went into the kitchen and soon returned with two of

the mugs that Howard hadn't deigned to take. They were the only ones left out of a set given as a wedding present, and were dark blue with white stripes. Kate had loved them to begin with but now they just made her realise it was time for a change.

'Go on then, open the pressies,' Sophie said, handing Kate a mug.

In seconds, Kate was delving into the basket, as excited as Elsie had been on her last birthday. First she unwrapped a journal, bound in sumptuous red leather. It had a glossy crimson fountain pen to match. 'This is beautiful,' Kate breathed. 'I'll start writing in it tomorrow, I promise.'

She carried on opening her gifts, finding a pack of felt-tips for decorating the journal, a large flagon of ruby-red bubble bath, a scarlet lipstick and two glossy mugs that were the reddest items of all.

'Are you sensing a theme here?' Sophie asked, grinning. 'I'm determined that you're not going to let the indigo back in, or the black or grey. There's one more.'

Kate lifted the last present out of the basket and peeled off the shiny paper. Inside was a knitted drawstring bag in every shade of red imaginable.

'Did you make this?' she said, feeling the warmth of the soft wool as she undid the string.

'I did, hence the dropped stitches. Knitting isn't really my bag... ha ha, see what I did there... but this is a special gift and it's to use right now. I've brought the rest of my kit and I've got a couple of hours before I need to make Aunty Beryl's lunch.'

While Sophie was talking, Kate had dipped into the bag and found it contained a new hairbrush, some products to enhance hair shine and texture and a voucher, handwritten on red card, saying:

This entitles the recipient to a once-only hair makeover of the donor's choice. It must be used immediately.

Kate looked across at Sophie, who was already rummaging in her hairdressing bag. 'And what might the donor's choice of the day be, if I'm allowed to ask?'

'You're going to be Golden Brown. It's a technique I've just started using called balayage.'

'Huh?'

'It's all about painting the colour on so you get a very subtle range of shades. I know you don't want to go blonde, although I have to say your mum looks amazing, but this is going to be different enough to liven you up without freaking you out, okay? Trust me.'

Kate wasn't sure if she could do that with complete confidence, especially as Sophie didn't seem very experienced in this thing, but there didn't seem to be a choice in the matter and she told herself firmly that it was very kind of her friend to give such thoughtful presents.

'Right then, let's do this,' she said. 'But I warn you, if the birthday visitors start coming, you'll need to pause.'

'They won't,' said Sophie, and then put a hand up to her mouth.

'What do you mean? My godchildren always call round on my birthday, and a few others too. What's happened? Is it something bad?'

'Oh, damn it,' said Sophie, very flushed now. 'I never could keep a secret but to be fair, I did tell them you hated surprises and they wouldn't listen.'

'Who's *they* and what are you talking about?'

'Look, let's get started on your hair and I'll fill you in, but you must promise to act shocked later on, okay?'

Kate was beginning to get the picture now and the dark cloud that had engulfed her when she thought her friends had all forgotten her birthday was lifting. She listened as Sophie wrapped her in a plastic cape and got to work on her hair.

'It was Pat's idea,' she said. 'Chin up, pet, or I'll end up painting your neck. Pat wanted to give you a huge surprise party because this is a big one. All your regular customers are in on it and she's contacted the godchildren-gang and lots of other people.'

'Well, that's kind of sweet, I guess,' said Kate. 'But didn't anybody think I might be sad if I had not got a single visitor?'

'You've got *me* to come and see you,' said Sophie. 'I'm here. You've got a point though and I did tell them that. The trouble was, the whole thing had gained momentum by the time I got my invitation, and it was too late to cancel the party, even if they'd have let me. It's actually much better this way, now I've let it slip out. You're not feeling abandoned any more, you've got time to get that really great dress out of your wardrobe – the red one your mum bought for you will be perfect – and you can manage to act surprised, can't you?'

'Where's all this merriment happening?' Kate was undecided whether to feel touched or alarmed. Big parties had always thrown her. She never knew who to chat to and when she did find someone friendly, she was constantly worried that they were bored with her and were sneaking looks over her shoulder to see if there was anyone more interesting available.

'Oh, it's going to be at the café. They're getting it ready as soon as Pat closes for the day. Her ex-girlfriend Michelle's back on the scene for a couple of days to help out. I'm not telling you anything else but at least now you can lose that forlorn expression and enjoy getting ready. It's my job to get you there. I was meant to say we were going out for a meal with Aunty Beryl. Please tell me you're not angry about the party.'

'Not angry. A bit nervous, though. Let me practise my shocked face before we go and I think I'll be fine.'

Sophie breathed a sigh of relief and carried on with her work. They'd moved to the kitchen this time and without the usual big living-room mirror in front of them, Kate had no idea what was going on with her hair. She'd just have to have faith in her friend's skills.

A while later, after much painstaking tweaking and scissor craft, Sophie was ready to show Kate her handiwork. Kate wasn't sure which of them was the most edgy as they moved through to stand in front of the mirror. When she saw the results of all this effort, Kate gasped.

'Oh, Sophie,' was all she could say.

'Do you like it?' There was an unusual wobble in Sophie's voice and they stood side by side, gazing at this new-look Kate. Her hair was much shorter now, trimmed into a style that emphasised her heart-shaped face and graceful neck. The shining fall of the sides perfectly showed off the delicately graduated shades of mahogany, chestnut, caramel, dark blonde and gold.

'You're so clever, Soph. I absolutely love it,' Kate breathed, turning to enfold her friend in an enormous hug. She released Sophie and moved her head from side to side. 'I look...' Words failed her and she brushed sudden tears from her eyes.

'You look amazing,' said Sophie. 'If you're going to have a fiftieth birthday party, you need to do it in style. I'll have to go round next door and see to Aunty Beryl now or she'll be banging on the wall for her lunch. She's so looking forward to the party. The Saga Louts have all bought new dresses. There hasn't been a do like this for years.'

Kate was still staring at herself in the mirror, transfixed by the glowing colours in her new asymmetric bob. Mousey Brown was no more.

'I'll come back early and do your make-up, okay? Then we three will get a cab to what you're meant to believe is our secret dinner date,' said Sophie. 'See you later, pet. You are going to be the star of the show tonight, which is just as it should be.'

'Thank you so much,' said Kate. The words sounded feeble, but she was too overwhelmed to wax lyrical. Sophie blew her a kiss.

'See you around five o'clock,' she said. 'This is going to be a night to remember.'

38

Sophie arrived back at Kate's with plenty of time to spare for their party preparations. By the time the taxi arrived to collect them, both were in such a state of anticipation that they could only manage one glass of the champagne that Beryl had sent round with her niece to have during the make-up session.

'We'll finish it tomorrow when we do a big recap on the night. It'll be just like our post-mortems in the old days,' Sophie said, handing Kate her sparkly red evening bag to borrow and standing back for one last check.

The dress had only needed the lightest of pressing. It clung to Kate in all the right places, cherry-red folds swinging down to almost floor level. The neckline hinted at a cleavage but left most of it to the imagination and the elbow-length sleeves emphasised Kate's slender wrists, now decorated with a set of silver bangles, also sent round by Beryl.

'Aunty Beryl wanted you to have these. She said she wore them for her first ever dance,' Sophie said.

'But shouldn't they be yours, in that case?' Kate looked down at the delicate twisty bracelets, dotted here and there with bright jewel-like crystals.

'Not my thing,' Sophie said, holding out her own arms to display much chunkier versions. 'I like to clank as I walk. Come on, get your dainty feet into those skyscraper heels. I need to fetch Aunty Beryl, she still thinks the party's a surprise. Don't let on. Oh look, the cab's here. Let's get this show on the road.'

Beryl was soon being helped into the taxi, sending forth wafts of Estée Lauder Youth Dew and resplendent in her new dress, a flowery number in many shades of pink. She handed Kate a gift bag and gave her a kiss.

'Dinner out, eh?' she said. 'I hope I manage to use all the right cutlery and don't spill soup down my front.'

'Thanks so much,' Kate said, getting ready to look innocent and un-knowing, and pretending not to see the large wink Beryl directed at Sophie. 'Where are we going to eat? It's really kind of you two to organise this for me. It's been kind of a quiet day so far.'

'Your hair looks fabulous, dear,' Beryl said, neatly dodging Kate's question. She grinned. 'You'll have to give me the name of your hairdresser.'

Kate grinned. She was beginning to enjoy this now. 'Funny you should say that, she's here sitting next to me. You'll have to talk terms if you want yours doing. Erm... are we heading out of town now? I thought we'd be going to one of the restaurants in the centre.'

'Wait and see,' said Sophie and Beryl together.

'I tell you what, why don't you close your eyes and we'll give you a nudge when we're there? That way it'll be a complete surprise,' Sophie added.

'Okay,' said Kate, trying not to giggle. Mad hysteria would

really give the game away but she was teetering on the brink of it now.

A short time later, the taxi pulled up onto what sounded like gravel and Sophie said, 'Keep your eyes closed and hold my hand.'

Kate inched her way out of the car as Beryl paid the driver, and soon found herself being guided by the other two who had her by an arm each and were propelling her along at some speed. The scent of roasting meat came to greet them.

'Are we having a hog roast?' Kate said, hearing her stomach giving a loud rumble.

'Not exactly. Right, you can open your eyes now,' said Sophie.

As Kate blinked and tried to focus, she was met with the most amazing sight. They were round the back of the café where row upon row of tables were covered in golden paper cloths. To each one was attached a large gold helium balloon bearing the number fifty. As Kate opened her mouth to speak, a crowd of people poured out of the open patio doors, and as one voice shouted, '*Surprise!*'

'Oh, my life,' Kate said. Even if she hadn't been warned, the delight she felt couldn't have been greater.

Everyone was cheering now as Kate was swallowed up by the mob of friends. She turned full circle to see everyone. All her godchildren had turned up with their parents in tow. There were colleagues from her teaching assistant days, all clapping wildly, Pat, Michelle, Sam and the regulars from the café were together on one side and through the middle of the crowd came a group that caused Kate to stand very still.

'Mum?' she whispered. For there, in one of her trademark flowered tea dresses, was Kate's mother, flanked by Jamie, Davina and their three children.

In seconds, Kate was enveloped in a massive family group

hug. She couldn't tell if the tears were hers or her mum's but when they stood back, both of them needed to dab at their mascara.

'I'm glad I got the waterproof kind,' said Kate. 'However did you all keep this quiet?'

A babble of voices answered her. Everyone seemed to have a story to tell about how clever they'd been to protect the secret. Gifts were being showered on Kate from all sides and looking down, she found several children trying to wrap their arms around her waist. Elsie jumped up and down on the spot, shouting, 'Guess what we bought you, Aunty Kate. Go on, have a guess.'

Gradually, the initial madness abated and Kate was able to find a seat under a nearby oak tree. Its branches were festooned with fairy lights, as were all the others around. The whole effect was magical. Music began to play now, and Kate craned her neck to see a DJ and his decks just inside the café doors, with large speakers set up so that the partygoers could enjoy being outside for as long as the weather allowed. The rain from the morning was long gone, and the afternoon sunshine had dried the grass enough for the older children to be able to start a crazy game of rounders on the other side of the fence while the food was being laid out on long tables.

Pat came over to Kate after supervising this operation, weaving her way through the gaggle of guests who were still trying to give her presents and cards. 'You okay, love?' she said. 'Is this what you wanted? I got a job lot of decorations from that shop in town. Michelle put it all together. I think they're meant for golden weddings, really, but hey, they liven the place up, don't they?'

'They so do. I didn't know I needed a party at all, to be honest, but this is fantastic. Oh, good grief, imagine if I'd still been married to Howard after fifty years. I'd have been totally bonkers by then. Pat, you're so lovely. I can't believe you did all this without me knowing. And everybody's here.'

'Nearly everyone,' said Pat. Her attention seemed to have been caught by something, or someone arriving by taxi. 'I'm just going to tell people to start eating. See you later.'

Mystified, Kate turned to see where Pat had been looking, and her heart skipped several beats, because coming towards her was Milo and with him a tall, auburn-haired teenager who must be his son. The two newcomers stopped in front of Kate's table and the people nearest moved away slightly to let them come closer.

'Happy birthday, Kate,' Milo said shyly, proffering a large bunch of yellow roses. 'I hope you don't mind me bringing Luka. He wanted to meet you.'

The boy was blushing now. 'I didn't say... or at least... I mean...' he mumbled.

Kate's heart went out to him. It was a difficult age, halfway between child and adult without the innocence or confidence of either. 'Of course I don't mind,' she said, trying to get to her feet without cascading presents onto the ground. Sam spotted her problem and came over to gather them up and add them to a pile on a nearby table.

'It's lovely to see you both,' said Kate. Whatever had gone on between her and Milo would need addressing at some point but for now, the sound of the music was making her want to dance, and the guests hadn't even started eating yet. She hoped Pat had her eye on the DJ. He didn't seem to have got the usual party memo about quiet music to begin with.

Milo leaned towards Kate and whispered, '"Blue Savannah". This was one of Frankie's all-time favourite songs. She was only about two years old when it first came out, but I was always playing it so it was kind of in her blood. We wore my CD out in the end.'

'Me too,' said Kate. 'I loved Erasure. Still do.'

The music swelled, and someone called out, 'On your feet, guys, let's dance!'

In seconds, a Mexican wave of guests leapt up and started to sway to the beat. Some spread out across the grass, others danced just where they stood, and everyone who knew the words sang along. Kate could feel the tension that had gripped her in the taxi ebbing away.

'Are you joining them?' Milo asked. Luka rolled his eyes and wandered away, presumably to find someone less embarrassing than his dad.

'Do you like dancing?' As she asked the question, it occurred to Kate how little she knew about this man.

'I can manage a waltz at a push, but I'm terrible at the disco stuff,' he said, grinning ruefully. 'I tread on toes, I knock tables over, and once at a wedding I actually tripped and landed on a passing waiter. I broke his arm. So I tend not to risk it very often these days.'

'Wise move.'

Kate decided to sit this one out, and watched happily as the crowd boogied, with a variety of quite unexpected moves going on in some quarters. It was no surprise that Beryl still had it in her. She was now doing a weird version of a rumba with Sam, and Anthea and Winnie were performing some kind of rock and roll routine involving spins and twirls. The song ended and Pat could be seen muttering in the DJ's ear. As if by magic, a playlist of gentle background music began. Soon, the dancers were milling towards the tables, ready to see what treats the staff had conjured up. Kate and Milo followed more slowly.

'Can we talk sometime soon?' Milo asked before they could be swallowed up by Kate's friends.

'I've no idea when all this will end,' said Kate. 'Maybe tomorrow. But I'm warning you, I'm in a different place now.'

'How do you mean? Have you moved house too?'

Kate laughed. She was going to have to spell it out. 'I'm fifty and I'm starting again,' she said. 'I was kind of going under when we first met, and I hadn't realised how sad I was. My friends Sophie and Beryl and Winnie and Anthea pointed me in the right direction and it's early days, but I think change is in the air.'

'Funny you should say that. I'm in exactly the same situation. Look, can I message you tomorrow when you've had time to recover from all this fun? We could go for a walk... or something...'

Kate wasn't sure if meeting him alone would be a good idea when she'd decided to avoid any more entanglements for a while, but Milo looked so anxious that she put her misgivings to one side and nodded. 'Okay, you do that. Now I'd better go and be sociable,' she said, smiling up at him. 'And in the meantime, please don't ask anyone to dance. Willowbrook Park's a long way from the nearest A&E department.'

An hour or so later, Kate flopped down in a chair next to Beryl, who was sitting with her two sidekicks all holding glasses beaded with condensation.

'I don't usually drink lager because it goes straight through me and I have to keep running to the loo, but after that last dance with your new man, I need this,' Beryl said, putting the glass against each of her flushed cheeks in turn before taking a huge gulp. 'He told me he doesn't usually take to the floor but I find that hard to believe. He's a sweetie, that one. He only trod on my feet a couple of times and it was well worth it.'

'He's not my man,' Kate said.

Beryl eyed her beadily. 'If he's not yours yet, he wants to be. I know we said you had to get to grips with your other baggage first but now I've actually met the gorgeous Milo, I'm having a rethink. Winnie says the same, don't you, dear?'

'Ooh, yes, sex-on-legs, that one,' said Winnie. 'He can park his slippers under my bed any time.'

All three hooted with laughter as Kate tried to get this picture out of her mind.

'Talking of sex, Maurice has been super-keen lately, darling,' said Anthea, downing her glass of fizz. 'I've booked the two of us in for a relaxing spa weekend for his seventy-fifth birthday next month, with some extra treatments. I need him to keep his strength up. You were exaggerating about the octogenarian part, Beryl – he's still a spring chicken.'

'Excellent news, and it's a good idea to keep him in working order,' said Beryl. 'As for Kate's chap, he's got plenty of go in him, by the look of it. I do like a tall man, and he's got very big feet too. Always a good sign.' She winked at Kate, who cringed inwardly and felt her face flame.

'You're a wicked woman, Beryl,' she said, giggling.

'I know. That's why my Len liked me so much, I suppose. I've never had much in the way of inhibitions. They just give you wind.'

'So what's your advice now?' Kate could hear the introductory bars of 'Agadoo' and had a horrible feeling the gang of her godchildren heading this way were going to make her join in with the pineapple-pushing and tree-shaking actions. 'Spit it out, Beryl, I think I'm going to be dragged away any minute now.'

'Right. Well, Winnie and me are all for keeping that air of mystery as a rule. Don't give too much away too soon, that's been my motto. If I'd let Len have his way with me before the wedding, I'd never have got a ring on his finger. That was nowt to do with being inhibited, it was just tactics. But we reckon you should just go for it with this one and let him help you work through whatever muddle you've still got in your head, dear. Get him into bed. Worry about the rest later.'

Elsie appeared, towing two of the other godchildren, just as Beryl's words caused Kate to blush from head to foot and take an overlarge sip of her drink. Beryl patted Kate on the back helpfully and then the three children hauled her to her feet. As Kate was just about to be pulled onto the dance floor, Beryl grabbed her arm and leaned closer. 'Don't leave it too long, or somebody else'll snap him up. Remember what I said about the feet...'

Kate snorted with laughter as she had a sudden image of Milo on a shelf at the supermarket with eager housewives queuing to take him home after clocking the size of his shoes. Beryl shouted after her, 'It's no laughing matter, my girl. Get in there before it's too late.'

'Agadoo' morphed into 'The Macarena' and then one that Kate had never heard before which involved much more complicated actions. Eventually she escaped her flock and made her way to the outer door, receiving several rather sweaty hugs on the way. Everyone looked to be having a wonderful time, although she couldn't see Milo anywhere.

Outside, the blissfully cool evening air hit her just as the DJ changed tack and began playing a more mellow set. Now, she heard the familiar sound of an old Van Morrison song that she knew her dad had loved. 'Brown Eyed Girl' playing on the radio had always made him pick the small Kate up and swing her around, both of them singing the lyrics inaccurately at the tops of their voices.

Before Kate could experience the wave of melancholy that this tune usually triggered, Milo moved towards her out of the shadows.

'I thought it was you. Excellent timing, brown-eyed Kate. I asked the DJ to fit this song in somewhere, because that's what you are. Except they're more hazel, aren't they?'

Milo was standing right in front of Kate now and she had to tip her head back to see his expression. His own eyes were gentle but full of an emotion she couldn't quite read in the dusk, even with all the fairy lights that twinkled around them. 'It was always one of my dad's favourites,' she said huskily.

'Mine too, but I didn't know I was actually going to meet an amazing brown-eyed girl. I must have known you were out there somewhere, though. I've been waiting for you for a very long time, but I didn't realise.'

Kate frowned. This seemed like a giant leap from *just friends who had their own lives to sort out*. 'Have you been drinking?' she said doubtfully, trying to tell her heart to stop racing.

He laughed. 'Well, that wasn't quite the response I was hoping for when I finally plucked up my courage to get romantic. No, I've been on the soft drinks because I need to get Luka home and I was hoping we could drop you off too, if you haven't made other arrangements.'

Kate didn't answer. She was stuck on the word *romantic*. Had Beryl told Milo to *get in there* too? As she wondered, the song changed to one that made thinking impossible. A river of gold swirled into Kate's mind as the DJ played 'Band of Gold'. Not her dad's favourite this time, but her mum's. Through the open door she could see Caroline shimmying onto the dance floor with Sophie and starting to strut her stuff. Milo took her hand and led her inside. 'This song is all about disappointment in a marriage,' he said. 'You and me, Kate – we're going to dance to it and then leave all that behind us, okay? I'll try my best not to damage anyone this time.'

Moving to the music, enfolded in the golden moment, Kate

listened to the words. She'd already sold her own band of gold and Milo wasn't wearing one either. They were both free, the night was still young, and Milo's dancing was perfectly fine, if a little daddish. Just for once, she made a pact with herself to live in the moment, even if it was short-lived. She could see Luka watching them, his expression unreadable. As she danced, Kate saw Sam sidle up to Luka and lean across to whisper in his ear. As the music changed to a more recent, much funkier tune, the two of them moved to the centre of the floor and began to find each other's rhythm. Before long, the nearby guests were standing back in amazement, and Luka and Sam were in perfect harmony.

Milo smiled down at Kate as they stood watching. 'Good party?' he asked.

'Oh, yes, the best kind,' said Kate, wondering how it was that Milo's son could be flinging himself around the dance floor and locking eyes with Sam but could still manage to throw her some very enquiring looks.

The dance ended and Sam and Luka, arms linked, made their way towards the bar.

'Shall we go and talk to them?' Milo said. 'I want you to meet Luka properly.'

'Let's leave it for now,' Kate said. 'I've got a feeling meeting me is the last thing on his mind right now.'

'Don't worry, he's only just getting used to the idea that I might want to have a new life. And then there's the way he feels about the situation with his mum and your ex. It's tricky, isn't it?'

Kate sighed. She really didn't want to think about anything stressful right now. 'Let's put all that on hold and just enjoy ourselves,' she said. 'Tonight's for partying. Tomorrow can look after itself.'

39

The headache that woke Kate the next morning wasn't nearly as bad as the one she probably deserved, considering the amount of champagne she'd drunk at the party. It had been two o'clock when she finally made it home, and now, peering blearily at the clock on her bedside table, she could see that she'd barely had six hours' sleep.

Padding downstairs, Kate made herself a pot of coffee and took it back to bed, along with a very expensive-looking tin of chocolate biscuits which had been one of her presents, possibly from one of the café regulars, but it had all turned into a blur by the time she'd got to opening a few. The rest were still downstairs in a wonderfully multi-coloured heap. Kate vaguely remembered Milo driving her back to Fiddler's Row. He and Luka unloaded all her gifts and cards but then left abruptly before she could say a proper thank you. As she drank her coffee, random memories of the night before chased each other through Kate's mind.

Wincing as she remembered Milo's swift departure with his son, Kate decided to focus on the more positive memories from the previous evening. The warmth of the party guests' welcome still made her want to cry happy tears, and the way she'd danced the evening away accounted for the throbbing of her feet this morning. The music had been amazing, somehow tailored for everyone. When Luka had danced with Sam, displaying some very funky moves, Elsie had watched wide-eyed, clapping madly. By the time they'd finished dancing, Sam and Luka had put their respective shyness and natural reticence to one side, taking themselves off to a corner table and chatting for over an hour, while Elsie joined the rest of the children for a last game of rounders before she was spirited away to bed by her beaming dad.

Beryl had danced herself to a standstill and eventually had to call it a night, reluctantly accepting a lift home with Winnie and Anthea. As she'd said goodbye to Kate, Beryl whispered, 'Remember what I said. Feet first, my girl. Life's too short to fanny about. Just get on with it now, and wish me luck too. Anthea's only had one small tipple tonight so we stand a chance of making it home unscathed, so long as she remembers which one's the brake.'

Kate made herself more comfortable on her pillows and thought about how ecstatic the party had made her feel. For someone who'd always detested surprises, this was a major admission. Maybe she was changing in more ways than she realised. The new golden-brown hair, the wonderful red dress, the 'Band of Gold' moment on the dance floor and the outpouring of friendship had gone a long way to healing some of the hurt inside. Regrets were seeming ever more pointless these days, and forgiveness and acceptance were still the words that kept coming to mind.

She'd even managed to ask Pat for more details about the memorial tree-planting project and been given the number of the person to contact about it. On the whole, it had been a magnificent evening. Now all she had to do was find out exactly what sort of person Milo was underneath his dependable, charming exterior.

Their dance had unleashed a kind of feverish longing in Kate, try as she might to squash it. Was Milo as lovely as he appeared to be, or were there hidden depths that would show him up in a very bad light? Kate dreaded the latter, but a conversation with him had to happen, and soon. She sensed there were things he wasn't telling her either but it wasn't so much Milo's possible secrets she was afraid of, but her own. A new relationship couldn't even begin to happen if knowing about that black, desperate day in her past was going to put him off. It was time to call for help.

Kate reached for her mobile. This was going to feel like one of those *phone a friend* moments on *Who Wants To Be A Millionaire?* Something had struck her afresh as she'd watched her party guests letting their hair down. A lot of them must know that elusive secret to finding and keeping happiness in life, love or any other way possible, and if they did, they shouldn't be allowed to keep it to themselves. She quickly formulated a text that would do for all the recipients.

> Hi there, it's the morning after the night before and I want to thank you for sharing that fabulous party with me. As an extra birthday gift, I'm asking for one more thing from you. I want to know what you think the key to happiness is, so, please, please tell me your tips for making the next fifty years the best ever! Thanks in advance, and much love,
>
> Kate x

As she sent the message out into the ether, Kate wondered

what response she'd get, if any. Would people think she was incredibly nosy or just plain ridiculous and needy? Maybe they'd all be too busy or hungover to answer. Just as she was starting to regret the impulsive move, the replies began to ping into her phone.

First came her mother.

> Morning love – it was a great do! Here's my answer. Togetherness. Either with friends, family, lovers or all three. Xx

Kate was just pondering on this when the next arrived.

> Good question. I'm going to say kindness. Find your tribe and your man if you want one, but their kindness and yours comes first, always. Winnie

> P.S. Could you pop me some paracetamols round when you've got a minute? Ta x

The others followed thick and fast. Jamie went for *have some adventures*, his wife Davina plumped for *sharing the love*, Anthea voted for *rumbustiousness* and Beryl's one-word answer was, predictably, *bedroom*. Only one person hadn't replied by the time Kate had finished jotting all these wise words down in her new red journal. Eventually Sophie's answer appeared.

> Hi, darl.

I tried to do this in one word because I feel a bit fragile this morning but it's bloody impossible. Relationships are way too complicated for that. Here's what I think (and I texted Paul too, because he's still working away. He agrees). I know you want a general answer but I'm talking specifically about what happens if you decide you want to choose a partner.

You need boundless trust, a good sprinkling of sheer fun, lots of laughs, as many hugs and kisses as you can fit into every day, honesty, and shared morals. But the most important thing, we reckon, is that right from the start you need to be aiming in the same direction, dreaming the same dreams, on the same wavelength as to what you want from the relationship.

You and Howard definitely never had that. You wanted the babies more than you ever needed a husband, he wanted a career and a brilliant golf handicap more than a wife. If you'd both given yourselves a chance to find those facts out, you might have made different decisions.

So, what I'm trying to say is, if you ever jump in again, make sure you read the small print first.

Love you squillions,

Sophie xx

Copying this out into her journal along with all the other answers took a while, but Kate was determined not to waste what felt like the best advice ever, even if the words filled her with a deep sense of regret and a lot of foreboding. Milo couldn't have read the small print either. He didn't know the secret of happiness any more than Kate did. It wasn't a hopeful sign that they'd both probably started out on the road to long-term contentment with very little regard for what they or the other person needed. Still, the past was another country, as the saying went, and the only way to find out more about what made him tick nowadays was to talk to the man.

Kate waited hopefully to see if Milo would still want to go for a walk today. The more she thought about him, the more she wanted to have the chance to see if there was still the same buzz between them in the sunshine of the morning when she wasn't influenced by party lights and champagne. Milo's own message, shortly after this, suggested that he should collect her at eleven o'clock, by which time Kate had showered, forced down a piece of toast and made herself as presentable as she could in her new Levis, bearing in mind her hair wouldn't behave exactly as Sophie had instructed it to yesterday and the bags under her eyes made her feel nearer seventy years of age than fifty. Even so, Milo's face broke into a wide grin when he saw her.

'You don't look as if you'd been dancing the night away,' he said. 'I like the yellow sweatshirt. It's so bright I'm wishing I'd brought my sunglasses.'

'Is it too much? It was a present from Beryl,' Kate said.

'Not at all. It really suits you. I didn't get a chance to tell you yesterday how much I love the new hairdo. And that amazing dress last night too. You're really going for the whole spectrum now, aren't you?'

'Trying to.'

Milo glanced sideways at Kate as they got into his car. 'Sorry I rushed away last night.'

'Did you?' said Kate, raising her eyebrows. 'I hardly noticed.'

He laughed. 'Of course you didn't. That would be because Luka's so subtle when he's in a grump. Anyway, that was yesterday. Maybe he'll wake up in a better frame of mind. I don't think it's even anything to do with us.'

'Really?'

'No. He's totally smitten on the blond boy at the party and I reckon he's having an attack of nerves because he's never done this sort of thing before. I left him snoring into his pillow. Shall we walk by the river? I... I'd like you to see the place where my sister spent her last moments. Is that too morbid?'

Kate wasn't sure, but she was touched by the fact that he was willing to share such a personal location with her. 'Let's go,' she said.

Ten minutes later they were negotiating a rutty track that wound its way down to the water's edge. The river was flowing quickly today, thanks to another heavy rainstorm in the night. It bounced over rocks and swirled its way round tree roots on the bank, taking loose twigs and even a few bigger branches with it. The rushing sound was exhilarating but also unnerving, as if the river had a power and an urgency of its own. There was danger in the air. Milo held out a hand to steady Kate as she skidded on a patch of mud.

'It was like this the day Frankie died,' he said. 'The weather had been awful for days but at last the clouds lifted. She was a keen runner and we all thought the worst of the asthma was behind her. She seemed to have grown out of most of it as the years passed, and the extra "rescue" inhaler she was supposed to carry must have slipped her mind, I suppose.'

'So what do you think triggered it?' Kate had been reluctant to go down this road, but Milo obviously wanted to talk about the fateful day.

'Nobody knows for sure, the doctors said it could have happened at any time.'

'Like Dad,' said Kate sadly.

'Yes. Different causes but just as shocking. Life's short and we need to make the most of it. And that kind of brings me to what I wanted to say to you.'

'Go on.' Kate tried not to hold her breath. Going blue in the face would definitely ruin the moment. She waited.

'It's about my job. I'm selling my share of the partnership I'm in. My business partner's been behaving like a knob lately and I'm done. I can work from home a couple of days a week as a financial advisor. I'll keep some of my existing clients and carry on focusing on helping people to get out of debt. Some of the money from the house sale can be a deposit on a decent flat. So I'll have a lot more free time, if anyone happened to want to spend some of it with me.'

'Right. And I'm guessing there's more?'

'Ah. This is the trickier one. Marianne called me a couple of days ago in floods of tears. Apparently she suspects that Brad... Howard... is regretting leaving you and he wants you back.'

Kate jumped up and turned to face him. The river roared in her ears. It sounded almost as if it was laughing at her. 'Whaaat? You're kidding? And how would she know something like that? He can't have told her? Even Howard's not that crass.'

Milo leaned forward and took Kate's hand. 'Sit down a minute. Let me finish?'

She flopped back onto the seat and turned to face Milo. 'You'd better explain.'

'Marianne says she heard him talking in his sleep. He was saying your name over and over.'

At this, Kate burst out laughing. Relief made her giddy. 'Oh, Milo – he's always done that. It doesn't mean anything. He says really random stuff in his sleep. It never makes any sense.'

Milo didn't look convinced. 'Well, if you say so. It gets worse, though. Marianne said it's made her rethink the whole situation and... she wants us to try again, for Luka's sake.'

This time Kate stayed sitting down. She couldn't look at him.

'So... what are you trying to tell me?' she said quietly.

'Nothing. Nothing at all. Don't look so stricken... except... actually, do, because that must mean you care. I told her there was more chance of hell freezing over. We're finished for good. She needs to knuckle down and make it work with Sleeping Beauty instead of doing the knee-jerk thing and looking to me for a quick fix.'

Kate felt her heart leap with joy, but then just as suddenly remembered that life was never this simple.

'I've got something I've got to tell you too,' she said, trying to stop shaking.

Milo seemed to sense Kate's anxiety and reached for her hand. 'Okay,' he said. 'I'm listening.'

'You remember the night at the pub when we played the game and I blurted out my secret? I pretended it was just a joke?'

'About stealing a baby?'

Kate nodded and Milo turned to look at her. 'You're going to tell me it was true, aren't you?'

Kate's stomach was churning so wildly that she thought she might be sick. That would really put the top hat on this morning. 'Yes,' she managed to whisper.

'I think I rumbled that, really,' Milo said. 'You looked so horrified as soon as you'd said it, and it was a very strange thing to joke about. Do you want to tell me more?'

It was now or never, Kate decided. 'I was desperate to have my own baby but it didn't happen. I miscarried four times, and I couldn't bear the pain that day. The little boy was crying in his pram. I only meant to take him home for a little while to make him feel better. I would have taken him back.'

'Would you?'

Kate swallowed hard. 'I... don't know. Maybe I had some

bizarre idea of keeping him. I was... kind of unstable at the time. Anyway, Howard managed to avert a real crisis by getting him back to where he came from and we soldiered on with the marriage, but he refused to try again. That was it for having children. It wasn't to be, he said. We gave up then.'

Milo was silent for a while. The babbling of the water rushing over rocks and the faint sound of birdsong were soothing. Even in the midst of her shame at having admitted all this, Kate felt a huge sense of relief. Now it was up to him how he dealt with the revelation. She could do no more. Milo's next words surprised her.

'You both must have had a terrible time,' he said. 'I'm guessing that Howard spent a lot of time feeling like a failure too.'

Kate stared at him. 'It was me that failed,' she said. 'Howard was never that bothered about having a family.'

'Wasn't he? Look, I'm not sticking up for the bloke, he ran off with my wife, remember. It's just that I've been thinking a lot about marriages lately, mine mostly, and I've come to the conclusion that when a relationship fails, everybody tries to shift the blame. Maybe unconsciously, but it's easier to deal with if it's not our own fault that it all went pear-shaped.'

Kate let this point of view sink in, still unable to quite process the feeling that Milo wasn't judging her for what she did that day. 'You're absolutely right,' she said eventually. 'And what worries me now is that you and me... well, we're damaged goods. Are we going to be bad for each other? It looks as if we can't even escape from our disastrous partners properly and neither of us ever found the secret of getting it right in a relationship.'

'How do you mean?' Milo sounded genuinely baffled. 'There's a *secret*?'

'I think there must be. We've made mistakes in the past and

been hurt. Can we get over that? We've both got a long way to go when it comes to getting the hang of forgiveness and letting go of regrets.'

'True enough, but we're on the way there and it'll happen in the end, I'm sure, especially if we're in it together. We can be a team.' He grinned. '*Team Battered Survivors.*'

'I think our name needs work, but yes, the general idea's good. I mean…' Kate struggled to find the right words. 'We *can* be a team. Not partners as such, but…'

'Friends with benefits? Whatever are you suggesting, Ms Brown? I hope you don't have designs on my virtue?' Milo chuckled and pulled Kate closer.

'Well, I…'

'Joking. Take that horrified look off your face. I know exactly what you mean and I think we'd make a great pair, in whichever way we choose to take it.'

'Do you?'

In answer, Milo gently turned Kate around to face him and stroked her cheek, looking into her eyes until her head began to swim. Milo's gaze was hypnotic in its intensity. He waited until Kate was almost bursting with anticipation. Then he kissed her so thoroughly that she completely forgot about the remains of her hangover. She kissed him back, sliding her hands up into his hair and revelling in being close to a man who could make her senses reel like this. It had been a very long time since a kiss had been so magical, if it ever had. They clung together, Kate revelling in the warmth and passion flowing through her body. She could feel her heart thumping and her skin tingling, picking up on Milo's excitement as her own mounted to fever pitch.

Eventually they broke apart, and stared at each other before starting to laugh. 'Well, at least that's something we're good at together,' Milo said. 'Although to be fair, I think we'll need to keep practising to make sure we don't let standards slip. What do you say?'

'I thought we were just having a serious conversation today. That's thrown all my sensible thinking up in the air. I suppose sometimes following your instincts can work better than hours of agonising about what's the right thing to do.'

Later, as they walked slowly back to the car hand in hand, Milo said, 'Was it wrong for us to have such a great moment at the place where Frankie died, do you think? I completely lost track of where we were, but at last I'm starting to feel as if I don't have to punish myself for her dying.'

'Is that what you've been doing?'

'I think so. Brothers should be able to look after their little sisters, shouldn't they?'

Kate stopped and turned to face him. 'You reminded me earlier that we're grown-ups. It's hard to let those feelings go, but Frankie was a fully-fledged adult too. We're all responsible for ourselves when it comes to the crunch. We can help each other as much as we possibly can but we can't run each other's lives. Let your sister rest in peace. There, those were my wise words of the day. Don't expect any more, okay?'

They strolled on, oblivious to everything but this brand-new feeling of rightness.

'This wasn't how I expected today to pan out,' Kate said at last, 'but finding the big happiness secret was always going to be a work in progress.'

'Do you really think there is one? A secret, I mean?'

'I've got a few possibles to run past you, I've been doing a survey.'

Milo laughed and pulled Kate close to kiss her again. Just before their lips met, he murmured, 'Well, it can't happen overnight, but I think we're well on the way to making a start.'

40

'So you told Pat you were happy to take over the running of the café?'

Milo and Kate were both wrapped up snugly against a chilly breeze and sitting on Frankie's bench, holding steaming mugs of coffee. She glanced across at Milo, alarmed. 'Yes, I did tell her that. Why, do you think it's a mad idea?'

'No, not at all, and I'm so glad you did. She asked me to come in and meet her this morning too.'

'Did she? What for?'

Milo slid an arm along the back of the bench. Kate felt the warmth of him spreading through her shoulders and moved slightly closer. He'd studiously avoided touching her so far today, apart from a hug when they met. This was the first time they'd been together since the day of the kisses by the river and she was desperate for it not to be awkward.

'Pat had a proposition for me,' Milo continued. 'Hey, don't look like that, it was a business one. She explained that she'd decided to sell the café. She's moving back home to South Wales to try again with Michelle.'

'She told me about that.' The familiar anxiety clutched at Kate's stomach. 'I've been worrying about who'd take over. It never occurred to me to think I could do it, but she obviously thinks I've got it in me.'

'Well, you can stop fretting right now. Pat's idea is for me to either rent or buy the building from her and then for you and Sam to take on the running of Pat's Place between you, with me helping out if you need me. I told you I've been planning to drastically reduce my working hours.'

'Can you really afford to do that?'

'Yes, I didn't expect Max to agree to my proposal so easily but he's all for us both retiring early and, to be honest, I've lost all respect for him lately. He's been letting things slide for quite a while. We can sell the business as a going concern. It's got a great reputation so there shouldn't be a problem. I'm going to work from home. We're very sick of the hotel now, Luka and me. Time to move on.'

'It all sounds too good to be true. Pat honestly thinks that would work?'

'She does. And it will.'

Kate watched a family of ducks waddling along the path in front of them as she tried to take this in. Was it possible? Surely they'd flounder without Pat in charge, but before she could say anything, Milo carried on.

'Pat's prepared to stay and supervise for a couple of months to make sure it's working out and Sam's up for it. He wants more hours now Elsie's well settled at school. I'd be free, Kate. Or almost completely free. We both would. It's a brand-new start for us both. And then there's the flat to go with the deal, the icing on the cake.'

'You mean you'd actually live on-site?'

'Do you think that's feasible?'

Kate imagined the scene, Milo comfortably settled upstairs while they both worked, Luka... well... probably away at uni for most of the time but he'd get used to her being in his dad's life eventually, and being in close proximity to Sam in the café would definitely be a plus for him... It sounded wonderful.

'Yes, you could definitely make it a home, I reckon,' she said. 'The rooms run the whole length of the upstairs part of the shop but it's still a tip in there. We've been using most of it as a store-room with Pat living in a small part of it. I think she always hoped she'd go back to Michelle and it didn't seem worth her making the flat cosy. She put all her energies into the café. You and Luka could soon make it a decent place to live. But...'

'Don't say *but*, just think about it. It's a fantastic opportunity. You need a fresh challenge and I've found out where I really want to be. I... Kate...'

Kate waited. *Go on, just say it*, her mind screamed, but she made her face impassive, just in case she'd read him wrongly. It would be so awful if he just wanted to be friends and business partners.

'Look, I'm going to spell it out,' said Milo, a sheen of sweat on his upper lip now despite the slight chill in the air. 'I want us to be a proper couple. Working with you in the café now and again would be great, but I can't keep pretending being friends is enough. Is there more? Kissing you told me there could be. Shall we give it a go?'

This sounded awfully unromantic to Kate, and she felt her hopes plummeting. Milo took one look at her expression and slapped himself on the forehead.

'I'm so rubbish at this. What I really want to say is... I love you, Kate Brown. I've wanted to be with you right from the moment I saw you sitting on this bench on Frankie's birthday. You shot off so quickly and I guessed you'd seen my flowers so you'd moved away to be tactful. I thought that was wonderful but you looked so... kind of self-contained, and I was still in a mess after Marianne and... I... anyway, I'm telling you now. I love you, and I want to see you every day and have dinner together at night and... stuff.'

Milo was bright red in the face now. He couldn't even look at Kate any more, so she touched his face gently until he gave in and turned to meet her gaze.

'Tell me more about the *stuff*,' she said, grinning.

His arms went round her as if they were meant to be there and the kiss that followed seemed endless. Finally they drew apart and looked at each other.

'So, I take it that's a *yes* then?' Milo said, beaming at Kate, his eyes shining.

Kate smiled back. 'It's a yes from me. Separate houses... for now, at least,' she added, when she saw his face fall. 'I'll give the café my best shot with your backing, and we'll give each other the same. I think we're on the verge of something very special all round. Let's go over and see Pat right now and talk about the details.'

Milo seemed to be waiting for something else. He stared at her, as if willing her to go on. Kate thought she'd covered all the bases, but then the vital part she'd missed dawned on her.

'And I love you too, Milo. I should have said that before, shouldn't I? It's just that I wanted to get all the fine tuning right from the very beginning.'

Milo laughed with relief. 'Thank goodness for that. I was beginning to think you just wanted us to be business partners with benefits.' He got to his feet and held out a hand to Kate. His fingers curled round hers again as if they belonged there, warm and energising.

'We were right in what we said before. We're going to make such a great team, Kate,' Milo said, bending to kiss her again.

They carried on towards the café for Kate to get ready for her shift and for Milo to grab another quick meeting with Pat. Kate was already imagining what it might be like to have choices about the way things were run in the future. Maybe they could introduce an after-school session for children, with story time and snacks while their parents relaxed with a hot chocolate. Elsie would help her organise that one. Kate could at last have a chance to bake for the morning coffee gang and the tea-time rush. Sam would blossom with more responsibility and longer hours would mean he wouldn't be stony broke all the time. Kate's mind whirled with plans and dreams. From feeling stuck in a rut earlier, she'd leapt to a place where anything seemed possible. Milo, and the café. It sounded blissful.

Overcome by a rush of happiness, Kate tugged on Milo's hand to stop him in his tracks and then put her arms around his waist. He responded immediately and bent to kiss her again, holding her so closely that she could feel his heart thumping. The connection was there again, and her whole body fizzed with her own reactions and Milo's waves of sensual pleasure too.

'This is magic. Is it really happening?' he murmured when Kate finally released him.

'Yes, it really is,' she said. 'And it's going to keep on happening. We'll make absolutely sure of that.'

41

20 MARCH 2024

It's taken a while for the tree-planting scheme to take effect, but now Kate and Milo are standing with Luka in a clearing overlooking the top pond, together with a small group of people who'd also elected to join them, because Milo had felt very strongly that a tree in Frankie's memory right next to the one Kate had commissioned for the lost babies and her father would be a great way to cement their bond.

Wrapping her new red coat around herself more snugly, Kate thinks back to those first sticky days when she and Luka had circled around each other with excessive politeness, making sure they were never alone together anywhere. It had taken all Kate's patience and a lot of encouragement from Milo to get over his misgivings about their shared and ongoing link with Marianne and Howard. In the end, making everything easier had been Sam's doing, and all because he made the decision as early as October that he wanted them all to spend Christmas together.

'You're making the past kind of leak into the future, and that's a complete waste of energy and time,' he'd said, when he'd managed to get Kate and Luka in the same place on Luka's first flying visit home from university. 'I'm leaving you in here and when I come back in ten minutes, I want to see you both smiling and telling me that this Christmas is going to be the best ever.'

Sam had stalked out of the room and there had been an awkward silence. Then Luka said, 'Can you imagine falling for someone that bossy? I must be insane.'

After that, they'd laughed and sat down together to make a list of how they wanted the festive season to pan out for their family and friends. The first time Kate and Luka had formed their own small team was in the run-up to the school Christmas Fair. Once she'd plucked up her courage to offer to take over the running of the committee, Kate had confided in Luka that she hadn't realised what a huge task it was going to be. He'd been surprisingly interested in helping her to revamp the programme of events, regularly emailing and messaging with numerous new ideas for stalls.

On the day of the fair, Luka, home from uni for the holidays, had offered to help Sophie run the face-painting stall for most of the time so that Kate could dip in and out keeping the ball rolling with everyone else involved and Sophie had kept Luka motivated with mince pies and mulled wine. Consequently, some of their very last clients of the day looked a little blurred when they returned to their parents, but everyone was so impressed with the resulting huge amount of money raised for the school that nothing was ever said about Sam's later, more uninhibited style of artwork.

Christmas hadn't been completely plain sailing, especially when a tearstained Marianne turned up on the doorstep of the flat, but Luka and Milo had persuaded her to go back to Howard and try again and, since then, peace had descended, to Kate's boundless relief.

Now, on the hill above the café, Luka holds up the sapling

that he's been given. 'Who's going first?' he asks. Kate gestures for Frankie's tree to take precedence and the organiser helps as Luka and Milo dig out the final spadefuls of soil and settle the little tree into its new home. Next, Kate plants her own memorial, and bows her head for a moment. Finally, all three stand back.

The organiser of the scheme has already asked them if anyone wants to say a few words but both Kate and Milo have decided that just being there is enough, so with their permission, he reads out the words on the beautiful stone plaque that's been put in place, in readiness for all the other saplings that will be planted here in the future.

These trees will flourish, growing tall,
In sunshine bright or evening shade.
With love, we stand here and recall,
Deep within this peaceful glade.
The silence brings comfort for all.
Our memories will never fade.

In the moments of silence that follow, Kate knows that Milo will be thinking of his charismatic, often unreliable but always loveable sister. She has a feeling that now, at last, he's starting to come to terms with her death. She looks at her own sapling. Her wedding anniversary will now be superseded by this new event. It's time to try really hard to let go of the worst of the sadness for the babies and the sometimes unsettling memories of her dad and think to the future. The little glade is indeed very peaceful and many more trees will follow these two. It's a good place to come and remember but not to be too sad. To be thankful for good times past instead and celebrate what's happening now.

Kate, Milo and Luka stroll down the hill together, lost in their individual memories. Pat and Michelle have come back from Wales to visit for the occasion, and Kate knows they will have the kettle on, and the hot buttered teacakes ready and waiting at the café. There's a chilly breeze blowing the leaves around, and they'll all be glad to get indoors.

'The café's looking great,' says Luka. 'You've done a good job, Kate.'

Milo beams at his son, clearly relieved that the atmosphere is so much easier. The road might still be bumpy at times, but on the whole, life is good.

'It's not been easy,' he says. 'But we've always known it would be worth the effort. The new sign was Kate's idea. She wanted it to be a place where everyone can feel at home, especially if they need a friend or they're feeling a bit lost.'

They look up at the sign, gleaming in the hazy afternoon sunlight. 'Golden Brown', it says proudly, the letters picked out in gold in an arc around a picture of a traditional brown pottery teapot, a plate of perfectly golden-brown scones and a dish of yellow farm butter, with the smaller words 'Come on in, you're very welcome' underneath.

'We did it, Milo,' whispers Kate, slipping her hand into his.

'*You* did it. And you haven't finished yet,' he says.

They go inside and the warm, steamy atmosphere enfolds them. The tempting smell of toasted teacakes is in the air and the tables are already filling up with customers waiting for one of Kate's special afternoon teas, but the tree-planting party soon colonise all of one side of the room. Beryl, Anthea and Winnie are waiting, sitting at their favourite table with Sophie, plus a good handful of the regulars. They all applaud as Kate comes in.

'We look like one great big family,' says Luka.

'And that's just what we are now. I wish Mum could have come over for this, but they're all going to be arriving soon for

Easter. I'd better order a leg of lamb. We can have dinner here on Easter Sunday,' says Kate. 'That way we can all fit in.'

'This is my favourite place in the whole world,' says Elsie, rushing over to flop down in her usual seat next to the friendship table, the one where people are encouraged to sit if they're in need of a listening ear.

'You and me both,' says Kate. She looks around at the yellow and white gingham cloths, the madly eclectic collection of chairs and the pretty, mismatched crockery. 'It doesn't get much better than this, does it?'

As the few remaining tables fill up, Sophie gets to her feet and comes over. She draws Kate to one side. 'No regrets?' she asks quietly.

'Not a single one,' says Kate. 'We've all got our memories but we've got the future to look forward to now and I'm pretty sure Milo's made his peace with himself about his sister at last.'

'What about the secret of happiness and the perfect relationship? Do you still think it exists?'

Kate shakes her head. 'There isn't just the one, is there? You were right. But what you said about making sure both of you want the same things and dream the same dreams... that was spot on. All of the tips were useful and they made a great start to my journal. You'll need to get me another book. I've been writing in it nearly every day.'

Kate stops talking as Beryl joins them. 'What a lovely atmosphere you always make in here,' Beryl says. 'Are you still having a good time with the gorgeous Milo?' She cackles loudly and nudges Kate in the ribs. 'I know he helps out here in more ways than one.'

'You make him sound like some sort of randy kitchen boy.'

'Oh, no, he's way too big and scrumptious for that. He looks totally blissed out too. You must both be doing something right.' She wiggles her eyebrows.

Sophie tuts. 'Oh, behave yourself. Not everybody thinks about sex all day long.'

'Don't they?' Beryl looks mystified.

'I'm really proud of you, Katie,' says Sophie, ignoring this remark. 'You've come such a long way since the day I told you to ditch the navy.'

'Indigo,' says Kate.

'Whatever. You've revamped your image, ticked everything off your list, made your peace with your mum and started to get your head around dealing with the sadness. Excellent work, buddy. It's a properly colourful world you live in now.'

Kate looks around at the eclectic mix of happy customers and her heart swells with gratitude. 'This really is a place where everyone's welcome,' she says. 'Golden Brown's the way forward for us all. Friends, scones, a warm place to get together and lots and lots of love and laughter. Keep an eye on everyone, Soph, would you? I just need to run up to the flat for five minutes.'

Kate lets herself out of the kitchen door and hurries up the stairs. Looking into the newly refurbished kitchen and living area, she breathes a sigh of relief. A large golden Labrador crossed with a few other random breeds is curled up on her dog bed and tucked snugly into the curve of her tummy is the newest member of the family, a small black cat with one ear missing.

'I knew you and Smudge would get along, Flo,' Kate whispers. The dog wriggles luxuriously in her sleep and the little cat growls a protest at being moved.

The sound of footsteps on the stairs makes Kate turn. She smiles and puts a finger to her lips as Milo enters the room.

'You're checking on them too?'

'No, no, I just came up to fetch...' Milo sees Kate's expression and laughs. 'Okay, yes, you sussed me. I wanted to see if these two were still settled. It's quite noisy downstairs and I thought it might have disturbed Smudge. She's probably still getting used to us.'

Milo slips his arms around Kate's waist and she leans against him. 'I think we can safely say they're settled,' Kate says. 'I thought she would be coming to live with me in Fiddler's Row. We only brought her up here from the refuge while we bathed her eyes but as soon as she saw Flo, I had no chance of getting her away.'

'It makes us feel even more like a proper family, doesn't it? And you know that you can move in any time with Smudge and me and Flo and Luka when he's back, don't you?' says Milo hopefully. 'You only have to say the word.'

Kate looks down at the contented animals. 'I think we're fine just as we are for now, don't you?' she says.

Hand in hand, they tiptoe away and head down the stairs to the café. As they pause in the doorway, Kate turns to Milo and reaches up to kiss him. 'At long last, I'm getting the feeling that this is exactly the way life should be,' she says. 'And that's more than good enough for me.'

'Me too,' says Milo. 'So for now, let's stand back and let life carry on doing this great job of ticking over. We've still got hungry people to feed, including ourselves. Come on, my lovely Kate Golden-Brown. It's time to eat cake.'

ACKNOWLEDGEMENTS

There's always a wave of excitement and a tingle in my fingertips when it's time to begin the development of a new fictional community. This one is particularly special to me because part of it is loosely based on a real place, one where I've spent many happy hours caravanning with the gang, eating cremated sausages and drinking questionable wine, riding my bike, falling off my bike (not so happy) and generally enjoying the fresh air and birdsong. Although the village of Willowbrook and the town of Meadowthorpe are completely fictitious, Willowbrook Country Park bears a strong resemblance to Ferry Meadows, Peterborough. The memorial bench featured in the story is sited there but although some of the wording is the same, the name and dates on it have been changed. Ferry Meadows is a very peaceful part of the world, and it was firmly in my mind while I was writing this book, so I'd like to thank all the staff who work so hard to make their own country park a joy to visit.

Not only is Willowbrook a completely fresh setting, I'm thrilled to be just as new to Boldwood, and have already found out what a warm and welcoming publishing company this is. Thanks go to my lovely editor, Francesca Best for all her encouragement and enthusiasm, to Amanda Ridout, Nia Beynon and all the team. Looking forward to working with them in the future as they continue to go from strength to strength. I'm enormously grateful too to copyeditor Cecily Blench, proofreader Candida Bradford and cover designer Rachel Lawston. Also very importantly, huge thanks are coming over to my brilliant agent, Laura Macdougall and her assistant Olivia Davies at United Agents, who are endlessly helpful, deal calmly with any crises, both personal and work based, and always have my back.

Finally, I'm giving a big shout out to my family and friends. It would take too long to name them all, but their endless love and support has been valued much more than they realise, especially over the last few months. And especially as this book is published, we'll all be remembering my wonderful, witty Ray; chief cheerleader, writing inspiration, provider of chilled sauvignon blanc at the end of a long day and excellent giver of hugs. He will never, ever be forgotten.

ABOUT THE AUTHOR

Celia Anderson is a top ten bestselling author of women's fiction. She writes uplifting golden years fiction for Boldwood.

Sign up to Celia Anderson's mailing list here for news, competitions and updates on future books.

Follow Celia on social media:

facebook.com/CeliaAndersonAuthor
instagram.com/cejanderson
x.com/CeliaAnderson1
goodreads.com/CeliaAnderson

Printed in Great Britain
by Amazon

44558256R00185